Hot Stuff

KIM KARR

Cover designer: Michele Catalano-Creative

Cover model: Andrew Biernat

Photographer: Wander Aguiar Photography

Editing: Nichole Strauss, Insight Editing Services

Proof reading: iScream Proofreading Services

Interior design & formatting: Christine Borgford, Type A Formatting

Hot Stuff

Prologue

Lucas Carrington

EACH SPRING BROUGHT hope for National Football League teams, especially for those that had poor win-loss records in the previous season.

The NFL draft was an opportunity for the organizations to improve their roster by adding those college players considered to be the most talented in the world.

I was among those.

It was crazy to think the winner of the Super Bowl in 2019, 2020 or even 2030 could very well be determined by the decisions a bunch of executives were making right now.

This year's draft was about to commence, and trying to accurately predict the outcome was a nearly impossible feat for anyone. The true fans, the players, and even the board had a knack for getting it wrong every time.

Nothing was guaranteed.

It was just before 8 p.m., and I was sitting in front of the television staring at the outdoor theater steps that led to Philadelphia's Art Museum on the screen. Those were the very same steps from the movie Rocky, where Sylvester Stallone famously triumphed at the top.

I knew it was my turn.

An odd excitement flowed through my veins as soon as the sign above the stage began flashing, "THE FUTURE IS NOW."

With my elbows resting on my thighs, I held my breath when the football commissioner took the podium, and then, along with everyone else, I booed him.

It was tradition.

Once the crowd settled down, the commissioner made his annual speech, and then the draft was on. Since the order of player selection was determined by the reverse order in which the teams ranked at the end of the previous season, the suits predicted I would be the final pick.

I was in for a long night.

Because of the importance of the position I played, there was no doubt I would be selected as a second-string quarterback. *It was cool.* All the teams in the league currently had capable quarterbacks, and I knew this going in.

If things went according to plan, and I was selected last, that would mean ending up with New England.

Chowder and champions, baby, chowder and champions.

Grooming under their current elite quarterback wouldn't be a cakewalk, but I was looking forward to the challenge. Really, really, looking forward to it . . . that, and getting the hell out of Chicago.

The buzzer sounded. Excitement was in the air. Every team had a table set up in the venue and the ten-minute clock had begun to tick for the 49ers.

Time seemed to pass so slowly. Impatient. Anxious. Unable to interact with anyone in the room, I slouched back on the sofa and took a large gulp from my glass of water before setting it down on the table beside me.

Cutting it close to the wire, the 49ers announced their pick, and the tight end selected was as predicted. This had me gripping my knees tightly with my sweaty palms in anticipation.

Things were going according to plan.

The clock was just about to be reset, but this didn't stop the CNN sportscaster from interrupting with breaking news.

"Earlier today, Quarterback Dan Bailey of the Chicago Bears was let go from his contract for misconduct. Without him, it only makes sense that Jack Whitney abandon his original pick and draft someone to take Dan's place—"

I thought that was both an appropriate and unlikely assumption, since the Chicago Bears were next up for their draft selection, and they had little time to work any magic.

All of a sudden my cell phone rang. When I picked it up, the chatter in the room fell to a nervous hush. Not knowing if New England was calling me early or if it was going to be a crazy long lost friend, I answered with a simple, "Carrington here."

A voice came through the line loud and clear. "Lucas, this is Terrance Hines."

My entire body went cold.

No!

No!

No!

I wanted to hang up. Pretend I'd never answered. Change my fucking name. "Yes, sir," I managed to say to the General Manager, but he was not the GM for New England.

"Lucas, how would you like to play football for your hometown?" he asked.

My world stopped spinning.

Playing ball for a living and getting the hell out of the city I'd grown up in had not only been my dream, it had been all I'd been thinking about for years.

Growing up below the poverty line on the south side of Chicago, I'd spent all of my time training and staying out of trouble—mostly. I knew what it took to land the position you coveted, and I undertook the challenges, not once, but over, and over, and over again.

Yet it would seem, regardless of the amount of blood, sweat, and tears I had put into my future, luck would always be the dominating factor.

Luck.

One word.

Luck.

Four letters.

It turned out, after everything I'd put into football, I didn't have a fucking ounce of it. The worst part—*I never saw it coming.*

In a total state of shock, I sat with my mouth open wide and tried to figure out how the hell this had happened. It made no sense—the cards had been stacked in my favor in so many ways, or so I had been told.

Delusional as it was, I thought tonight was my time to rule the world.

Fuck, had I been wrong.

I ran a hand through my hair and tuned out the voice speaking to me in order to focus. Refocus. Figure things out.

The quarterback was considered the leader of the offense, and was responsible for calling the plays in the huddle.

It was a prime position.

An important one.

It was my position.

Just not on the team I wanted to be *it* on. It looked like there wasn't going to be a Boston tea party, after all.

Fuck!

"Lucas," I heard, but didn't answer.

I stared blankly ahead.

"Lucas, are you still on the line?"

While I remained in a state of shock, my brother, Nick did not. He was ten years older than me and had been more like a father to me than my own. He was also close enough to hear the conversation taking place.

When he lightly slapped me across the face to wake me up, I snarled at him. He ignored me and mouthed, "Say yes."

A cold sweat coated my forehead, my skin started to prickle, and my balls drew up tight when I realized that I had to give an answer.

That was when my gaze slid over to my old man. He was sitting in a chair with a beer in his hand. I didn't want him here, but Nick insisted on flying him up from Florida.

The diehard Bears fan had a smile on his face, and just because of that I wanted to say no.

Looking over at him, everything in me screamed, *say no. Fuck no.* I needed to get out of this town. But I knew if I said no, there was a very real possibility I would never go pro. More than likely the Bears had worked something out with the Patriots, and I was no longer the Patriots' number one pick.

It happened all the time.

Nick started nodding his head, and when that didn't work, he started nodding my head for me, and mouthing, "Yes. Yes. Yes."

"Son, are you there?" Mr. Hines said once again.

I was choked up, just not for the reason he might think I was. "Yes, sir, I am."

Just then someone else came on the line. "Lucas, this is Jack Whitney. We've got a group of people here who are really excited about you, and I'm one of them."

The head coach.

Fuck me.

The applause in the background.

Fuck me.

With him on the line, I dropped my head and squeezed the bridge of my nose. I don't think I was breathing, but somehow I found the breath to recite what I had rehearsed to say to the Patriots. "It would be an honor to be a member of your team. I can't wait for training camp. I'm going to give it all I've got, sir. You won't regret this."

Or I said something like that.

Honestly, it was all a blur.

After blinking a few times, I allowed my gaze to rise. When it landed on my brother, there were tears welling in his eyes.

Tears.

He never fucking cried. And with the smile on his face, I knew they were tears of joy. In those tears I could see all the pride, all the joy, and I could remember all the years of him giving up everything for me so I could end up where I had right now.

I.

Was.

Going.

Pro.

It was my dream . . . and I was about to start living it.

That would be what mattered to him.

Still, the Bears.

The fucking Bears.

A quick glance at the television was all I needed to prove this wasn't a nightmare. Up on the screen were my picture and stats with the Bears name flashing under it. The announcer at the podium said, "With the second pick in this year's NFL Draft, the Chicago Bears select quarterback, Lucas Carrington."

There was no going up on stage. I wasn't there. I'd opted to stay home and be with my brother and his family.

I glanced down on the floor where the Patriots' jersey and hat were neatly folded. Those were going in the trash.

In some twisted turn of fate, I was going to be a Chicago Bear. It was a team I didn't want to be on, one I didn't even like, and I would be living in a city I didn't want to stay in, but I'd be playing professional football.

Talk about bitter fucking sweet.

One

Lucas Carrington

YOUR LOCKER BECAME your little sanctuary in the NFL.

Today though the mood in this space was somber, and the air was filled with more than sweat and heavy breathing.

There was a strange mixture of sadness, tension, and apprehension. Guys stood in front of wooden lockers contemplating the end of this three-day excursion and what it meant.

The truth was, we were all waiting to see who was the next to be cut, and hoping it wasn't us.

Mini-camp was supposed to be geared solely toward acclimating rookies to the playing schemes of the team.

However after three days, stored on hooks and shoved in corners were more than sweaty shorts and worn helmets . . . there was also a piece of each of us.

As each day passed it seemed like orientation was a well-oiled machine meant to work out the kinks. Cut the sludge. Get rid of the waste. It felt more like an initial evaluation, and for some it had become the end of the road.

Even though I had a contract, I immediately started to feel on edge when I saw someone I knew had a contract, shoving the contents of his locker into a black trash bag. Shit, he was out before he had even begun.

More than likely he wasn't the first or the last.

No mistakes, one mistake, two, three or four, it didn't matter. You were out when Coach said you were out, and that was all there was to it.

"I can't fucking believe what's going on," I barked, to no one in particular, as I watched the black trash bag dangle over the player's, no ex-player's, shoulder.

"Yeah, me either," the guy next to me responded under his breath.

I flung my locker open. "I am so close to packing my shit and leaving on my own."

"Why don't you?" the barrel-chested giant standing across from me remarked. "It will open a spot up for someone who actually wants to be here."

"I want to be here," I bit out, offended.

Brown hair curled from beneath a gray skullcap. "Yeah, right," he muttered, yanking his pants down.

"You don't know shit." I stared at him, ready to put this argument to an end, and not with any more words.

Showing me his bare ass, he raised both hands high in the air and gave me two middle fingers as he strode toward the shower.

Just as I was about to jump the bench and go after him, good old Johnny Dwight, my quarterback coach, hollered into the room, "Carrington, Coach Whitney's office, now!"

In that one moment the earth cracked beneath my feet. Feeling like I was about to be forced to take a step on unsteady ground, the blood rushed to my head and I broke out into a cold sweat.

Was I about to get cut?

I couldn't be.

I had a contract. Then again Coach had just cut a player with a contract. What were the legalities? Was his contract different from mine? Did it even matter?

With my mind spinning, I closed my locker and looked up to catch the dude who I was just going at it with, turn around. The smirk on his face was one I instantly wanted to punch off.

Kotch or Catch or something that sounded a lot like crotch, crossed his huge arms over his bare chest and stared at me in disdain.

Fearless, I stared right back. When the corner of his lip twitched up, I'd had it with that tattooed motherfucker.

The two of us were oil and water. We hadn't gotten along since day one. No reason really. Sometimes it happened.

Just as I lunged for him, Thor, the guy who called himself my locker mate, pulled me back by the shirt collar. "Dude, don't. It's not worth it."

I glared at him and considered going after *him* instead.

His hair hung to his chin, and through the strands I could see a genuine look of concern in his eyes. That was when my gaze softened.

It was a look I couldn't deny to be the truth.

He was right of course. Getting into it right now with this prick of a tight end would only make what was going to happen that much worse.

Being late when Coach called would only serve to irritate him, but showing up banged up would surely piss him off.

Shaking off my ire, I spat on the ground and then turned and walked away. Stalking out of the locker room, I passed the Bears gear as I did, and for the first time I wondered if I would actually be wearing one of those jerseys in the fall. Had I screwed it up already with my *I-don't-give-a-fuck* attitude?

Fuck!

Self-destruction had always been one of my biggest issues—you'd think I would have learned by now.

As I pushed through a set of double doors etched with the Bears logo on it, all I could do was hope when I returned it wouldn't be with a black trash bag in my hand.

Sunlight poured onto my face, and in the bright glow my pupils dilated. Soldier Field was gorgeous. Not a blade out of place. The yard lines and hash marks were even whiter than Thor's teeth. And the sideline looked like it was just waiting for champions to fill it.

A glimmering navy blue helmet dangled from my hand as I made my way around the field to Coach's office. I hadn't changed yet from practice, and my cleats clacked on the tile as I entered the building.

The place was practically empty since it was a Saturday. I walked at a slow pace, looking at the grandeur of what could be mine—could have been mine.

Who the fuck knew anymore.

Just outside Jack Whitney's office stood an eight-foot photo of himself from at least twenty-five years ago. The life-sized image was taken when he was the star quarterback for the Bears.

It was meant to remind everyone who saw it to strive for greatness, but all it did was intimidate the shit out of me.

His door was open, and he took no time at all to beckon me in. "Come in, Lucas," he called.

Slowly, reluctantly, I stepped over the threshold.

Jack Whitney was at the other end, standing near the large window looking out at Soldier Field. He wore a standard coach's outfit: navy Bears shorts and an orange Bears t-shirt, white cross-trainers, and yet he looked lethal.

When he whirled around, he said sternly, "Sit down."

I sat immediately and put my helmet on my lap. Unsure why I'd brought it with me, now I was glad. It suddenly felt like a security blanket.

I glanced around.

The office was plush. A large wooden desk with tall, towering bookshelves behind it took up most of the space. There were pictures. Tons of them. But I couldn't focus on a single one through the white haze of my vision. There was also his chair. It was huge. Then again, so was he. Chiseled and in shape, I bet even though he was more than twice my age, he could give me a run for my money.

In his late fifties, Coach wore his blond hair short, was always cleanly shaven, and had the most chiseled jaw I'd ever seen. "Great job at practice today," he started.

I nodded, staying quiet. Suddenly feeling like my time here might be coming to a finish and instead of being happy about it, I felt like this could be the end of my world. Talk about a turnaround. "Thanks, sir, I appreciate that."

Coiled like a snake, Coach circled his desk and flopped in his chair. "I'm not a sir, don't call me that again."

I nodded, swallowed, felt like I was going to vomit. "Yes, Coach."

His gaze drifted over me. "Better. I'm sure you won't mind if I get right to the point."

"I'd appreciate that."

There was no hesitation when he spoke. "You have a bad attitude, Lucas, and I want it gone before you head to training camp in July."

Again, I nodded.

Until very recently, I had mistakenly thought I had nothing to worry about. That my contract with a team I didn't want to be on, in a city I had grown to despise over the years, was ironclad. So yeah, that was true, I might have had a bit of a bad attitude.

He pushed back in his chair to steeple his hands. "You understand your contract isn't final, right? It's unsigned, and won't be signed until training camp is over."

I'd signed.

They hadn't.

A fucking incomplete contract. And no further ink would be put to that piece of paper until after training camp.

This meant only the signing bonus was guaranteed.

That stare of his was deadly. "This is a tough-assed game," he told me. "Do the things that matter, and even those that don't, the right way, and you might just make it, Lucas. Stay on the destructive path you're on, and there's no way you will go anywhere but out the door. Do. You. Understand. Me?"

Cold sweat covered my entire body. Talk about being scared straight. "I understand," I answered, swallowing the prickly lump in my throat.

His voice was smooth and deep when he spoke again. "Good. Now, I'm going to give you some departing advice."

I waited, and didn't say a word.

He stood up and leaned over his desk. Reiterating what he had just told me, he didn't beat around the bush. "Know this Lucas, no position in the NFL is guaranteed. If you don't prove your worth at training camp, you're out of here, no matter how important you think you are. It's that cut and dry. Got it?"

The only thing I could do was blow out my breath in a deep exhale. I wouldn't be getting cut, not right now, anyway. "Yeah, I got it."

"Great, then get the fuck out of here."

I couldn't move fast enough.

Back on the field, I stood alone and looked at the quiet stadium. This was the NFL. The fucking NFL. And I was on a team that I'd just come so close to being cut loose from.

As my gaze circled the empty stands, I began to understand the look I saw in my brother's eyes the day I was drafted.

This could be mine.

And I wanted it.

Fuck, I wanted it.

Still, I had a lot of work ahead of me. It didn't matter that I'd once proven myself. I had to do it all again.

Back in college I had notoriety. I was the *it* guy. Now I was *trouble*, and what I had to do was prove I was *football*.

I would bleed football, eat, drink, and sleep football.

I would be fucking football.

At training camp, not a shit would be given that I was a rookie drafted in the first round. I was just another player who either performed or risked being cut. That wasn't a problem for me though, I knew what I had to do. I planned to dominate the field.

To show I was hot stuff.

Two

Training Camp

Lucas

PLAYING NAKED WAS going to be the key to making it through the hot and humid days of training camp.

Any pervert might be thinking that meant gracing the field without clothes. But a player would know what I meant immediately. Understand that wearing no protection beyond the rulebook minimum was how to play naked the right way.

Quarterbacks typically wore padding on their legs, but until the official season kicked off, I'd be skipping the thigh pads. The risk of injury associated with this practice seemed unimportant, but speed—that was key. Then again, playing it safe had never been my style, and it was a good thing.

When it turned out football contracts weren't as ironclad as I had so naively thought, I got a new and improved attitude, and fast.

Roster spots were vast, but the sheer number of bodies vying to fill them was even greater.

With my cleats strung over my shoulder and in sweats, wearing no pads, I contemplated my disposability factor. I had to admit, I was more than freaked out that everyone's head was on the chopping block, even mine.

Nearly ninety of us wore navy blue or orange jerseys without numbers. We were spread across two practice fields like ants scrambling from our hills as we moved.

It was hard to believe that in forty-two days we'd be cut down to fifty-three. That at the end of all of this, our team would be formed. That we'd be ready for our first pre-season game. That with me on board, we would be a winning team.

I wasn't being cocky. I was being realistic.

Still, I was getting ahead of myself. First, I had to go through hell. And this was without a doubt, going to be a blazing inferno.

The training camp was located sixty miles south of Chicago at Olivet Nazarene University. The place boasted four practice fields, a fairly new air-conditioned locker room, dining facilities, a weight room, and of course dorms. This was where I would be spending the next six weeks.

For the first fourteen days, practices were closed, which meant fans weren't invited to watch. Therefore, there would be no ice cream truck set up between the concrete bleachers, no autographs to sign, and no show to put on.

Whether closed practices were good or bad, I had no idea.

Although players wouldn't even be in pads the first week, practices were still going to be split into two-a-days. Early morning and late afternoon, with every minute in-between occupied as well. Typically the morning practices would be spent walking through the newly discussed plays and the afternoon practices would be all-out physically grueling play.

The sun had only been in the sky for about an hour and we'd already eaten breakfast and were now strutting around the campus.

Per the email sent last night with our daily schedule attached, it was time to head to an administration building in the west quad for a meeting on team rules and then we would be settling in for a talk on sensitivity.

Interesting topics.

Not.

Not that my opinion mattered in the least because all of that had to take place before we actually could get on the field and play some football.

As everyone filed into the designated classroom, we were handed a pad and a pen to take notes. It was a lecture hall with chairs and whiteboards, but still I doubted any of us would be putting ink on the paper.

Already over this, I grabbed a seat next to the door. Standing by the back wall was a bunch of coaches—the safety's coach, the receiver's coach, and the special team's coach, but no quarterback coach for the quarterbacks. For me.

There were three of us quarterbacks, by the way, or there would be. Me, I was the starter, the primary backup, Isaac Swann, who was also new, and then there would be some dude from the practice squad as the reserve, but he hadn't been named yet.

And by the look of things, we would be coaching ourselves because Old Johnny Dwight wasn't here. He hadn't been here last night and as far as I could tell, he still hadn't arrived. He did like to hit the bottle. Wonder if he'd had one too many.

This past May in mini-camp, he was all up, down, and almost inside my ass telling me how my technique needed improvement and my attitude, an overhaul. He told me he'd be spending twenty-four hours a day with me at training camp. That he might even sleep in my room. He even went on and on about how much I was going to hate him. And then he hadn't even shown up yet. Go figure.

As soon as Jack Whitney walked in the room, the entire Bears staff hustled to sit right in front of him. There were seven coaches for offense, eight for defense, two for special teams, and three for strength and conditioning. Also present were the trainers and the equipment managers.

Everyone it appeared, except the quarterback coach.

Introductions came first, and then good old Jack ran his mouth on a gambit of need-to-know items, like how much Gatorade we should be drinking, mandatory Sunday dinners, and that this team was his team.

Next up was the operations manager, who explained to us the need to conduct ourselves appropriately on the college campus by using the Port-O-Lets by the fields to take a piss.

Good to know.

I guessed relieving ourselves somewhere on the four practice fields or behind the bleachers seemed like something we might do.

The head trainer got up and introduced his staff. He touched on the need to shower before entering the hot and cold tubs in the training room and how we shouldn't buy over-the-counter medication. After which he stressed the need to check with the NFL drug hotline before taking anything he hadn't approved.

"Performance-drug testing in the locker room starts tomorrow," he tossed out, "and photo identification is required."

A number of groans echoed around the room.

Ignoring them all, he went on. "If you test positive because you didn't realize what you were taking, I can help you, so bring the bottles of pills. If you test positive and you knew you were going to—well, you're just stupid."

That shut everyone up.

"Look," he said, "I've been doing this for a long time, maybe even before you *girls* were born, and let me tell you, every swinging dick in this room is counted on to follow the fucking rules."

The guy next to me glared at Dallas as he walked away.

Not my business.

Didn't ask why.

Once again Jack took front and center. This time he put on his reading glasses and read from a stack of index cards he had in his hands. "We have thirty team rules," he shouted. "Thirty, *girls*, do you hear me? Break one and you're out."

The room fell silent as he began to list them.

"Number one," he bellowed, "You must attend every meal."

I started to zone out as he spoke about refraining from vulgarity in front of the fans and no dorm room overnight guests.

"Number twenty," he said, "Don't chase too many women, it causes you to lose focus on what's important."

We had a lot of Goddamn rules. Minimal antics on the field unless you were just that fucking good, curfew, and no distractions . . . blah . . . blah . . . blah.

Jack removed his glasses and sat right on one of the tables, where he looked from one side of the room to the other. "Should you have a problem with any of these, I will be more than happy to personally explain their value to you."

I'd pass on that, thank you very much. I'd already had my share of *me time* with him, and I didn't want more—not ever again.

Coach went and took a seat in the front row and lucky us, it was sensitivity time.

"Hey, guys! How is everyone?" This came from a buff dude in his forties or early fifties with spiky red hair striding down the aisle.

No one answered. We all looked at each other with blank stares. Our reaction didn't seem to bother him at all. Probably used to it.

Taking the front of the room, he went on to tell us he was a former player and was now actively involved with the NFL. He stopped for a second to look at us, and I thought, okay, this is going to be really important. "One word . . . respect. Now give me another."

We all sat in total silence.

"All right," he pointed to a veteran offensive end. "Why don't you tell me what that word means to you?"

Preacher, the five-foot-eleven, one hundred and eighty-five pound cornerback, was speechless, probably for the first time in his life.

The calling on a player and waiting for his answer went on and on for forty minutes. He kept throwing words out, and we kept defining them.

So much fun.

After the meeting, we finally got to hit the locker room and then at last the field, where we ran the length of it six times before moving on to conditioning evaluations.

We were cooling down and I was deep in thought, spinning the football like a basketball on the tip of my left index finger, when Coach Whitney blew his whistle.

"Okay, *girls*," he hollered, "stop swinging your ponytails and show me how fast you can divide into two groups."

Jack was a real ball buster.

Then again, he was testing our ability to listen, wasn't he? Everything we did in training camp was a test and we were about to start another. Was this—who could follow instructions? Or maybe, who was able to line up in two even groups? Hey, I knew I could. Everyone else, I hadn't a fucking clue.

The offensive and defensive coordinators were over on the other field setting up more drills with the line coaches, which left just Coach over here.

And by the way, not only was the quarterback coach still nowhere in sight, no one had said a word to me about why he wasn't here.

I wasn't worried. I knew my shit, but the other guys, did they? I hoped they didn't expect me to teach them. That wasn't why I was here. Then again, why was I here?

It wasn't money.

It wasn't fame.

It wasn't because I was a die-hard Bears fan, although I had been for most of my life. Right, now I remembered. It was because I'd almost lost my spot, and now I knew how bad I wanted it.

And let's not forget I was here because I loved to play football. Because it was my life.

What I had to remember was now that my head was on straight—I had to prove it. Prove that I was here to play professional ball, and only that.

Hustling as fast as I could, I made it to the number two position in line. Right in front of me was the guy who'd called himself my locker mate. And he had somehow managed to get himself assigned as my training camp roommate.

Trace Wentworth, or Thor as he liked to be called, was a big six-foot-one, two hundred and seventy-five pound offensive tackle from Georgia. The guy was built like a tank.

Despite the fact that we'd become *friends*, we hadn't spoken at all during the three-month break. Come to think of it, we hadn't spoken that much since arriving, either. Even so, I knew more about him than he knew about me. I knew he had a girlfriend because he was sweet-talking her on the phone last night until I wanted to punch him. Oh, and I knew one more thing—the dude could snore.

Under the rays of the soon-to-be-blazing sun, I watched him, a little surprised. Despite his size, he moved fast enough to reach the head of the line before me.

Whatever.

With the smell of fresh cut grass in the air, all of us prepared for the *fumble ready* drill coming our way.

The pile of balls in front of Coach Whitney was the dead giveaway. Regardless of whether each player at the head of the line was ready or not, he tossed a football on the ground about ten yards ahead.

I watched as it rolled, bounced, and randomly flipped into the air, as footballs tended to do. The objective of this drill was for each guy to try to get to the ball first and recover the simulated fumble by any means necessary.

This was one exercise I could run in my sleep. I'd been doing it since I was ten, and often while water sprayed on me from a fire hydrant, which meant I had to dive for the ball into a cool puddle of mud.

Talk about slippery when wet.

The whistle blew and within seconds, those two hulking bodies at the front of the line were flying and colliding in awkward positions. Thor triumphed as he stood with the ball in his hand.

Way to go, roomie.

The opportunity to compete flooded my veins with adrenaline. Just then, the second ball was thrown across the field and the whistle blew.

As soon as it did, my cleats moved and my body shook as I took off at a dead run. At six-four and two hundred ten pounds, I had agility on my side. With my speed off the charts, I got to the ball first and was gripping it with only mild exertion way before a struggle ensued.

As I raised the orange oval, I knew I was going to dominate these drills. Then again, maybe I was just overqualified.

I mean come on; being a part of the second-to-last team in the league wasn't exactly going to be a challenge, now was it!

Who knew in the days and weeks to come, I'd be eating those words, and a lot more.

Three

HEAD GAMES

Gillian Whitney

I WAS LATE.

Very late.

And not just to practice, but also for my first NFL summer training camp as an athletic trainer intern. I'd missed check-in, the first big meeting, and even introductions.

Although I'd been through the routine many times in my life, it had never been in an official capacity.

My flight had been grounded due to hurricane-force winds. Then again, I supposed that was to be expected when you were flying out of the state of Florida in the summer.

Unfortunately, I hadn't had much of a choice. I was attending the University of Florida, and was one semester away from receiving my DAT. That's my doctorate in athletic training, and I had to present my dissertation to the board before I could leave. Obviously, that was super important.

Still, I really hated being late.

The day was almost over and I was just setting foot in the training room. Ready to put myself to work, I glanced around.

The training facilities at this college were nothing compared to those at Soldier Field. Back in Chicago, the Bears had massive hydrotherapy pools that were thirty feet long and eight feet wide. They ran both hot, for pre-practice, and cold, for post-practice. There was also a giant flat screen within viewing distance.

In addition, the training room in Chicago was equipped with the latest in rehabilitation equipment. Not to mention, there was a machine that could measure baseline concussion scores to determine if players were ready to return to practice after suffering head injuries, which could be missed.

With the lack of state-of-the-art equipment, the medical staff had to go back to old school methods, which was fine by me. I had just finished learning most of them and was ready to put them to use.

One more glance around had me feeling nostalgic. Everything looked the same. I was really glad to be back. I loved this time of the year. The hustle and bustle that came with training camp was something I would really miss.

Dallas Spears, the head trainer, wasn't anywhere in sight. He must have been on the field. He'd been with the team for more than twenty years and was not only one of the best around, but also extremely dedicated to the players.

I wasn't alone though, the first assistant athletic trainer, Aiden Brantley, was here, and of course hard at work across the room.

Aiden was in his thirties, single, wore his hair in a bun and a diamond stud in his ear. A bit on the wild side, he was the polar opposite of clean-cut, go to bed by nine, Dallas. Hey, Aiden liked to party with the players, and that wasn't necessarily a bad thing.

It just wasn't my thing. I left that to the cheerleaders.

Wearing a pair of cargo shorts and a tank top, he was standing at one of the tables, stretching out a player who looked extremely fatigued. The player was new to the team, either a draft or a free agent, I wasn't certain.

The sudden rush of running water had me turning my head, and a smile crossed my lips when I did. Drake was back. I didn't think he would be. He had interned last year and we got along really well.

Blowing his hair from his eyes, he wiped his brow as he cleaned the whirlpools. I knew first hand just what hard work that was. And I knew in the upcoming weeks, I'd be doing a lot of it.

There were three students interning under Dallas this year, but I was the closest to becoming fully accredited. I was also the only female. In fact, I was the first female in this role for the Bears. I wasn't ashamed to say I got the internship due to nepotism. Not to worry, I intended to do more than just prove myself to everyone on this team during training camp.

After all, it would be my last one.

This very real fact weighed heavy on my mind. It was a bitter-sweet ending. Growing up was so hard to do. Then again, this sport was like a part of my family. I'd been around football my entire life, and being forced to leave it behind felt like a loss. Something I knew I would mourn, and I wasn't looking forward to it.

You see, my father had been involved with football in various capacities since before I was born, and he still was.

He held the prestigious position of first-string quarterback for the Bears when I was born.

The circumstances surrounding my birth were nothing that he ever cared to recall. Because of this, he hardly ever talked about his days playing for this team, but I knew the story, or the condensed version, anyway.

It was the middle of winter.

The Bears were scheduled to play the Colts in Indianapolis. Because the

NFL mandated that players be on the ground for an away game eighteen hours prior to kickoff, my father was already there when my mother decided to surprise him and drive to the game.

Six weeks from her due date, she told him she was staying home, so he had no idea she was coming.

My mother was driving on Interstate 65 when a tractor-trailer jack-knifed and hit her car. After being airlifted to the nearest hospital, I was born early by emergency C-section.

I survived.

She, however, died before my father even made it to the hospital.

I never knew my mother, but I know I got my strawberry blond hair from her. And my father says I have her drive and tenacity. But I think I got those traits from him. He's dedicated his entire life to football and me. He's been through a lot, and still, he's the most driven man I know.

After being traded to the Rams when I was two, my father played for six more years on the roster of three teams before he hung up his cleats for good.

The plan had been to go back to Chicago and lead a normal life, but then he was offered an assistant coaching position for Houston, and our plans changed. This job was one he couldn't turn down. He said just a few more years, and then we'd go back to Chicago. Have a normal life. We moved four more times before I turned sixteen.

That was our normal.

At seventeen, I left for college, where the only time I ever took off was the six weeks before Labor Day to be with my father during training camp.

I hadn't missed one—ever.

Sadly, like I said, this would be my last. After graduation in December, I'd have my doctorate, and it would be time to join the workforce, which meant no more six-week summer breaks.

It would be that normal life my father always spoke so fondly of.

He hoped I would get a job at either the Mayo Clinic Sports Medicine Center or at the Northwest Sports Center.

I wasn't sure what I hoped for.

Football wasn't an option, though. Even if I could get a permanent job in the field, my father insisted I stay away from it. He didn't want me spending anymore of my life on the road. The guilt he felt for the years we'd done just that was enough to make me agree, even if begrudgingly so.

Personally, I'd loved every minute of it.

But he wanted us to put down some roots, which was why he took the head position for the Bears two years ago. But if he didn't turn out a winning record this year, he would probably be let go. He said if that happened he'd retire for good because he feels like he's come full circle, and Chicago is in his blood.

I dropped my stuff on the table and hurried to where Aiden was now using his shoulder to apply pressure to the player's upright leg. "Hey. Sorry I'm late," I said.

He glanced over his shoulder and gave me a huge smile. "Hey, Gillian, good to see you. Welcome back."

I was watching as Aiden tried to relieve the tension. "What happened to you?" I asked the player.

"My leg cramped up," he scowled.

I raised a brow. "Already?"

"Tell her why," Aiden said.

"Dehydration." He was clearly annoyed, and obviously with himself.

"Yikes."

"I already got the lecture," the player said, a little dejected, and then he held his hand out. "I'm Dylan Kutchner."

"Hi, nice to meet you, Dylan," I said.

"Girl, call me Kutch. And before you start in on me, I'm sure

I'm not the first rookie to get his ass chewed out for eating two bananas for lunch and losing ten pounds."

Raising a brow, I took his hand. "No, I promise you, you're not."

He was pretty tall and big all around. Over six-foot five, was my guess, and probably at least two hundred seventy-five pounds. I could see how he had dropped that weight.

"I'm Gillian," I said. "And you'll be back on the field tomorrow, but I bet you'll never get dehydrated again."

It was common, and it only took once.

He shook his head as if disgusted with himself. "Girl, you better believe it."

With a smirk, I refocused on Aiden. "What can I do?"

Before he could answer, Drake interrupted. "Waters need to be filled up at least two more times before practice is called. And guess what? You're up, Whitney."

"Whitney?" Dylan echoed.

I nodded, hating the fear in his eyes, but more than used to it. Ever since I developed breasts, small as they were, it had been that way. No longer the cute ball-cap-wearing little girl, it was as if the team saw me as off-limits. Even at twenty-three years old, players were still going to see me as the forbidden coach's daughter, and that was never going to change.

Turning toward Drake, ready to scold him, I couldn't help but notice his grin. There was no fear there, but he had missed me.

Last man or woman out on the field every morning got assigned water cart duty for the day. It had been that way since the beginning of time, and much to my dismay, I would be the last one on the field.

"Sure, I'm on it," I responded, not scolding him for referring to me by my last name . . . for now.

In my orange *staff* t-shirt, khaki shorts, and Nikes, I twisted my long hair back and headed down the hallway for the cart, where I eagerly pushed it out the tunnel.

At four in the afternoon, the second practice had only started about an hour ago. The players looked fairly fresh still as they did various drills in groups across the field.

Holding the cart like a wheel barrel, I started to jog down the center of the practice field, picking up speed once I'd made it half way.

To my right a group of players were sidestepping cones, nothing out of the ordinary. To my left another group of guys had started running through a series of agility tests, some of which at times could be downright funny to watch.

The offensive coordinator loved Taylor Swift and sometimes he'd blare her music over the field and make the guys do some kind of dance to facilitate their balance.

Right now, the music was more hard rock, and I knew the defensive coordinator was running the show. None of that pop music for him. His words, not mine.

I knew everyone pretty well.

This was, after all, my third summer on this campus, with this team. Sure, there were some new faces, but I'd get to know them soon enough.

Looking around, I spotted defensive tackle Warren Gerard right away—all three hundred and thirty pounds of him. He had a wife and two kids, who my father and I spent Thanksgiving with last year.

Over on the sidelines stood the team's general manager. Terrance Hines was wearing a baseball cap that was severely bent and sucking on a red lollipop. As he observed the first day of practice, it was hard not to notice the way the pockets of his cargo shorts bulged with what could only be more candy. More than likely the waxy wrappers of those he'd already finished were packed inside there as well. The players joked he had an oral fixation. In truth, he had a nervous habit.

Up ahead of me a guy broke out of one of the drill patterns

and started side stepping in my direction. With that messy, dark, sexy-as-hell hair that fell over his forehead and flipped out at his ears, he was hard not to notice. But with the tight coil of muscles that marked his arms and legs and made him look as if were made of steel, he was impossible not to gawk at.

I think a bit of drool slid down my chin.

Normally, I was immune to good-looking players. In a setting like this, they were everywhere, all the time.

When I was in my teens, the old adage you can look, but not touch seemed appropriate. Now though, I was the same age as a good majority of these guys, so technically I could touch.

However, I was no longer a teen. I had grown up, and my career mandated I come in contact with the players. So now when I looked at them, I didn't take notice of anything except abilities and injuries. It was much safer that way. After all, my professional reputation was on the line.

The player smiled at me, and when he did, I felt the strangest pitter-patter of my heart. Ignoring it, I nodded, and slowed a bit. That smile didn't waiver. It was an easy smile, one that made me a little weak in the knees, and I felt a blush creep up my neck.

The truth was I wasn't used to players paying attention to me. Nor was I used to them actually looking me in the eye. Most avoided eye contact—the whole fear thing. This player obviously had none of that.

It was refreshing.

When his lips tilted further, I couldn't help but notice just how good-looking he was. Paired with that smile and those penetrating blue eyes, he made me a little breathless.

"Hey, there, Strawberry Fields," he said, with a wink.

He was flirting with me. Players never flirted with me. So shocked by this, I smiled back. But when I felt that thump of my heartbeat go a little crazier, I picked my speed back up. This worried me, and I knew I should hurry past him and forget I even noticed him.

It was about that time that he'd stopped right where he was to bend over and tie a shoelace.

That's when everything went terribly wrong.

Unable to slow fast enough, I couldn't stop what was about to happen, not even with my horrified scream of terror. "Watch out!"

It was too late, and I hit him with the tremendous force of the three-hundred-pound cart. The point of contact was the crown of his head, and he was propelled backwards, landing flat on his back.

At first, my heart stopped beating, but then my instincts kicked in and I dropped my hold on the cart to hurry over to him.

His eyes were closed.

This was bad.

Very, very bad.

It might have been a freak accident . . . but it would be one that would change both of our lives.

Forever.

Four

First Down

Lucas

TALK ABOUT BEING knocked off your feet.

This was not what I had in mind when I moved in her direction. Not by a long shot. For being blindsided though, I wasn't in terrible shape. Sure, my head was killing me, and I was seeing stars, but at least I wasn't out cold. Not only could I hear the sound of players doing drills, I could feel the breeze and the hot sun, and I could smell the wet dirt.

There was however, an iron taste in my mouth that really sucked. With no mouth guard, I hoped like fuck I still had all my teeth in place. I'd been sacked by some of the fiercest defensive ends, but never had I gone down like this.

"Are you okay?"

I tried to nod, but couldn't.

"I'm sorry. I'm really sorry." The voice was sweet, like honey.

It must be Strawberry Fields.

Small hands with the smoothest of skin held my shoulders still. "Stay right here. We're going to move you off the field."

After another second or so, I lifted my lids and found myself looking into two very green pools of concern.

Trying to prop up on my elbows, I stopped right away because those damn stars came back. "Don't move," she whispered, so close to my face I could feel her warm breath on my skin.

I probably should let her know I was not seriously injured, that I was not compromised in any way. With that intention, I moved my arms and my legs in a way that indicated I was trying to get up, but she kept a firm grip on me, holding me in place. "I said, don't move," she ordered.

I wasn't going to say I was unhappy that she was holding me down, but I didn't really like it either. Then again, I wasn't sure I was going to be able to get up.

I grimaced and reached for my forehead. "What just happened?"

"I hit you with the water cart," she said, panic clear in her voice.

"The water cart," I groaned, dropping my arm to my side.

"I'm so sorry," she said again.

Hearing the apology in her voice didn't sound right. "I'll be all right," I reassured her, and hoped like fuck that was going to be the case.

Behind her I could see the medical wagon heading my way, and both Dallas and Coach Whitney were on it.

Shit!

They came to an abrupt stop and rushed from their seats.

Jack Whitney stood six-foot-three and with the span of his shoulders, he looked like one intimidating motherfucker, even to me.

Dallas was much smaller than him and had dark hair, but was also neatly dressed in khaki shorts and a polo shirt and cleanly shaven.

"I think he might have a concussion." It was Strawberry Fields, and whether she knew it or not, she was about to fuck me.

And not in the way I wanted her to.

"No, I'm fine," I argued, and immediately popped up.

If Dallas enacted the concussion protocol, I would be off the field until I underwent a full evaluation and then put through the rigors of the return-to-participation protocol.

Can you say fucked for the season?

"Did he lose consciousness?" Coach Whitney asked.

"No, but—"

Strawberry Fields was standing up in order to get out of the way while trying to relay what she saw, but I cut her off. "I'll be all right. I just got the wind knocked out of me," I said, and somehow got to my feet before she got to her own.

Coach Whitney eyed me with speculation. "Do you know where you are, Lucas?" he asked. He was starting the evaluation that I was sure Dallas would complete to determine the extent of my injuries.

I wiped the sweat from my brow. "Yes, I'm mid-field, Coach."

Satisfied, he nodded, and then immediately turned his attention to Strawberry Fields. "Gillian," he barked, "please explain to me what just happened?"

Right there, I knew at the very least she was about to get her ass chewed out, but more than likely, regardless of what job she held, she was going to get fired on the spot.

She opened her mouth to speak. "Da—"

"It wasn't her fault," I blurted out. "It was mine."

This caused his head to dart in my direction, and I knew I was now the one about to get my ass chewed out. "Your fault? Care to explain to me, *Quarterback*, why the hell you would go barreling into a water cart? Are the drills we're putting you through not challenging enough?"

"Yes, sir, I mean no, sir."

He narrowed his eyes at me.

"Coach," I corrected.

His gaze grew fierce.

So I shut the fuck up.

"Jack," Dallas said, "I'd like to take him to the training room for further evaluation."

"Do you think that's necessary?" Coach asked Dallas.

I started to argue, but Coach put his hand up silencing me, and gave his full attention to Dallas.

"Yes, I do." Dallas's response was matter-of-fact. There was no hesitation or waiver in his voice.

Strawberry Fields, or Gillian, I guessed was her name, handed me a bottle of water from that fucking cart. "Drink this," she said twisting the cap off.

Coach was shaking his head in disgust. "Fine," he muttered. "Send him back out to the sidelines in an hour unless you find an issue, which if you do, I want to be notified about immediately."

Dallas nodded and motioned me toward the medical wagon.

"I'll be in to help as soon as I get the waters filled," Strawberry Fields said to him, and it became obvious she was an athletic trainer in some capacity.

My neck felt like it was stiffening by the minute, but I said nothing as I sat where Dallas insisted.

The players weren't staring though, and I was certain they were told to pay attention to their shit.

Thank fuck.

Still, the ridiculing would come, I was certain.

Fuck me.

Coach Whitney pointed his finger at me. "I want to see you in my office immediately following breakfast tomorrow morning."

"Yes, Coach" I said, swallowing a lump in my throat.

When he wheeled around to face Strawberry Fields, I caught sight of her face, and it was filled with concern.

Our gazes held for a moment too long because Coach moved

to his left a little to block my view. "Gillian," he bit out.

Unsure why I felt I had to see her, I shifted so I could get a glimpse of her face. She tried to speak, but he put a hand up, and instantly I could see her dejection.

Gently, he lifted her dropped chin. "And you, you'll join me before dinner, alone, in my room, and explain everything to me then. I don't have time right now."

The strangest surge of adrenaline burned through my veins. It was a flame of jealousy I couldn't control. Everything I'd heard about Coach Whitney was what a stand-up guy he was, but was he tapping Strawberry Fields?

Then, she threw her arms around him and I almost went flying off the wagon until she said, "Yes, Daddy, I'll be there. And I'm really sorry."

Daddy! Strawberry Fields was Coach Whitney's daughter? She was Coach Whitney's daughter!

What the hell?

I had just thrown myself under the bus for her, and she hadn't even so much as tried to warn me that it wasn't her head on the chopping block . . . *it was mine.*

Five

SIDELINED

Lucas

THIS WAS SERIOUS shit.

During the previous offseason, the NFL had added a measure that would punish teams who failed to properly enforce the concussion protocols. Any violation could cost a team fines or even the forfeiture of future draft picks.

For years nothing had worried me. I lived recklessly, fearlessly, taking each day as it came. Right now, though, I wasn't sure I felt that invincible.

The future, which hadn't looked so bright since the day of the draft, suddenly didn't seem so dim in comparison to what could happen in the next few minutes. If I were to be diagnosed with a concussion, it would be signing my camp death warrant. I'd be replaced as first-string quarterback faster than I could blink.

What a humbling way to be knocked down a few pegs.

The training room was empty, and I was glad for that.

As soon as the tech moved the portable x-ray machine out of the room, Dallas closed the door. The report would go to the doctor, but Dallas had looked at the x-ray taken of my neck, and he was certain there wasn't anything to worry about, at least when it came to any possible neck injury.

"I don't have a concussion," I told him with insistence. "Like I said, I was just caught off guard. I should have been more on my toes."

He pointed to the table. "Shirt off and hop up. How about you let me determine the extent of your *mishap*?"

Grimacing because it was apparently obvious I had been on the hunt, I did as he instructed.

The muscles around my shoulder blades and just above them were starting to tighten, and that slightly worried me. I made light of it and told Dallas the pain was an ache from the way I landed, which more than likely it was.

He raised a brow and told me to look up, to the right, to the left, and then down. This I did with a mild amount of discomfort, but I knew my range was slightly limited.

During his exam, Dallas found a bump that was forming at the base of my skull just above my neck. "This is to be expected since a hard, blunt metal object practically bludgeoned you," he said with complete seriousness.

There was no way to describe the anger I was beginning to feel. For the past four years, on weekend afternoons, I ran around a field pursued by eleven men who wanted to hammer me, and what could end it all for me was a fucking water cart.

A light knock sounded at the door before it slowly swung open. Strawberry Fields walked in, apprehension written all over her features. "Is everything okay?" she asked softly.

Dallas looked back at her, a little more than concerned. "I'm not sure. I think I'm going to try a little electric stimulation to see if I can't break up the spasms he seems to be having."

Suddenly she looked more than nervous, she looked terrified, and for some reason this pissed me off even more.

Anger flashed in my eyes when her gaze met mine. It was misplaced. I knew this wasn't her fault—it was mine.

After all, I'd been the one unfocused.

She moved gingerly around the edge of the table. Nervousness and uncertainty were evident in her body language, at least until Dallas put her to work. Then she moved in a manner that told me she knew what she was doing, which helped put me a little at ease.

Together, they manipulated the tight area around my neck. When that didn't work, they moved on to traction, which provided enough relief that Dallas was no longer furrowing his brow.

I did the best I could to ignore Strawberry Fields, or perhaps I should refer to her as the Coach's off-limits daughter, but it was hard. The way she smelled. The way her skin felt on mine. The way her breathing picked up infinitesimally as she stared at my chest when she thought I wasn't looking.

There were moments I had to close my eyes and block all the white noise out, which had the added benefit of helping me relax.

Although Dallas couldn't determine with certainty any definitive diagnosis of a concussion, something didn't sit right with him. "I think we should call the team physician in," he said.

A pang of fear raced through me. "Please, Dallas, don't do that. If you do that Coach will put me on watch. Today is only day one of training, and contract or not, you know not being at practice will keep me off the field come game time. And that will end my career before it starts."

Strawberry Fields handed me ibuprofen for the inflammation and ice for the swelling, and then cleared her throat to speak. "Lucas," she said, and I swore my name on her lips made me shudder. "That isn't necessarily the case."

After downing the pills, I stared at her.

She was staring right back.

That was when I drew my brows together in consternation and leaned toward her a bit. I was dying to hear what she had to say. Sure, I was being an ass, but come on, look what I had at stake. "Go on," I said.

She took a step back and went on. "He could give you a steroid injection. Dexamethasone is a fast acting, anti-inflammatory and will stop the spasms."

"I know what a steroid shot is," I bit out. "And contrary to what you might think, I prefer to avoid putting chemicals in my body whenever possible."

"That is not at all what I was inferring," she said in a husky voice that sent shivers down my spine. Her voice alone would have seduced me under any other circumstances.

"I agree we should wait on any injections," Dallas said, trying to ease the building tension in the room. "For now. Just remember it is an option and will get you on the field if need be. Let's give it enough time to see if the ibuprofen and ice work, first. That could be all you need."

It's not like I'd never practiced or played with pain, because I had. "Then you'll give me until tomorrow before calling the team physician?" I asked him, or better put, pleaded with him. I would have got down on my knees and begged if I thought it would have worked.

Thankfully, he nodded. "Come in here before you hit the field tomorrow. I'll have one of the medical staff put you on the stationary bike or treadmill and monitor your cardiovascular activity to determine if there are any signs or symptoms we need to be concerned with."

Strawberry Fields moved closer again, but kept her gaze on Dallas. "I can meet him in here before breakfast, so it doesn't interfere with his meeting with my father or his training schedule."

Surprise gripped me at the earnestness—and urgency—in her tone.

Dallas arched a brow. "That's pretty early, Gillian."

She smiled indulgently at him. "I know. It's not a problem, and it's the least I can do."

She had that right . . . didn't she?

There was another thought in the forefront of my mind, and it wasn't very gentleman-like at all.

But then she looked my way. "If that is okay with you?"

Fighting the darkness that threatened to erupt within me, I was just about to tell her to go to hell when I caught her wide-eyed gaze. I took a moment to take her in. Her strawberry blond hair and that beautiful face with those striking eyes, and I couldn't believe it, but that darkness was gone, and so was the only noise in my head.

This was my fault.

Not hers.

Classic Lucas.

Shit like what happened was my normal. Like always, I had been on the hunt. Looking for a challenge. Being reckless. Unsatisfied with what I had. Wanting more. Interested in what I shouldn't be interested in.

If hitting on a girl at NFL training camp bled all kinds of wrong, then going after the coach's daughter screamed insanity. And yet I wasn't exactly ruling it out when I looked at her and said, "That would be great. I really appreciate it. I'll meet you down here in the morning."

So yeah, she had it all wrong. She didn't owe me anything. In fact, she'd be smart to stay the hell away from me. I was the devil wearing a Bears jersey. She just didn't know it. Not yet, anyway.

No worries . . . she would.

Six

A Hail Mary

Gillian

IT WAS A bad idea.

No, *he* was the bad idea, but there was little I could do now except go.

My breath hiccupped, and as I reached for my phone to turn my alarm off, I once again recalled every second of the conversation I'd had with my father last night.

Lucas Carrington was the player I'd run over. I still cringed just thinking about it. The only thing making it worse was finding out who he was.

This insanely hot, flirty, bold player with a brooding side was my father's golden egg. The quarterback he'd eyed long ago, watched countless interviews with, and in the end decided he wasn't worth the risk, but then at the last minute dire circumstances caused him to change his mind. He'd decided to draft Lucas because he said it was fated. That losing his quarterback the very day of the draft was some kind of sign he couldn't ignore.

The truth was Lucas Carrington was my father's Hail Mary.

And the crazy part was it wasn't like my father didn't know what he was getting into. He did. He knew that Lucas wanted to get the hell out of Chicago, that he had attitude issues, and that he had yet to learn the meaning of having real respect for his team.

And so it turned out, my father ignored all the warning signs that screamed *pass*, and instead picked up this Notre Dame elite player because he saw something in him.

With a sigh, I sat on the edge of my small bed and placed my feet on the linoleum floor. That was my father for you. He saw something in someone and stopped at nothing to bring that person to his or her potential.

In Lucas's case, though, I worried that not only was he more than he could handle but this time his expectations might have been unrealistic. Perhaps he'd bitten off more than he could chew.

Shoving my phone in my bag, I stood and hurried to the dresser that was mere feet from my bed. The room I stayed in was small, but at least I didn't have a roommate. Then again, it wasn't as if I ever did when I was here. There were never girls my age around to share a room with.

That hadn't changed.

I'd been awake for hours and had already showered and dressed before I'd laid back down to wait for the time to pass.

For some reason I couldn't stop thinking about Lucas and the strange attraction I felt toward him.

This was the first time I'd ever thought about one of my father's players that way, and I couldn't stop thinking. Thinking about what would happen between us if I weren't an intern, or if I wasn't the coach's daughter? Would he kiss me, run his rough hands over my body, or maybe more?

Would he still . . . even though he shouldn't?

Would I let him, knowing he shouldn't?

My mind had become a flurry of upheaval and I had yet to comb through the mess.

Forcing a last-minute glance at myself, I looked in the mirror and winced. My face showed evidence of my early rising. There were dark circles under my eyes that no amount of makeup could hide and my hair had refused to do anything I wanted it to, so it went into a braid.

No more time to fret. It was time to go.

Taking a deep breath, I pulled my braid over my shoulder and hurriedly left my room. I was on the fourth floor of Chapman Hall, and my father stayed across the hall from me. Technically speaking, he had a number of rooms—one he used as a living space, one as an office, one as a viewing room, and the other as his bedroom. Still, I didn't want to run into him.

The rest of the staff occupied the fifth and six floors, and the players were spread out across the top three floors. Last year we were split among dorms, some of which didn't have air conditioning. This year we'd been relocated to the newest and largest dorm. And not only did it accommodate all of us, it also had air conditioning.

Downstairs at the door, I closed my eyes. I could do this. I knew how to take care of injuries like his. I was more than qualified. And yet, I had a sinking sensation in my belly that I couldn't expel.

Once I pushed the door open, I had to squint against the wash of the early morning summer sun and then I finally ventured out.

Olivet's grounds were beautifully landscaped. The sidewalk paths wound their way around the buildings, which were nestled into the trees.

The team practiced on the four grass fields at the very east end. They also used the fitness facilities and meeting rooms in the Douglas E. Perry Student Recreation Center, which was located on the Northeastern side of campus directly across from the practice fields.

I wasn't in a hurry.

Yet I walked as fast as I could across the grounds.

When I found myself inside the large brick building and heading down the hall to the training room, my palms began to sweat. After I wiped them on my gym shorts, I unlocked the door and scolded myself for being nervous.

I could do this.

I could absolutely be in the same room as a hot guy with ripped abs, sinewy muscles, and broad shoulders.

I'd been around men like him my entire life.

So why was he different?

It was dark inside the room, no one was here yet, and I took a moment to breathe deep before flicking on the lights and then emptying my bag.

This room was about half the size of the Bear's Training Room in Chicago, but it was still state-of-the-art. Remodeled a few years ago, it had been designed with the Bears' needs in mind.

"Hey," a deep voice said. "I'm reporting for duty as ordered."

I jumped, turning to see Lucas in the doorway.

His blue gaze practically drank me in and instantly I felt my nipples harden. I was wearing a tank top and feared their protrusion was more than evident. It was just so hard not to notice how gorgeous he was. Even in his grungy state, there was so much raw power emanating from him. Unshaved, and his hair a sexy mess, he wore sweatpants and a Bears T-shirt. A duffle hung from his shoulder in a lopsided way, and it was the first thing I noticed about his condition.

Something about it wasn't right, and I snapped right back into work mode.

"Good morning," I said. "How do you feel today?"

He dropped his duffle to the ground. "Terrific."

"No headaches, nausea, or dizziness?"

"Nope," he said. "How long is this going to take?"

Grabbing a water bottle from the refrigerator and a heart rate monitor from the drawer, I slowly started toward him. "Less than thirty minutes, as long as everything checks out."

His expression grew pensive. "Great. Then let's get this over with so I can get back to what's important."

There was something in his tone that was off. Sure, he was being a smart-ass, but I was used to dealing with that from disgruntled players. It was their coping mechanism. There was something else going on. "This is important, Lucas."

"Yeah, right, of course it is." His voice was cool.

I strode past him and went directly across the hall to the weight room, where I flicked on the lights.

Lucas was obviously in a hurry because he was on my heels.

I tossed him the monitor and then pointed to the treadmill. "Strap that around your chest and then hop on."

Okay, it sounded a little dirty.

At that, he shot me a glance, and I tossed one right back. But then I was momentarily stunned when he stripped his T-shirt off to affix the monitor to his chest. Lucas had the body of a god, and by the smug look he wore, he not only knew it, but he also knew *I* knew it.

Climbing onto the treadmill, he tossed his shirt over the rail. Then he pushed the speed button, and the machine roared to life.

I placed the water bottle in the cup holder in front of him. "Get to a pace you're comfortable with, one you can sustain, and if you start to experience any dizziness or headaches, tell me right away and we'll stop."

"And if I have none?"

With the monitoring device in my hand, I watched his heart rate increase and his blood pressure remain steady. "We'll go for the full twenty minutes."

"And then what, I get a prize?"

I ignored his comment. "No, then, although I can't diagnosis you, I would say you are non-symptomatic."

Giving me a nod, he drank some water from the bottle and after he'd put it back in its place, he programmed the timer. From beside him, I noticed he still appeared to have some lingering neck spasms. Not that unusual after what happened.

About ten minutes later he looked over at me. He didn't speak around his huffing and puffing. That was fine by me because every time his abs and pecs rippled, I couldn't stop myself from thinking about how his sweat would taste if I ran my tongue along the ridge of his ribs or around the concave cup of his belly button.

It was wrong on so many levels.

By the time eighteen minutes passed, his mouth had set into a tight, hard line of determination. Sweat had also coated his entire upper body, but it was far from disgusting.

Ridiculous as it was, I couldn't stop flicking my gaze from the monitor to his muscled thighs and occasionally to the incredibly mesmerizing set of dimples on his back.

God was he sexy.

"Everything cool?" he asked.

No, everything was not cool.

It was hot.

He was hot.

The treadmill beeped, and I blinked out of my very inappropriate thoughts. As the belt slowed, he grabbed his T-shirt and wiped his face, and then he climbed off. Standing with his back to me, he drank thirstily from the water bottle. I was just about to tell him he had the all clear when he bent to touch his toes.

That's when the question came to me. Had I actually hit him in the crown of the head? Or had I hit him at the top of his spine, and that was why those neck spasms were still occurring? Although much milder than yesterday, it appeared it was his shoulder at risk, not his head.

He looked up with a small grin. "Looks like I passed."

"Yes, I would say a concussion isn't the issue."

"Great. I'm out of here. Thanks."

"Lucas?" I asked, distracted, "Where exactly did the water cart come in contact with your body yesterday?"

There was confusion in his stare. "My head, I think. I'm not really sure. It all happened so fast."

I walked over to one of the pieces of equipment meant to strengthen shoulder muscles. "Do you think it could have been your neck or shoulder area, and not your head?"

He shrugged. "I have no idea, but it doesn't really matter. I'm fine."

"I'm not so sure you are. I think we should take a look at the range of motion in both of your shoulders before you go."

"Not necessary," he hissed and started for the door.

"Lucas," I called, "I saw your file."

He whirled around, like he was ready to strike. "And?"

"It states you dislocated your shoulder twice in college."

"So what?"

"The Bears' doctors spotted it during the pre-mini-camp physical."

His glare was ruthless. "It wasn't like I was trying to hide it."

I closed my eyes for a second to recall what it said and then I reopened them. "I understand that, but it was noted." I glanced down at the chart. "In fact, it reads,"

"This 23-year old right-hand dominant quarterback from Notre Dame has a history of dislocating his right shoulder. He is currently asymptomatic. This patient was examined and no waiver is required at this time."

His bottom lip pushed out, as if he was pouting, but he said nothing in response.

"If you don't let me do this," I continued, "I will be forced to voice my concern to Dallas. In turn, he will bring it to my father's attention. And then he will, more than likely, make you sign a waiver. And then your file will read,"

"This 23-year old right-hand dominant quarterback from Notre Dame has a history of right shoulder issues. He is currently symptomatic. This patient was examined and appears to have range of motion debilitation. A waiver is required at this time."

His entire body went taut.

This was hard. I didn't want to do that. I wished none of this had happened. But it had. And I needed to make certain he was okay. So I took a breath and then spoke. "I don't want to be put in a position to have to do something that very well could permanently alter your record. It might not matter to you right now, but if you ever get traded or want to play for a different team, it will matter. So please come over here."

The hard stare wasn't unexpected, but his question was. "Why do you care?"

Turning around, I adjusted the weight on the machine, and then glanced over my shoulder. "Because you wouldn't be here if it wasn't for my carelessness, and because I genuinely want to help you."

Begrudgingly, he strode toward me and took a seat. With only a slight hesitation, he reached for the bar above his head. I saw it immediately, the lack of follow through in his right shoulder compared to his left—in his throwing arm—and I knew he felt it as he pushed the weighted bars out to the side.

"Do it again with a lighter weight this time," I instructed, watching for the aftermath and muscle recovery.

He did so without a word.

While he performed this movement, my fingers probed the spot on the back of his neck that was still slightly swollen. It was right between the third and fourth vertebrae, and the inflammation was definitely causing him some discomfort in his shoulder.

This time he didn't remain quiet. In fact, his voice turned a little husky when he said, "Feel free to move your fingers around the front and then a little lower."

It's hard to explain the mix of fury and desire I felt in that moment. Part of me wanted to do just that, but the smarter part of me felt disrespected, and luckily I was always more analytical than emotional.

I put my mouth right near his ear. "Stop being a colossal dick," I whispered.

His laugh was stealthy, hearty, and so full of himself. "I've been called worse."

"I don't care what you've been called. Talk to me like that again, and I'll be the one walking. And Lucas, trust me when I say, I'm on your side and you don't want that."

For a few short moments the tension between us was off the charts. He stood as if he was about to leave, he even took a step, but then he whirled around with a cocky grin on his face. "Sorry."

That was not an apology.

That attempt at a charming smile more than likely got him what he wanted whenever he used it. And it probably worked on every female, but I wasn't just any female. And I wasn't charmed, not really, well, maybe a little bit. Still, I wasn't going to give him the satisfaction of knowing what his charm did to me. "Does that really work for you?"

He furrowed his brow, and even that was charming. "Does what work?"

I fought the urge to laugh. To scream. To run over and kiss him.

"That wide-eyed innocent smile," I said.

There was no point in denying it any further, so instead he grinned. "Yes, usually, it does."

With the frown that I had to force on my face intact, I placed my hands on my hips. "Don't use it on me again. I don't like it."

This set him back a step, both literally and figuratively, but not for long. A moment later, he lurched forward and then frowned right back me. The look he gave me was fierce and hard.

"I mean it," I added, squaring my shoulders.

In his head I knew he was calling me a bitch and telling me to fuck-off, but I had to set boundaries between us. "I'll try to remember what you like and don't like," he muttered, and I could tell by his tone that he'd started to soften toward me.

Blowing out a breath, I sat where he had been seated not that long ago. "Look, Lucas, you have a range of motion impairment in your right shoulder, more than likely a result of old scar tissue that is now inflamed. With some minor rehab and no further impairment, the inflammation should go down and it should be fine in a week or so. *Should,* being the key word. You could wait and see, or we could be proactive about it."

His smile was slow and deliciously arrogant, but at least it wasn't cocky. "What exactly are you *offering?*"

Just the way he asked sent a shiver down my spine. I chose to ignore his innuendo, otherwise we would get nowhere. "My help, and you should take it."

"Has anyone ever told you that you're very bossy?" he asked, and it was his roundabout way of answering, I supposed.

I snorted soft laughter and nodded my head, giving him an amused glance. "Yes, as a matter of fact, all the time. And?"

"No *and,*" he said. "Just an observation."

This time I smiled. "So are you in or out?"

Okay, that sounded really dirty.

With the sexiest raised brow I'd ever seen, he said, "In. I'm always in."

I let it pass. I'd started that one. "Great, I'll let Dallas know there's nothing to worry about, just a minor shoulder issue and we're working on it."

I hoped that was the case, but I wasn't one hundred percent certain.

"Are we?" he asked.

Still thinking about possible complications, my face went blank.

"Working on it," he grinned.

I nodded and pulled my braid back over my shoulder. "Same time tomorrow. I'll meet you here."

"Yes, ma'am."

I made a face. "Don't call me that."

"Okay, Strawberry Fields, whatever you say," he quipped instead, and then turned on his heel before I could say anything else.

After he was gone, I lingered for a long while remembering my hands on his back and how good he felt under my touch.

Shaking off what could never be, I went back into the training room. There I stared at the bottles and jars of nutritional supplements that cluttered the shelf. Green fuel, protein shakes, vitamins, and antioxidants—all things to help players get stronger, faster, better.

Too bad they would be of no help for what I'd done to my father's star player.

Seven

PUNT

Lucas

I HAD NEVER been one to shy away from contact.

In fact, sometimes I might have even initiated it by lowering my shoulder and barreling into oncoming tacklers, which very well could have been how my shoulder ended up dislocated two years ago, twice.

Hey, I didn't become a football player to act like a pussy and run out of bounds.

Nerves have never been anything I had to worry about. Or at least that had always been the case. I wasn't so sure anymore. I tried to focus on the positive as I pushed open the glass door.

This injury wasn't that bad.

I still had a lot of time to get my arm in top shape before the season.

And yet staying positive didn't help as I walked down the gray hallway of Chapman Hall feeling like I was headed to the gallows.

Then again, I had to remember that I was in better shape than most of the guys. My locker neighbor needed three Tylenol PM capsules to close his eyes last night. I only needed two. Another player lost ten pounds yesterday from stress, exhaustion, and loss of appetite. I only lost five.

See the trend.

Better.

Stronger.

Faster.

Then again, yesterday had been chaotic, and not only for the players. The trainers had a rough time of it as well. Even with their belts on, they couldn't keep track of their scissors and kept running out of athletic tape. When Dallas wasn't glued to his notepad, he was giving us all rehab tips, taping pointers, and injury prevention suggestions.

It didn't help that the coaches were blowing their whistles on top of one another and the players were confused as fuck.

Everything was out of control.

The bottom line was we were all trying to perform at our highest level and doing the best we could to make sure of it.

I wasn't the only one with a slight injury. Problem, I mean.

Sure we all trained during the offseason, but it took being here for it to become glaringly clear we hadn't trained enough.

Yesterday there were countless muscle strains and sprains—hamstrings, ankles, hips, glutes, calves, knees.

So it seemed, it sucked for everyone, not just me.

My sneakers thumped noisily on the linoleum as I took the stairs and practically raced up them. When I reached the fourth floor, I paused for a moment.

A feeling of déjà vu washed over me. I'd done this once before, but that was when I didn't have my head on straight. Now that I did, it didn't seem fair for it all to be taken away.

Because of my actions yesterday, this mandated meeting with Coach could change my entire life. And now that I'd had a taste, I wanted to stay and wear an official NFL jersey . . . for the Bears.

The Bears.

Things had changed over the past few months, and I'd grown to realize how much I really did want to be here.

The dorm room that served as Jack's office was closed. I stood there for a minute or two before I nervously knocked on it. "Come on in," he bellowed from inside, his voice already intimidating as fuck.

Slowly, I opened the door and looked around.

The room was so different from that at Soldier Field. It was empty except for a desk and a few chairs. The college-sized furniture looked dwarfed with Jack behind it. He had an iPad in front of him and he was eating. "Sit down," he said through a mouthful of food.

I did as instructed. "Those look good." I pointed to the plate on his desk. "What are they?"

"Fish tacos," he answered, pushing his food aside.

"For breakfast?" I was trying to ease into whatever this was about.

He nodded briskly. "I eat them whenever," he paused. I didn't say anything because he looked as if his mind had wandered far away, then he blinked and went on. "Whenever I . . . need to remember that day."

"What's *that day*?" I asked curiously, now just putting off the inevitable.

He shook his head, dismissing my question, and got up from behind his desk. "Look, Lucas, as you already know, I'm the sort of man who doesn't like to bullshit around, so I'm going to get to the point."

Like father like daughter, I thought, but kept that little ditty to myself. "I appreciate that."

Coach Whitney sat in the empty seat beside me. "I asked to see you for a reason, and it's because I have a few important questions to ask you."

I swallowed hard. "Okay, shoot." I tried to sound calm, but I was anything but.

His face darkened and he looked between his desk and me as if trying to figure something out. "Are you stupid?"

My fists clenched at my sides. "No!"

"Do you not understand English, then?"

"I do!"

"Then, you should comprehend, that when I said you needed an attitude adjustment, I meant it. You. Need. An. Attitude. Adjustment."

"Coach, I—" I tried to explain I had changed. Saw the light. Found God. However the fuck he wanted to say it.

He cut me off. "Did I make a mistake taking a chance on you?"

My eyebrows popped up. "No," I said immediately. "Why do you think that?" The confusion was evident in my voice because not only was I in top shape, but also I was throwing like a seasoned pro.

He cut a hand up in the air and glared at me. "I'm asking the questions!"

I nodded, keeping my mouth shut.

Reaching across the desk, he grabbed his iPad, which he had paused at one of my interviews from Notre Dame. It was the one where I told the sportscaster that if it weren't for football, I'd probably have ended up in prison.

Coach played that snippet for me. It's not like he had to. I knew it well. Knew the facial expressions I made and the mood I was in when I gave the interview. Remembered the look on my brother's face and the regret I immediately felt afterwards, too.

When the video ended, I looked over to Coach and flat out told him, "What I should have said was that if it wasn't for my brother, Nick, I would have ended up in prison. Nick is the one who taught me how to channel my aggression, to use football as my outlet."

This confession caught him off guard, and it took him a moment to speak. "Look, son, football is supposed to give your life structure and meaning. But you have to want it, I mean *really* want it."

"I do."

His expression softened. "You might not know this about me, but I grew up not far from where you did. When I heard you talking about what it was like for you, I knew exactly how you felt. Shit, I was you. The only difference, I didn't go around bad mouthing Chicago."

"Coach—" I tried to say.

With a fierce expression, he threw a hand up again.

I shut the fuck up.

In his khaki pants, he crossed one leg over the other. "If I'm going to be honest with you, I saw a bit of myself in you. The hunger. The need. The fearlessness. I thought all that bullshit you were spewing about Chicago was just that, bullshit," he said with a sigh.

He wasn't wrong.

He went on. "I thought that I could be the one to change your mind. Make you realize the best way to come full circle in your life was to prove yourself in the city that tried to bring you down. Even after mini-camp, I still had hope."

Hope?

He shook his head. "But after yesterday's little stunt, I'm not so sure."

I chose my words carefully. "I promise you, Coach, you didn't make a mistake."

He nodded, solemnly. "Another question."

This time I nodded.

"How bad do you want this?"

This answer came straight from my heart. "It's the only thing I've ever wanted in my life."

Setting the iPad down, he uncrossed his legs and turned his body in my direction. "That doesn't answer my question."

"Really bad!" I answered loudly.

"Bad enough to let all of your bullshit go? Put your mommy and daddy issues aside and focus on that ball?"

Had anyone said anything like that to me in the locker room, they would have gotten a fist in their face. As it was, I could feel myself getting worked up, but somehow managed to grunt through it. "Yes, Coach."

He shook his head. "Say it, Carrington. Tell me what you're willing to do. Tell me you're going to stop all the whining and crying and boohooing, and make yourself the best Goddamn quarterback there ever was."

All I could do was stare at him in fury. "I put that behind me months ago."

His voice rose. "After that little stunt yesterday, I'm not so sure. So I want to hear it! Tell me!"

Fuck, I wanted to punch him. Punch the desk, or the wall, or window. I didn't make a move, though, instead I stared at him stonily.

In an unexpected move, he jumped to his feet and took me with him by the collar of my shirt. "Tell me right now, or get the fuck out of my camp."

Rage smoldered through me like wildfire, and it took everything I had to bite out each word because I wasn't going anywhere. "I will focus on the game and put my mommy and daddy bullshit behind me, Coach," I yelled. "I will put my team first, and I will do everything I can to bring the Bears all the way."

His expression was still uneasy, but he was somewhat pacified because he rounded the desk and flopped back in his chair. "Now that that is settled," he said firmly, "there's one more thing."

Fucking great, here comes the *stay away from my daughter or I'll have your balls for breakfast* line. I heaved in a breath, ready to be sucker punched, and I wasn't even sure why it mattered that much. There was just something about her and I knew no matter how hard I tried, I wasn't going to be able to stay away.

"I know you've been cleared for training," he said.

Okay, anticlimactic or what. Not at all what I was expecting, the shock must have shown on my face as I sat back down.

He pointed his finger at me. "And I don't want to know anything else that I absolutely don't have to know. Do you understand me?"

Shit, Gillian had said something; then again, of course she did, but not enough to flag me. I should thank her.

I nodded.

I got it.

If my injury wasn't severe, I shouldn't discuss it with him because that would force his hand. Make him do something about it, like bench me. We all knew if Coach knew something that should be reported but wasn't, and the Commissioner found out about it, the entire team would suffer.

"One more thing. I need to talk to you about training," he said.

"What about it?"

"Johnny isn't going to make camp."

Frustration lined my face. Although I would never admit it out loud, I needed a coach.

Jack pushed his chair back. "His wife was recently diagnosed with cancer and she has been given less than a year to live. That means he won't be coming back this season. He wants to spend as much time as he can with her, and then be there when the Lord calls her home."

"Jesus," I whispered, and instantly regretted it. Obviously Coach was a religious man. "I mean that sucks—" I attempted to say more, but just shut my mouth.

He was shaking his head at me. "That means I'm taking over his role for camp. I should have his replacement in place before the regular season begins."

My eyes bugged out of my head. Old Johnny was a ball-buster, but he also knew when to let up and when to let us have fun. Coach Whitney, shit, all I knew was that I, no *we*, were in for it. "That sounds . . . great."

This made him laugh, loud and hearty. "Get the fuck out of here, will you, I have work to do." That was one order I wasn't going to argue about, not that I would be arguing about anything with Coach, any time soon.

Hey, big tough guy or not, when your head was on the chopping block, you learned when to reel your shit in.

And fast.

Eight

HUDDLE

Gillian

SOMETHING VIBRATED IN my bed.

Not an unusual occurrence for a woman who had been single for nearly a year, but this time it wasn't my Rabbit. I heard the buzzing from my bathroom as I was brushing my teeth, and I raced toward it with my heart thundering.

Typing out the text message should have been a no brainer. Composing exactly what to say to a guy who did crazy things to your body when he was around though, proved to be much more difficult than I thought it would.

Then again, with each sentence I tried to compose, I had trouble. I kept picturing his hard, lean muscled frame, the heat of his skin beneath my fingertips whenever I touched him, the flash in his eyes that I would catch every once in a while, and then there was that easy smile. It was the one thing I could never look away from.

For absolutely no reason, my hands trembled as I typed,

backspaced, typed again, and then once again backspaced. At that pace, it had taken me so long to get the message just right I never hit send until nearly nine thirty.

And after I did, I had gone into full out panic mode.

Everything I was thinking, feeling, wondering about—it was wrong. Lucas was a player for the team I was interning with. It might not have been written in my contract to maintain platonic relations with the players, but I had been around football my entire life. To pretend I didn't know it would be stupid. And I was anything but stupid.

What had I done?

I wished I could delete the sent text.

After having tossed my phone on my bed, I had rushed into the bathroom to see if the girl staring back was still me, and not some smitten version of myself I didn't understand.

Thank God, I only saw me.

That's when I grabbed my toothbrush and figured I'd go to bed, this way when he answered me, I wouldn't be awake to respond.

It was nine forty and curfew was at eleven fifteen. If it was Lucas responding to my text, it wasn't like we'd have much time together, so it couldn't really hurt, could it?

But what was his response?

Yes.

No.

Kiss off.

When hell freezes over.

After I'd put him in his place the first day we met in the training center, things had been easier between us, but not exactly easy. There was a constant push and pull, and the space between us was filled with an odd electrical charge.

I think we both liked it that way.

Digging through the sheets, I found my phone right where I'd tossed it and closed my eyes, not ready to look at the screen.

I was being completely ridiculous. It wasn't like I was asking him if he wanted to go on a date. This was work.

We'd met the past three mornings in the weight training room. His range of motion was improving. While discussing our progress with Dallas after dinner tonight, he gave me an off-the-books suggestion.

What I was doing with Lucas wasn't anything anyone wanted to know specifics about, Dallas included. But he did know, kind of, since I posed it as a hypothetical the day I discovered Lucas's shoulder problem.

He suggested I see Lucas's arm in motion, real motion . . . like as he threw the football. That's when I decided to ask him if he wanted to meet me.

The text that took nearly an hour to compose read:

> *Me: Lucas, this is Gillian. I was wondering if you wanted to meet at Ward Field and throw the ball around. I think it would help if I could see you in action.*

His response had me rolling my eyes. It read:

> *Him: In action?*

> *Me: Yes, as in, in motion.*

> *Him: Are you asking me out?*

Even with no one in the room, I felt my cheeks blaze, but then I regained my composure and replied.

> *Me: No, this isn't a date. Stop being a dick. Do you want to meet or not?*

> *Him: Tell me you miss me and you want to see me, and then*

I'll answer you.

Me: Never.

Him: Then at least stop calling me a dick.

Me: Never.

Me: ☺

Me: I'm giving you five seconds to respond with a yes or no.

Him: Or what? You'll spank me?

Me: Four seconds until I turn my phone off.

Him: What are you going to wear?

What was I going to wear?

Me: Three seconds.

Him: Will you wear your hair down, at least?

It was down. I could do that. I just needed to fix it.

Me: Two seconds, and I'm going to bed.

Him: I could join you.

Me: Goodnight, Lucas.

Him: Relax. I'm trying to have some fun. I just got out of the shower. I'll be there as soon as I get dressed.

At that, I smiled to myself and didn't respond. Instead, I scrambled to the small accordion closet and rummaged through it to find something to wear.

Even though this technically was work, I didn't want to wear work clothes. Those tended to make me look either frumpy or young, depending on which version I chose.

Not that I should care.

This was going to be physical. I had to be able to move around. So jeans were out. Shorts might be too much. Obviously a summer dress wouldn't be practical, even a T-shirt one, and besides, then this really *would* look like a date.

Which it absolutely was not.

In the end, I settled on a pair of lightweight black yoga pants and a matching cropped exercise top. With a thin white T-shirt over the top and my Converse, I felt comfortable.

I had the clothes because I taught yoga, and in fact, very soon I was going to be teaching the football players downward dog. In all honesty, I couldn't wait. It was going to be so fun.

Before leaving I looked in the mirror. Turning my chin to one side, then the other, I caught my profile. Yes, it was still me looking back in the reflection. I hadn't morphed into someone I didn't know. I wasn't one of those girls who got all dolled up for a boy.

Not yet, anyway.

I still had the same strawberry blond hair as my mother and the same green eyes as my father. I still had the same narrow hips and the same skinny legs as I always had. Sure, my arms were more toned, my belly flatter, and I was much taller, but none of that seemed to matter.

I had grown up, but when I was at camp, I still felt like that pigtailed little girl my father kept close.

That hadn't changed either.

He was across the hall, and if the door was open, I'd have to tell him where I was going. I hoped it wasn't.

Just before I was about to leave, I couldn't help but catch a glimpse of the way my nipples pushed through the fabric of both thin layers. Even with the sports top that acted as a bra, it was noticeable.

I had no doubt he'd notice. His eyes would go right to my chest, regardless of how very small it was. His eyes. On me.

I didn't change.

All of the doors across the hall were closed, and when I saw that, I wanted to run, but settled on walking fast and taking the stairs.

The weather was so much nicer at night than during the day. The air was light and clear and warm. Bearable, as opposed to unbearable. Because of this, I took my time as I made my way toward the college's football field.

It was south of campus, and rather isolated, so I was fairly certain no one would stumble across us.

I looked up to the clear sky with its shining stars and full moon. I was going to miss all of this. Not only the hectic days of training camp, but the quiet nights that followed as well.

When I walked through the metal gates, he was already there. He wasn't looking my way. What he was doing was gripping a football with his right hand, and standing tall on the perfectly manicured turf like he owned it.

He looked like he did.

A slow, tumbling roll of sensation centered in my belly. I considered walking away and not even letting him know I'd come because this really was a bad idea. I already knew I couldn't do that, though.

I couldn't.

The moment my feet hit the plush blades of grass, he turned toward me with a smile so wide and bright and genuine that I felt the strangest pitter-patter in my chest.

I didn't like it.

I liked it.

I was so confused.

Lucas was wearing cleats, gray sweats, and a Notre Dame jersey.

Nothing out of the ordinary. What was different though from our morning therapy sessions was he had shaven and it actually looked like he might have styled his hair.

I wanted to lick his jaw and run my fingers through his locks.

That would be wrong on so many levels though. Wouldn't it? Instead of doing anything even close, I gave him the barest hint of a smile. "Hi."

It was then I noticed the half dozen balls on the field.

He had gotten here quick, and right to work.

"Watch this." Scanning the field as if in the middle of a game, he pretended to lock on a receiver, and then he fully cocked his arm and pushed the ball away from his body in what was almost a perfect throwing motion. *Almost.*

"That was great," I called as I continued to walk toward him.

He shook his head in disgust. "It was short." He picked up another ball. This time he dropped his arm back like a fulcrum, and then circled around making a bit of an overhead swinging motion.

I wasn't certain where exactly he was aiming, but it didn't look quite right. "I've seen better," I said.

That comment pissed him off, and he picked up the last ball at his feet. This time he managed to get a great extension behind his body and he came up and over in a nice arc. The problem was, that type of delivery was slow and not as accurate as the tight motion he should have been using.

Then again, he couldn't, not yet.

It wasn't that I was trying to be a quarterback coach, but I'd watched my father for years, and he was one of the best quarterbacks, after all.

I gestured to the field where the last ball sat. "That one wasn't bad."

He crossed his arms over his chest. "It wasn't great, either."

There was this look of vulnerability about him I'd never seen, and I wanted to hug him.

Do. Not. Touch.

Changing direction, I jogged out onto the field and gathered the balls in an armful, and then hurried back to drop them at his feet. "Do that first one again, but with more power."

"You're lucky I don't get insulted easily," he told me, narrowing his stare.

"Sorry, just being honest," I said without remorse.

His gaze grew even more piercing.

"Please," I added to pacify him.

The sucking up seemed to work because he bent that powerful body of his down and picked up another ball. I shouldn't have been watching him the way I was. Looking at his physique like I wanted to eat him, but he was so damn beautiful. The tight coil of muscles that marked his arms, the way he moved, the power he had. It was intoxicating.

Heat shot into my cheeks, and I took a step to the side. With some distance between us, I blinked those thoughts away and concentrated on watching the movement of his shoulder. Just like a slingshot, he pulled his arm back, released, and the ball propelled downfield.

With my blush gone, I clapped my hands together. "That was so much better."

Ignoring me, he picked up another ball, and another, and another still. Using the same motion, he continued to arc the ball, but on the last one, the pullback wasn't quite there. The swollen tissue was obviously impacting his range of motion.

When he was done, he turned to face me. "What? No more comments from the peanut gallery?"

I looked sideways at him. "I don't have to say anything. Your eyes are saying it all after every throw."

He snorted. "Uh-huh. Right."

"They are," I insisted, trying not to giggle.

Giggle.

How pathetic.

"Then tell me what they're saying."

The response was blurted out, meant to challenge me, and I was going to bite. "What I see is that you want to do better. That you know you can do better. That you will do better. You just have to keep trying."

After shooting a quick glance at the balls on the field, he looked over at me and grinned. "That sounds a lot like therapist mumbo jumbo, but it's not a bad assessment."

"I'll take that as an apology," I laughed.

He stared at me with uncertainty.

"You doubted me."

"No, not you."

He didn't say *me*, but I felt like it was on the tip of his tongue. "Don't worry . . . I'll get you there," I said.

"What are you? Eeyore?"

This time, I burst into laughter. It was loud. Unfettered. And I stifled it with my hand when he grinned at me. "You know the lines from Winnie The Pooh?"

His blue eyes bore into mine, and for half a minute nothing else existed. There was something primal in his gaze, and it made me feel extremely vulnerable. If there had been any doubt this was dangerous, the doubt was gone. He stepped closer. "Does that surprise you?"

I swallowed hard, nodding. "It does."

He purposely slid his gaze lazily down my body. "I wish it didn't."

My heart rate picked up, the blood rushing in my ears. "I'll keep that in mind."

With each passing moment, it felt as though he was stripping me naked. When he reached and took a piece of my hair to twirl it around his finger, I wondered if he felt the same crazy chemistry that I did. "You wore it down. I like it."

That pitter-patter in my chest turned into a thump. "I did, but just so you know, I didn't wear it like this because you told me to, it was already down."

"I'm sure it was." The grin he gave me was sly, knowing, charming. Before I could remind him not to use that on me, he slid his free hand into the open side slit of my shirt, right onto my bare skin beneath my cropped top. "I like this too. It makes you look—sexy." He let the word hang in the air.

Again I submitted to laughter and reveled in it. "As opposed to when I'm not."

His gaze had turned thoughtful, probing. "You are never, not."

Just then a mosquito landed on my arm, and I stepped back to swat it away with a slap. This put some space between us, but not much.

He lifted the hem of his shirt to wipe a trickle of blood from my arm that puddled from the bite. I was closer to his bare torso than ever. Sure, his belly was tight, taut, with a light single line of hair trailing from his navel into the waist band of his low-hanging sweat pants, but this close, his belly button looked like pure perfection. I wondered how a dip and hollow could be so perfect.

"Thank you." My breathing was loud.

His was too. "You smell good. What is the scent? I can't quite place it?" he asked, coming closer once again and breathing in the air around me.

"It's called Clementine California. I get it from an organic skin care boutique in Gainesville."

He pressed his nose into the long strands of my hair. "It's really nice."

The first time I saw him I had been attracted to him. I'd thought it had been because I'd been away from football for almost a year and I was craving anything to do with it, or even perhaps because I hadn't been with anyone in so long, and he had turned me on so easily.

Here, though, now, I knew neither of those were the case. I knew I wanted him because of *him*, and I also knew I shouldn't.

Yet, that didn't stop me from leaning into him as he leaned forward. That didn't stop me from looking into his eyes. He swallowed, meeting my gaze, and breathed out without saying anything.

My pulse was racing.

All of a sudden it was really bright as each and every light turned on. "Hey!" a bellowing voice boomed from somewhere up in the stadium. "You shouldn't be down there!"

Lucas grabbed my hand in a flurry and started for the gate. "Come on, Strawberry Fields. Time to get out of here."

"But your balls," I said, without thinking of how it sounded.

He laughed heartily as he interlocked our fingers. "No worries. I got the only two I need."

"You are too much," I gasped, as my legs moved quickly to keep up the pace.

He shot me a coy glance over his shoulder, and looked like he wanted to say something, but didn't.

Lucas was a good six inches taller than me, and he was also so much bigger. Not that I was worried. I trusted him. Still, heading into the woods with someone I barely knew wasn't something I would normally do. Then again, none of this was.

In the years I'd been around football, the only players I ever hung around were the married ones with kids. That was probably because those were the only ones my father wanted me around.

Before I'd gone to college, I was too young to be interested in any of them anyway. Once I went to college, I was only around for training camp, and everyone was busy then, including me. I always had some kind of odd job, unofficially, to keep me busy.

Being with Lucas now like I was, it was a first. Here, in this setting, with my father so close, anyway. In college I'd dated more than a few guys and even had a couple of boyfriends. None I ever brought home. None that made my heart flutter the way Lucas did. And none that had a body anything like Lucas's.

They were boys.

He was a man.

The path he led me to wasn't one I'd ever seen. It was south of the field and once we cleared the blinding lights of the stadium, he stopped.

Winded from our escape, I bent down with my hands on my knees and attempted to catch my breath. When I did, I heard the sound of rushing water. "Where are we?"

He pointed to where the noise was coming from. "Let me show you."

At first I didn't move.

"Come on," he said, and then walked toward the sound.

I followed him through some trees and brush. A few times he pushed limbs out of the way, holding them for me to pass.

This did feel like a date, but I would never tell him that.

Soon we'd reached an outcrop of rock, big slabs of it poking from the clear water.

Lucas bent to untie the laces of his cleats.

"What are you doing?"

He pulled his shoes off. "Getting ready to walk through the stream."

"The stream?" I asked.

"Yeah, it leads to the Kankakee River."

Surprised I never knew it was here, I watched him as he pulled his socks off and tucked them inside his cleats. "How'd you find this place?"

"Stumbled across it when I went for a run the first night of camp.

Take your shoes off and follow me. I want to show you something."

Toeing off one of my Converse, I reached back to pull my sock off and found myself a little off balance.

Lucas lunged for me, but I landed on my ass, first.

"I'm fine," I said.

Knowing this, he laughed, and offered me his hand. "Have you been drinking? Is that why you asked me out?"

I made a face at him, and batted his arm away, hopping to my feet myself. "I did not ask you out."

He raised a brow that I easily saw with the gleam of light still spilling over from the stadium. "You sort of did."

"Whatever," I huffed and brushed the dirt from my rear before I began to remove my other sneaker and sock, more carefully this time.

With a shrug, he said, "Don't you teach balance classes?"

"Balance classes?" I asked.

"Yoga, whatever."

I snickered. "I do teach Yoga. How'd you know that?"

He looked a little sheepish. "Your father's secretary stopped in his office during one of our quarterback meetings, and asked him about it. She was preparing his schedule, and wanted to know if he would be participating in your class."

My mouth opened wide. "My father in yoga class?"

Lucas snorted and took a step in the water. "Yeah, right? Don't worry, he said no."

"Thank God," I blew out.

"Yeah, Old Jack in a downward dog might be a little disturbing." He said this while he took his first step in the stream.

The stream appeared narrow and not very deep. "How about you? Can you do that yoga move?"

He waved me toward him. "You'll have to wait and see."

Something that felt like anticipation rushed through my veins as my toes sank into the warm water and I headed in his direction. "Where are we going, anyway?"

"Keep your pants on. It's right up here."

How could I not laugh? This was so far from a date. I mean he was talking to me like I was a dude. Through my snicker, I followed close, and I knew we were there before he said anything. Up above was a rickety wooden bridge that spanned the widest part of the stream. It looked like an old relic someone had forgotten about long ago.

Lucas stopped walking and held out his hand. "Come on, I'll help you up the rocks. You can practically see the entire campus from up there."

Light shone from the road somewhere ahead, and I used the glow to step carefully up the rocks until I could reach his outstretched hand. A spark of electricity jolted through my body when our fingers touched, and it gave me a moment of pause. When I glanced down, I spotted something shiny and bent to pick it up.

"What's that?" Lucas asked, leaning down from his place above me.

"I'm not sure. I'll check when we get to the bridge."

With a shrug, he turned back and led me up the side of the quarry and then across the rickety old bridge. There was a green rope for a railing and he was careful with his steps until we reached the very center, where he plopped down and let his legs dangle over it.

I did the same.

"See, look over there." He pointed to the campus, where the stadium lights continued to cast a glow over the field.

"Wow," I told him, mesmerized by the picture of rolling hills and old buildings that made the campus appear to be a magical place. "It looks so tranquil."

"Yeah," he said, his gaze on me and not where he had just pointed.

The bridge creaked, and when I went to hold onto the rope, I remembered the rock in my palm and opened it. The shiny piece of broken gravel had worn into a shape that looked very similar to a football. I traced the outline and held my palm out. "Look, it's a football."

He took it, and I thought he was careful not to touch my skin when he did. Then he held the rock up, examining it like it might have been a diamond. "Cool," he finally said, and I could tell he meant it.

When he went to hand it back to me, I pushed it back toward him. "You keep it. It's good luck."

There was a surprised look on his face. "I can't. You found it."

"And I'm giving it to you."

We stared at each other like we were each that magical place we had been looking at moments ago.

The bridge creaked in the wind again, and when I held onto the rope, so did he. I thought about holding on to him instead, but I didn't.

"Tell me something about you that I don't know?" I asked, glancing back toward the campus because all I really wanted to do was kiss him.

Somehow the movement of the bridge had shifted us closer together, and our outer thighs were touching. Lucas glanced down, noticing, but not moving away. "You first."

I didn't hesitate. "I love football."

He smiled at me. "You don't say."

I ducked my head for a moment, but then looked back. "No, you don't understand. I love everything about it from the beginning to the end of the season."

His gaze traveled over my face.

I wasn't finished. "During the off season I can't wait for the new season to start. I'm like a kid waiting for Christmas."

His voice was soft. "Really? I would think being the coach's kid, you'd like it when you didn't have to be on the road."

The shake of my head was more than slight. "Not at all. My father has always had this thing about us being normal. You know, sitting down for dinner at a normal time, going grocery shopping like normal people, even taking out the trash."

Lucas laughed. "Like normal people."

"I'm serious. The thing was I never liked normal. During the off-season he was around after school, and wanted to know why I wasn't hanging out with my friends. I couldn't tell him I didn't have any. No one wanted to be friends with the new girl. And I was *always* the new girl."

"Shit," he said. "You moved around a lot, didn't you?"

"We did, but here's the thing, I never cared about the moving. I can remember being a little girl sitting in the box with whoever had been assigned to watch me, and just watching my father play. Even though he would be charged at, pounced on, and sometimes tackled, I could never look away. I loved it. What I hated was going to school and being away from it all."

His head was down, but he swung his gaze my way. "I think everyone hated school when they were younger."

I met his gaze. "No, I loved the work, hated the place. When I was fourteen I told my father I was quitting and that I would get my GED. He went out of his mind. In the end, we compromised on a full-time tutor. At the age of seventeen, I graduated high school and started applying to colleges. By then my father was coaching and moving around a lot, so I had no choice but to leave him."

"How many places have you lived?"

"Too many to count," I joked. "And you?"

"Only two. Just Chicago and South Bend."

"But I bet you've at least traveled out of the country." I said this almost enviously.

He shook his head. "Never."

"Never?"

"Never. I haven't really ever gone on vacation to be honest with you."

This astonished me. "Me neither. Only where football took us."

"Where do you want to go?" he asked, and this surprised me.

I looked up at the stars and said rather dreamily, "Paris. I really want to see the Eiffel Tower. I'm planning on going after I graduate in December."

"Alone?"

I nodded. "During the off-season my father likes to nest." This I said with a laugh.

His brows furrowed. "Nest?"

"Yes, you know, make his house feel like a real home. He's always been that way."

"Interesting," Lucas snickered.

"He just bought a place in Lake Forest and is moving in after the season is over. He's having it decorated right now. This time I don't think he'll ever move again."

"That's almost an hour from Chicago."

"I now, but he has an apartment in the city for the days he doesn't want to commute."

"What about your mother? Where is she?"

There was this empty feeling I got whenever I talked about her. I never knew her, so I couldn't say I loved her, yet I know I would have. "She died the day I was born."

He looked down. "Shit. I'm sorry. I had no idea."

Our shoulders touched. "Most people don't," I whispered, and then I told him what happened. Something I rarely talked about with anyone.

"So is that what your father calls *the day*?" he asked, swinging his gaze back to mine.

"The day?"

"Yeah, you know, the reason he eats fish tacos?"

I gave him a blank look. Clueless. "I have no idea what you're talking about. I've never seen him eat fish tacos. Maybe you have the wrong person?"

"Yeah, probably," he said, looking away.

It was time to shift the conversation to him. "What about you? Where in Chicago do you live?"

This clearly made him uncomfortable. "My brother and his wife have a house in Lincoln Park. I've been staying with them and their two kids, soon to be three, whenever I come back to Chicago."

"Are you close with your brother?"

He nodded. "More than close. He practically raised me. My mother left us when I was a baby, and my father fell apart when she did. If it weren't for Nick . . . well." He shut up, and shrugged it off.

Noticing he didn't want to say anymore about it, I let it go. "I've always wished I had a sibling," I said, pushing my knee tighter against his.

His hand was squeezing the rope beside mine, and he slid it toward me. Now both our legs and hands were touching as we gazed over the campus. "Well, I owe my brother everything. It wasn't until I was fifteen that he started to make money. Before that, we had nothing. If I needed a new pair of cleats, he ate macaroni and cheese for the month. If I wanted to go to football camp, he worked two shifts at the construction site. He gave up whatever he had to for me."

I looked over at him. "Your brother sounds like a really special person."

Lucas's head turned in my direction. "He is."

We both leaned closer, and I knew he was going to kiss me. And I knew I was going to let him. To feel his mouth on mine was something I wanted and I wasn't going to turn away.

There was this look in his eyes, hot and consuming, and it made my insides feel like they were melting, all liquid, as if they were running hot and torrid.

Our lips were so close, not even a breath away. Just as each of us leaned in a little closer to make contact, the clock tower from the campus started to chime.

"Curfew!" I said in alarm.

Like lightning, he hopped to his feet, and when he did, the bridge rocked. I went to grab the rope for stability, but he took my hand. "I got you," he said.

And he did. That only made me melt all over again. "We have to hurry." He never let go of my hand no matter how much I protested. I didn't have a curfew. He did. I could run fast, but he could run much faster. Still, he wouldn't leave me behind. We reached the dorms with our shoes in our hands and only minutes to spare.

"You go." I tried to push him toward the door.

He stood solid. "You first," he insisted.

What I did next was impulsive. Stupid. I hadn't thought it through. Instead, I just popped up on my toes and kissed him right on the mouth before taking off. "I had fun," I called, looking back at him one last time before opening the door.

That wasn't so smart. Then again nothing I had done tonight was. Was it?

I didn't wait for him to answer. Besides, I didn't think he would. Inside the dorm, I ran to the stairs and up them as fast as I could. I was thinking the entire time . . . tonight did kind of feel like a date.

My father would blow a gasket if he knew. Twenty-three or not, he wouldn't like me hooking up with one of his players. Or any player for that matter. He had a thing about that. He always warned me to stay away from them. Told me he wanted me to marry someone normal, have a house, a yard, and two kids. *Be normal.* I always laughed and told him he was crazy. I had too much to accomplish in my life to let a man weigh me down. That always made him smile.

What I didn't tell him, what he'd never understand was . . .

I didn't want normal.

Nine

Rush

Lucas

NO SEX DURING training camp.

It wasn't a team rule for the Bears, not yet anyway. But after the Rams coach cut a player last season when he invited a woman into his dorm room, everyone around here was waiting for the addendum to be posted, the meeting to be called, the hammer to fall.

Hey, I got it. Rules were rules, and breaking a team rule was a fireable offense. After all, training camp was designed to give focus, and insubordination indicated a lack of discipline.

But did wanting to fuck a woman mean you weren't committed? *Fuck no!* Besides, how was having intercourse with the opposite sex any worse than staying up late watching porn and masturbating?

The answer was . . . it wasn't.

Not my place to point that out. And at least the whole no sex thing wasn't a team rule that I had to worry about breaking—not yet anyway.

But was what I wanted to do even worse than breaking a rule? I wanted to fuck Gillian, and she was not only the coach's daughter, but also an intern for the team I was now a part of.

She was forbidden fruit.

It didn't get more off-limits than that.

Did it?

The truth was, for the first time in my life, I was worried about doing the wrong thing. In the past, what I wanted I always went after one way or another. I knew I could have her, but what would that do to her reputation?

Ruin it?

I didn't want to put her in that position.

I'd asked a few of the returning players about her. No one said much, no one commented. Nothing negative. Nothing defamatory. Good thing for them too. She was quiet. Nice. Beautiful. And everyone around here seemed to respect her.

Perhaps I should do the same.

Seconds before the hall lights flicked off, I flung my door open with a million thoughts of Gillian scattering through my mind, and the feel of her lips against mine still burning in my brain.

What the hell was I going to do?

As soon as I shut the door, I made the mistake of looking to my left and found myself staring right at Thor's balls. At least his hand was covering his dick.

"Oh, baby, don't stop. Make it last all night," he gritted out with his phone lying beside him on his pillow.

"Fucking A, Thor!" I yelled as I whizzed by, flying into the bathroom. "Next time give me some kind of warning," I shouted before slamming the door.

Sitting on the closed lid of the toilet, I turned on the shower to block out the noise and then cradled my head in my hands.

She was pure temptation.

The way she spoke.

The way she moved.

The way she laughed and the way she made me laugh.

What she did to me.

The semi I was sporting from sitting so close to her on the bridge was throbbing in my pants.

Since I was stuck in here until Thor got his rocks off, which by the sounds of things was going to be never, I was left with no choice but to do the same.

Too bad I couldn't make a booty call, but I wouldn't even if I could. I wasn't going to do that. I was going to grow up and think of someone besides myself for once.

The mirror started to fog up and I still couldn't stop thinking about her and the way she made me laugh tonight. The way she called me on my shit. The way I felt so comfortable around her.

I'd had my share of girls, but I never talked to any of them like they were friends of mine. I had a goal, and I didn't let anything or anyone get in my way. Women could only drag you down. Look what happened to my old man. Ruined after my mother left. Because of this, I always kept the girls in my life an arm's distance away.

Fuck, I should be more like my brother. He'd tell me to fuck that shit and deal with what you have. And he wouldn't be wrong.

Stripping off my clothes, I was harder than a rock the moment I let myself think about her—her perfect body and how much I wanted to be with her. I stepped in the pint-sized shower with my cock in my hand, but I wanted it to be her hand curling around me and feeling how hard she made me.

It was wrong.

I knew it was.

The thing was, I couldn't stop myself. I closed my eyes and gently rubbed first around my cock, then my balls.

Fuck, that felt good.

I started to picture her with me—in the shower with me, us exploring each other's body for the first time. Fuck, I wanted to feel her hands gripping me. Her lips kissing me. Her legs wrapping around me.

My fist pumped at a quicker pace, and as I licked the water from my lips, I thought of her hair, her face, her body . . . the ways I wanted to touch her, where I wanted to touch her, how I wanted to touch her. Then, in a way I knew was so wrong, I imagined driving my cock into her sweet pussy and when I did, it made me want to come hard and fast.

The pressure welled deep, and a tingling radiated from my cock. As my orgasm started to build, so did the contractions—it felt like electricity shooting through me.

When my dick twitched, I couldn't hold on any longer. As I started to come, practically spasming in my hold, the incredible feeling built and I finally let myself go. That's when I crossed that threshold over and over until I was spent.

My chest rose and fell and I slouched back against the shower thinking about how many hours it was until I would see her.

Once my breathing returned to normal, I lathered up with soap, rinsed it off, and got out.

Wrapping a towel around my waist, I listened at the door and heard nothing from the room. Thor must have been done.

Ready for bed, I wiped the steam from the mirror and gave myself a quick look. Blue eyes and brown hair reflected back, and I tried to see the good in them. The part of me I had buried long ago, or maybe the part of me I never bothered to uncover.

I hoped it was there, because if not . . . I was so fucked.

And not in the good way.

Ten

FUMBLE

Gillian

IT WAS SUCH a girl thing to obsess over a guy.

In my freshman year of college, I had this roommate who was infatuated with this boy she knew from high school.

She talked about him all the time. I still remember his name. Mike Talone. That was how much she talked about him. She went out where she knew he'd be, just so she could run into him. She waited in front of the window in the stairwell of the academic building between classes until she saw him coming down the sidewalk, just so she could see him.

The whole thing was crazy.

It drove me mad.

If he liked her, he would have asked her out, taken her up on one of her dozens of offers to have sex, said hello to her for heaven's sake.

He never did.

I often wondered if she was still obsessing over him.

But now I felt like karma was being a real bitch because here I was unable to stop thinking about Lucas. It had been three days since our date, which wasn't really a date. Other than coming down for therapy each morning, I hadn't seen him. He hadn't said a word to me other than what was necessary, and nothing about that night. Not about the stream, or the bridge, or *the kiss*.

God, I really hated when I acted so much like a girl.

Feelings were so not my thing.

Shaking it off, him off, because I wasn't going to be like my freshman roommate and obsess, I got to work getting ready for the players' first week de-stress session.

Every year my father marked the weeks of training camp with a special event. The first one was always something to make the players laugh. The second one was a night off. The rest depended on where he was in the team selection process and what he had left to accomplish.

Marking week one last year, my father had a synchronized swim instructor come with her class of women, who were all in their sixties and seventies, to teach the guys how to do skulls, the egg beater, and even lifts.

It was really funny.

To mark the completion of week one this year, I would be teaching yoga to the players. As Drake and I pulled the mats from the cart and started setting them on the floor of the college basketball court, I took a certain satisfaction in knowing whom I was going to use to help demonstrate at least one of the moves.

I couldn't wait.

Payback.

The door swung open. "Who wants to take bets on how much junk is going to be hanging out all over this floor?" Austin asked as he strode in the room.

Austin was the third athletic trainer intern. This was his first year at any football camp and it was proving to be an experience for him, and us. To be honest, I wasn't sure he liked it very much.

I was busy arranging the college-owned yoga mats on the floor when I glanced up to speak. "None, I hope. The email that went out to the players was very specific. It stated they should not wear their baggy gym clothes. That tight clothes were recommended."

Austin grinned. "Yeah, like I said, let's see how many show up ready for their junk to fall out."

Drake shook his head. He didn't really like Austin and his carefree attitude very much. "Hey, Gillian," he said.

I looked over my shoulder at him. "Yes."

"What's the reasoning behind wearing tight clothes, other than Austin's concern?"

Straightening the corner of the last mat, I stood. "It makes it easier for me to see how a student's body is set all the way from their shoulder blades to their feet. That way I can easily help adjust the pose if I need to."

"Makes sense."

"You should come with me to a class. There's a studio in Bourbonnais that I really like. I go on Wednesday nights after dinner."

He made a face. "I want to, but I don't think so."

"Why not?"

He shrugged. "Are there any guys in the class?"

I laughed. "Sure, there are a lot more than you'd think. Come with me this week and if you don't want to take the class, you can wait in the coffee shop next door."

Drake glanced at the mats laid throughout the room. "I'll think about it."

"The coffee shop also sells boba teas."

He walked toward the front. "Sold. I'll go with you."

"What the hell is bobboo?" Austin asked.

"It's boba, and it's a tea mixed with fruit or milk, to which chewy tapioca balls and fruit jellies are added. It's delicious and really good for you."

Austin plopped down on one of the mats. He, like Drake, was here to help me with the class. Liam, the second assistant trainer, was supposed to join us as well, but he wasn't here. That was fine because other than Drake knowing a tiny bit, neither the interns nor the trainers were familiar with yoga, so it wasn't like they were going to be able to help.

"You should wrap your legs around your head while the players are walking in. That would totally freak them out," Austin said, while doing a few sit ups.

That wasn't a bad idea. In fact I was *totally* going to do that.

Drake shot him a glare. "Stop sweating on the mats and work out on your own time."

"Austin," I said, "why don't you get the water bottles and place one in front of each mat."

I wasn't in charge, but Austin needed someone to lead him. All the time. He got easily distracted, and this annoyed Drake. I chose to take Austin for what he was, which to be honest I hadn't quite figured out yet.

"Yeah, sure. I'm on it," he said eagerly.

Today was Sunday. My father always allowed for prayer time in the morning. Players were invited to attend a service at the college chapel after breakfast. It was strongly encouraged, although not required.

Lucas did attend after he met with me in the training center. He looked good in a suit.

There were no position meetings on Sundays, which allowed the guys to sleep a little later. And there was also only one practice, but it was an hour longer than usual. At least, the afternoons were free. However, all the players were required to attend the mandatory team dinner at six.

The clock struck three and Drake opened the gym doors to a horde of big players in various states of dress. Some sported cycling gear, some wore their football girdle without pads, others had on basketball shorts.

They swarmed in and found their places without me having to say a word. Lucas took a position on the end, third row back.

Was he hiding?

Keeping his distance on purpose?

I think he was.

Still, I had found him, and I allowed myself a second to look at him, but only one. He was wearing a tight white t-shirt and a black football girdle. God, the shape of his biceps and his quads were incredible. He wasn't huge, huge, like a lot of the guys. Don't get me wrong, he wasn't small. No, he was just right.

See, I was obsessing.

I couldn't stand it.

This had to stop.

Deciding against the Eka pada sirsasana yoga pose, or the leg behind the head move that Austin had suggested, I moved to the front center of the room and sat in Eka pada sirasana or easy pose, which was a basic seated yoga posture.

Everyone followed me, sitting down, but very few of them folded their legs. That was fine. "Namaste, Bears," I said loudly. "I'm Gillian, for those of you who don't know me. And welcome to Yoga for beginners."

There were some waves, a few groans, and a lot of laughs. All to be expected.

Austin's job was to video the class for playback during the season. These first week treats were always good for a laugh by the end of the season.

Drake was walking around the perimeter of the room. He

had no specific role except to help anyone who required it if I was otherwise occupied.

"Before we start, who here has taken a Yoga class?"

There were more hands than I expected, and Lucas's was among them. Of course I would notice his as one of the first.

Seriously, what was wrong with me?

"Good. Great. So for some of you this class might be too easy," I said.

The players laughed, and I did too.

"Yoga," I said, "is a bona fide science. One of the things it concentrates on is matching your movements to your breathing. Remember, with each breath you can let go of anything."

The music was quiet and peaceful.

Smartly, I had worn gray yoga pants and a black high neck tank top. It wasn't like I was going to wear what I normally would to yoga in front of ninety guys. I wasn't a cheerleader, after all.

And yes that was a dig. I really disliked the way they strutted around with their boobs and asses hanging out. Couldn't stand it, actually. Besides, it was distracting for the players. The girls would be arriving next Sunday, and I wasn't looking forward to it.

Uggg.

"Okay guys," I started, "we're going to begin today with a seated position on your mat. Starting with our seated cat/cow, inhale, open the chest, exhale, rounding the spine, tuck the chin down. Inhale, open, exhale, take it down."

The player closest to me went by the name Preacher. He was a veteran and really liked to talk, more like preach. Which was how he got his nickname. "Like this?" he whispered.

I nodded and smiled at him. "Just like that."

For the next ten minutes I added moves to this basic pose, and then we all lied down on our backs.

"No sleeping," someone yelled.

"Really?" I said, "I thought it was nap time."

The guys chuckled.

"Grab your right knee and hug it into your chest," I instructed.

I hadn't so much as looked at Lucas since the class started, but I did now, and when I did, I caught him looking at me. Of course I was teaching the class, and that could be why, but the smoldering look he gave me when our gazes locked wasn't one a student gives a teacher.

Barefoot, with his leg pressed to his chest and his blue eyes blazing in my direction, I wanted to crawl across the floor and lie down next to him. I wanted to roll on top of him and straddle him. I wanted to bend down and kiss him, using my tongue to taste him. Not anything like that childish peck I'd given him nights ago. No, I wanted full-on mouth and teeth and tongue.

Unable to resist, I smiled at him, and when he gave me that easy smile of his in return, not only did my chest do that pitter-patter thing, but this time my belly did too.

Focus.

I had to focus.

Although I didn't want to, I tore my gaze from his. "Warming up the ankle, we're going to roll it around," I told the class.

Ten more minutes passed before we got to our feet, and by now everyone was loose, and having fun. "Okay, who knows what a Mountain Pose is?" I asked the guys.

The rookie draft I'd met the first day, Dylan Kutchner, raised his hand.

I smiled at him, glad to see him back on his feet and in full recovery. "Dylan, come on up and show us," I smiled.

He was confident and didn't hesitate. "Girl, I told you before, it's Kutch," he said with a smirk as he walked toward me.

Some of the guys chatted among themselves. Some drank water. Others laughed. It was all good.

"Okay, *Kutch*, show these guys how it's done."

"Sure, girl," he said. "I got this down."

As if liking the attention, he made a show of stretching, cracking his muscles, moving his neck from side to side, and then he stood with his feet together and his arms at his sides. And stood, and stood, and stood.

"What comes next, Kutch?" I posed.

There was a blank look on his face.

I moved closer to him and took hold of his arms to show him. "Like this," I said. "As you inhale, elongate and extend your arms up, then out." I paused to look around.

Everyone was laughing now, but they were also trying to mimic the pose.

This session was doing what it was meant to do—help everyone unwind from a stressful week.

"Great," I announced. "Now, exhale and release your shoulder blades away from your head before you drop your arms back to your sides."

Drake was helping a few guys who were having trouble getting it.

"Good," I said, letting go of Kutch's arms and looking at the players. "Try this a few more times. It only looks easy. I promise you it's not. It requires a lot of balance."

Kutch laughed. For six-foot-six and over two hundred and sixty pounds, he had a lot to balance, after all. "Girl, all this time I thought I was doing yoga with that move I showed you."

One of my brows rose and I tried to laugh. "And where did you learn it like that?"

He gave me a shy shrug. "Probably best if I don't say."

Now we laughed together, and I gave him a shove. "Go back to your spot."

As I was bringing my focus to the front, I caught Lucas's gaze again. This time it was different. Fierce. Hard. He was deliberately tracing the lines of my body with his eyes. I felt that look as if he were touching me, and I shivered.

Quickly, I averted my stare.

He was too distracting.

I had to remember not to look his way.

Next, as a group, we did a few more poses. Then I brought some guys up front to demonstrate a series of my difficult moves before allowing the players to experiment themselves.

Some fell.

Some got stuck.

Some couldn't even comprehend how their body could move that way.

They were all having fun.

After we finished the more difficult moves, I clapped my hands together to get their attention. "Okay, let's do one more pose, and then you guys are free to go. Any suggestions?"

"Downward dog. Downward dog. Downward dog," they started chanting.

"Okay," I said, "Downward dog it is."

Taking a sip of water, I then asked, "Who wants to try this one in front of the class?" I had much fewer volunteers this time around, and although Lucas's hand was not raised, I picked him anyway. "Carrington," I said, purposely not using his first name so it wouldn't come across as intimate.

That blue gaze narrowed on me. I smiled and crooked a finger, trying to remain as playful as I had been with Kutch. He hesitated, but when someone gave him a shove in my direction, he started to walk to the front.

As soon as he was standing beside me, I could feel a ripple of lust explode through my body. Hoping like hell I wasn't flushing from head to toe, I tried to keep my voice even when I spoke. "This is one of the most recognizable yoga poses. It is a great way to stretch your back, shoulders, arms, hamstrings and well, just about everything, as well as keep you calm and centered."

Without waiting for my cue, Lucas got on his hands and knees, and the guys followed his lead.

"Okay," I said, "remember to align your wrists directly under your shoulders and your knees directly under your hips as you push up."

Damn him, but Lucas had gone into full position before I had even finished talking.

"Don't forget to point your middle fingers directly to the edge of your mat."

That was a huge hit and FU's were flying all around.

"Stretch your elbows . . . exhale as you tuck your toes . . ." I walked the players through each couple of steps. "Okay, now press the floor away from you as you lift through your pelvis. Draw your chest toward your thighs. Engage your quads."

I went on and on, stealing glances at Lucas, who was full on staring at me.

"Your gaze should be between your legs or toward your navel." I directed this to the class, but he knew it was at him because he looked away.

Bodies were moving in every direction.

"Don't forget to align your ears with your upper arms, and when you release, gently bend your knees and come back to your hands and knees," I said to everyone.

Some of the guys collapsed, some rolled onto each other's mats, others rolled over and stayed on their backs. They were all laughing. It was chaos. "If you couldn't maintain it, try again," I instructed.

While they were attempting to re-pose themselves, I got down on my knees and brought my mouth close to Lucas's ear. "Don't forget to breathe."

He glanced over with his blue eyes blazing. "Be in your room tonight at nine, and leave the door unlocked."

The warm buzz of his demand, of being so close to him, hit me quickly, and I had to swallow before I could even try to tell him that I absolutely would not.

"Answer me," he said, his voice husky.

"You didn't ask me a question," I responded in a low shaky tone. It wasn't what I should have said, but I couldn't form the words to reject him.

Collapsing to his hands and knees, he kept his gaze on me. "I want to see you, Gillian. Alone. Do you want to see me?"

Gillian. Had he called me by name yet?

I bit my lip, letting my tongue sneak out, and the sound he made was almost that of a growl.

His question got me, and I knew there was simply no other answer, so I whispered, "Yes."

He smiled at me then, and it was so damn seductive that I wasn't sure I could get up off the floor.

But I did, and so did he. And then he walked back to his spot without a backward glance.

I didn't care.

Class was over and I was feeling as fluttery as the teenage girl I never was. He wanted to see me. Alone. We both knew what that meant.

And in that moment I allowed myself to think it was okay. That what we were going to do was okay. But in the back of my mind, even I had to question my judgment . . .

Because I knew it really, really wasn't.

Eleven

Gillian

THE THOUGHT OF having to eat felt like a chore.

I wanted to stay in my room and have something brought up. At least that way as the time passed, I wouldn't have to force myself to focus, over and over again. I'm sorry but this obsessing stuff had to stop. I couldn't take it anymore. At least with my roommate all those years ago, I could shut her out.

Yeah, myself . . . not so much.

My thoughts were once again on Lucas and not the conversation at the dinner table.

It was hard to concentrate.

Then again, that was nothing new. It wasn't as if trying to plan family-style Sunday dinners for more than one hundred people who should be consuming almost two thousand calories in one sitting didn't have its challenges, add to it pushing tables together and passing bowls, and well, just picture it.

Chaos.

As head coach, though, my father had declared it a team rule, and no one dared to not show up.

Not even me.

Very aware of this team rule, the nutritionist tried to plan meals that lent easily to this type of serving.

Normally the cafeteria offered an extensive fruit and salad bar, whole grain breads, brown rice, chicken, or fish, and fresh fruit juices. There were never any institutional products normally found in a college cafeteria served to the Bears.

That wasn't allowed.

On the menu tonight was whole-wheat pasta with lean ground beef and salad. It was delicious, I was sure, I just couldn't taste it. Not only had I become used to eating this way, I knew it was good for me, so I never complained. Tonight though, I couldn't find my appetite.

I did, however, snag a Skinny Cow ice cream sandwich on my way out. I left only after trying unsuccessfully to locate Lucas. I hadn't seen him come in and I hadn't seen him leave. I hadn't seen him since yoga.

Was he still going to come see me?

It was close to eight-thirty when I got to my room. Tossing the ice cream wrapper in the trash, I collapsed on my bed.

At Sunday dinners everyone was required to dress nicely. Not necessarily dress up, but not in workout gear.

The summer dress I had selected was green. The shift style made it simple and easy. Dresses weren't necessarily my thing, but after living in Florida for so long, I'd gotten used to them to help combat the heat.

I peered down at it.

Should I change?

No, I thought, I'd keep this on, but I did toe my sandals off and let them drop to the ground.

The underwear I'd selected was done so with care. I wore a black wispy bra and matching thong. Even I could admit it was sexy.

The men I'd been with in the past weren't men, not like Lucas, anyway. Sure, they were the same age as him, and sure they talked the same, probably even liked the same things he did, but they weren't . . . I wasn't sure how to put it . . . *like him.*

They didn't make my heart race or my belly flutter when I saw them.

Perhaps that was because I'd stayed clear of athletes, heeding my father's warning without even realizing what I was doing. And maybe athletes were my type. If I had one. I didn't even know for sure.

Lost in my thoughts, I hadn't realized how much time had passed until I heard the turn of my doorknob.

My breath caught in my throat when I saw him.

He wore a pair of black dress pants and a white button-down open at the throat to reveal the smoothness of his chest. He'd slicked his hair back from his face and I instantly noticed the angle of his cheekbones that defined his good looks and those full lips.

That mouth.

Oh, God, that mouth.

It was perfect.

And that bottom lip, the way he pushed it out in a pout every now and then, I wanted to nibble it.

"Hey," Lucas said as he closed the door behind him and pushed the button on the knob to lock it.

"Hey," I said, sitting up and running my fingers through my hair.

He looked around the small space. "I didn't see you at dinner."

I swung my feet off the bed so I could sit up straight and placed my hands in my lap. "There were so many people, it was hard to see anyone."

There was a picture on my desk, and he walked over to it, and then picked it up. "How old were you here?"

The photo was of my father and me when his team won the Super Bowl. "I was thirteen when the Bucs won the Super Bowl. My father was the quarterback coach and I don't think I've ever seen him happier. It's the only time he's ever gone all the way in his career."

Lucas set the photo down. "So far."

I smiled at that. "Yes, so far."

He turned toward me and leaned against the small desk, pushing his sleeves up high on his elbows.

I took a satisfying look at his forearms, the tendons so very sexy, so very powerful.

When he was done, he shoved his hands in his pockets. "Maybe I'll be able to help him with that."

I cupped my elbows in my hands, uncertain why I felt so nervous. "I hope so."

We stared at each other for a few long moments until he cleared his throat. "So what's the story with you and Kutch?" he asked, innocently enough, but I knew he was wondering if I was into Kutch.

For some reason I liked that he was curious, that he had been watching me. I chewed the inside of my lip to keep from smiling. "We don't have a story."

"Girl," Lucas said mockingly, "it looked earlier like you had a story."

Ignoring the fact that Lucas used the name Kutch called me, because I was certain he called every girl he knew, *Girl*, I told Lucas, "We met the first day of camp, and I gave him some advice. Now we're friends. That's the end of our story."

Tilting his head, he gave me an assessing look, and muttered, "Friends."

"Yes, friends."

That bottom lip pouted out. "And you don't think he's after you? That he wants you?"

"No, I . . ." Lucas had stumped me. I hadn't expected this. "I don't know," I said matter-of-factly.

Lucas didn't seem to like my answer. "Are you interested in him?"

Frustrated with this conversation, I snapped. "No, I'm not. In fact, I have never been interested in any of the players on this team or any other team."

He put his hand on his heart and feigned being wounded. "Way to strike right where it hurts."

The way he seemed to know when to take it down a notch, made me snort lightly. "Well, that's not exactly a true statement. Not anymore, anyway."

His eyes drifted from the tip of my toes to my face, growing overheated as they did. "I think it's safe to assume you're referring to me."

My chest rose and fell with excited breaths. "I don't know. Am I?"

"You better be."

That's when we both burst into laughter, utterly companionable and uncomplicated. It wasn't long before my giggle fluttered into a sigh. He was watching me, and his blue eyes were alight. I couldn't interpret his long, studying look, or the half smile that accompanied it.

I scooted to the edge of the bed. "What?" I finally asked, wondering about his scrutiny.

He looked so full of himself. "Are you telling me that I'm the first football player you've ever—" He let the end of his thought hang there.

I didn't finish the sentence for him. Like him, I let the words dangle. Instead of speaking them, telling him he was the first, I got to my feet.

The pulse at the base of my throat was beating erratically, and I couldn't wait another minute for what was destined from that first glance a week ago. My breathing was ragged and tight with each slow step I took toward him.

It seemed like forever before I was standing in front of him and even longer before I reached up to pull him down to me. He groaned when my fingers tangled in his hair and practically growled when I nipped at his bottom lip, but he didn't strike.

Not yet.

He pulled back and stared down.

Searching.

Searching.

Searching.

For what . . . to do this? Not to do this? Did it really matter anymore? It was going to happen. He had to know that.

His hands clung to my hips. "Gillian—"

The sound of my name on his tongue might have stirred those butterflies in my belly, but even the thought of hearing it again wasn't enough to stop what I was about to do.

When he opened his mouth to speak, I covered his lips with my finger to silence him. "Don't say it. Don't say we shouldn't or it's wrong or anything else like that."

Those blue eyes blazed with the same uncertainty, and I think that was what made me feel like this thing between us was real. Sure, we were both torn. Sure, we were doing what we shouldn't be doing. But we both couldn't help ourselves.

I stared up at him. "Please, Lucas," I begged, "don't say anything. Just touch me."

He kept me trapped in his gaze.

Looking.

Watching.

Studying.

Deciding.

"Your father is right across the hall," he whispered.

"And both of our doors are closed. I'm not a kid. It's not like he's watching me."

Lucas took a step back. "Maybe we should put this thing on hold until training camp is over, and he isn't right across the hall?"

"We can't wait," I said. "I'm leaving Chicago as soon as camp ends."

He stared at me in confusion.

That was when I explained to him about school and my job path before I finally told him, "I won't be around anymore except to watch an occasional game."

Again he looked at me.

Watched me.

Studied me.

"It sounds like we don't have much time," he whispered.

"We don't," I whispered back.

"So this thing between us is short-term?" he asked, a slight hesitation in his voice.

"It has to be," I answered.

"And it stays between us?"

I nodded.

That's when his big, strong arms lifted me like I weighed nothing, and before I knew it, I was sitting on my desk and his lips found mine. "Then we better get going."

It took only seconds for my mouth to be so full of the taste of him, and took even less time for nothing else to exist.

No worries.

No rules.

Nothing broken . . . *not yet, anyway.*

He whispered my name, but didn't stop kissing me. His mouth moved with the same power his body did, and he took over what I had started. He was hard, heated, and demanding.

Oh God, I wanted him.

When his tongue pushed inward, hot and sensual, it glided over mine so effortlessly. I sucked in air as I fought for some equilibrium.

His hand flattened on my stomach and he smoothed it upward at the same time his lips moved down my chin, nipping and sucking along my throat. "I like this."

"Like what?"

In answer, he licked his way back up my neck. "The way you taste."

I think I stopped breathing.

This was him devouring me in a way no one ever had, and by the way he was eating me up, I think he knew that too.

With his mouth on mine, I pushed to my feet and started to edge back. He resisted though, not liking the fact that I was taking the lead.

That was okay by me. My legs were wobbling beneath me like they never had, and I suddenly found moving difficult. Not that I was going anywhere with his hard body pressing so tightly against mine.

It was warm.

Honed to perfection.

Sculpted like a piece of art.

And all I wanted to do was run my fingers over every inch of it.

I think I might have purred when I thought about it, and that's when he started moving back toward the bed. Him back, me forward, him back, me forward. I slid my hand to his face to feel his skin there, too. Like the rest of him, his face was chiseled with perfect lines and angles. I could have run my fingers all over him for days and never gotten bored.

All of a sudden his teeth were grazing over my lips and nipping at the fullness in the most delicious way, and still we were moving. Him back, me forward. Him back, me forward.

Our second kiss was harder, rougher, full of hunger. It was way more passionate than that childish peck I had given him nights ago.

This was the real thing.

The back of his legs must have hit the mattress because he

stopped for only a second before falling to it with me in his arms.

On his lap, I pulled my legs up to either side of his thighs and straddled him. Lucas pulled back and broke our kiss. I opened my eyes to find him looking at me. His gaze was unwavering as he pushed one hand between us and slid it up the hem of my dress, which had lifted to nearly expose my panties, anyway.

With my thighs already parted, he pushed his fingers up, up, up, until they were at the front of my panties. When he rubbed his thumb slowly over it, I bit back a moan.

Anchoring myself to him, I slid my hands from his face to shoulders. When he circled his thumb against the silk of my panties, I couldn't stop my blunt nails from digging into his skin. He groaned, and all the while, he kept moving.

Circle.

Press.

Circle.

Press.

I was going out of my mind and used my teeth as my outlet. I nipped at the sensitive part of his flesh at his throat, and when I did, he moved his fingertips up just a little to dip inside the edge of my panties.

"Oh, fuck," he hissed when he found me soaking wet for him.

Worried about who might hear us through the thin dorm door, I covered his mouth with my hand when he cursed again. When I did, he licked at my skin, and it sent a shudder of pleasure all the way through me. Now I was the one moaning loudly.

I couldn't believe I was going to come from just this little contact. I didn't want to come yet, and I wanted to come so badly, I didn't know what to do. Arching into his touch, I tried to push him down on the mattress.

Shaking his head no, he wouldn't let me take control, and I couldn't stop my low cry of protest. Silencing me, he slid his hands up my body and cupped my face. "Patience, Strawberry Fields," he whispered, and then covered my mouth with his in an earth-shaking kiss that left me breathless.

At last he rolled us both down onto the mattress in a twist of arms and legs that landed me beneath him.

In this position, it was difficult for either of us to move. He looked down at me with that easy smile. "This bed is really small."

I grinned up at him. "Or maybe you're just too big."

He raised a sexy brow. "Not a bad problem to have."

I reached up and nipped at his lip, hard enough to draw blood. "You really do think you're hot stuff."

That cocky look was too much. "What I think," he said, leaning down to kiss me, "is that you are the most beautiful girl I have ever seen."

Emotion clogged my throat. No one had ever said anything like that to me before.

Clearly, Lucas didn't want to give me time to respond because he shifted us again, this time ending with me on top of him and my knees gripping his sides. "Enough talking," he said.

I was fine with that. Like this, I moved my hands over his belly; pushing his shirt up to reveal the taut muscles beneath. And with shaking fingers, I traced the lines of each one, back and forth. I was mesmerized by the strength and power he possessed.

"Stop looking at me like that or it's going to get you into some serious trouble," he growled.

Doing no such thing, I lifted my seductive gaze upward. "How am I looking at you?"

"Like you want to eat me."

"I do," I said matter-of-factly. "All of you."

This stunned him. I think he was literally at a loss for words. I had to admit this thrilled me.

I became impatient with all the foreplay and started yanking at his belt buckle to find the zipper beneath it. It didn't take long to pull it down. For my hand to be in the front of his pants. For my fingers to be curling over the hot, hard bulge inside.

When I started to slip my fingertips inside his boxer briefs to free his erection, he bucked up and grabbed my wrist to stop me.

I gave him a challenging look. He gave me one right back. I wasn't strong enough to break free of him, but I kept the pressure of my grasp just enough that he had to make an effort to continue to stop me.

The push and pull only lasted a moment.

"Please," I whispered.

Lucas bit his lower lip and then repositioned my hand on the thick ridge of his erection.

Hiding my triumphant smile, I moved my palm up and down his boxer briefs. My skin slid so easily over the bright blue fabric of his Pumas, and just this slight touch of him electrified me.

As I continued to move with slow, deliberate strokes, Lucas pushed between my thighs and found my panties again. It took less than a second for him to dip his finger inside the edge and find me even wetter than moments ago, and even less time for him to push his finger inside me.

I bit into my own bottom lip as lust rolled hot through me, leaving me flushed, excited, desperate for more. I pushed myself up a bit to give him more room, and I used this motion to release his erection from the confines of his Pumas. There wasn't enough room for full access, but for now it would work.

He looked so incredibly sexy on my bed. I leaned down to kiss him again. The bed squeaked as we shifted and moved against each other. Frantic. Needing. Desperate.

The orgasm struck quickly. I closed my eyes and cried out his name as the first wave swept over me. Tumultuous and overwhelming.

The moans and quivers that escaped my throat didn't sound like me at all. When he reached up to gently cover my mouth, he didn't stop what he was doing. Not even as I sat back up and arched my body away from his touch because it was all too much. "Don't move. I want you to feel good," he whispered, his voice silky smooth.

And so I stayed still and let his touch carry me away. It was as if I had some inner pulse that his touch ruled over because more pleasure cascaded through me. And I lost myself in it. I used him as my anchor as I dug the fingers into the bare skin I found below the hem of his shirt.

He gasped, thrusting harder into my curled fingers that were still on his erection.

Our eyes met, and I had no idea what each of us saw, but it was something that seemed to erase any remaining barriers between us.

I pushed against him. "I want to taste you," I said, my voice strained and edgy as I stared into those intense blue eyes.

"I'm okay with that," he breathed out, his own voice husky.

Knock.

Knock.

Knock.

"Gilly, are you awake?"

My head jerked toward the door and I froze. Utterly horrified. *It was my father.*

At first I didn't move, and I didn't feel Lucas move an inch from beneath me, either.

"Gilly, you awake," he said again, knocking lightly once more.

Quickly, I glanced down at Lucas who looked both pained and amused. "Gilly?" he mouthed, "Like a fish's gill?"

In your teens, twenties, or even thirties, the last thing any girl ever wanted was for her father to catch her . . . well . . . in this case, literally with her skirt up. Worried that was just what was going to happen, I slapped my hand over Lucas's mouth even though he wasn't actually speaking loud enough for my father to hear and drew in a huge breath. "Yes, Dad," I answered.

"Do you have a couple of minutes? The decorator sent some paint samples over and I wanted to get your opinion on the wall color.

Lucas moved my hand away and his mouth opened wide in a huge grin. "Nesting?" he mouthed with wide, surprised eyes.

I supposed that for the head coach, who had a reputation of being a hard-ass, this was so out of character. To me, this was who my father was, a big softie on the inside that he only let me see.

With a narrowed stare, I shot Lucas a warning look that I didn't have to. By the way his brow had creased in less than two seconds, I was certain he was way more worried than I was. Him getting caught with me . . . well I had no idea what that would do to his position on the team, and I didn't want to find out.

This team needed Lucas, and I'd already been the cause of one possible setback. I wouldn't be the cause of another.

"Sure, Dad, give me a few minutes and I'll head over."

"Are you okay, honey? You sound out of breath."

I squeezed my eyes shut for a moment.

No.

No.

No.

How could I even answer that question?

I was more than out of breath. There was slickness between my legs, my core still throbbed, and Lucas's hard dick was beneath me. "Oh, yeah, I'm fine," I somehow managed. "Just doing a few sit-ups before bed. I ate way too much at dinner."

That was a lie, and I tasted the bitterness on my tongue.

I was a bad daughter.

"That's my girl," he said, and I cringed. "I'll be in the room I've been using to view play footage. Come over whenever you're done."

Done. I wasn't sure we could be *done* that quickly. But then again, judging by the pale, nauseated look on Lucas's face now, I was pretty sure we were done.

The ramifications of what we were doing must have sunken in.

"Okay," I answered, and waited to make sure he was gone before I dared move from the bed.

As soon as I was sure my father was no longer outside my door, I jumped to my feet. Lucas practically bolted to his.

"Fuck," he hissed, running a hand through that gorgeous hair of his.

Fuck was right.

"It's fine. He's gone. I'll leave first," I said. "The room he is in is down the hall, so give me a few minutes and then you can slip out unnoticed."

He nodded.

While he zipped and tucked, I stripped out of my wet panties and hurriedly pulled on a fresh pair. When I turned, Lucas had pulled himself together, clothing wise, but he looked anything but pulled together.

With swift fingers, I twisted my hair into a semblance of a knot instead of the sex-tangled mess I was sure it was, and then I shifted my dress back into its proper place.

I walked toward Lucas, who hadn't moved. "Everything is fine."

He said nothing.

I popped up on my toes and placed a chaste kiss on his lips.

He didn't kiss me back.

The sullen look he wore told me not to ask what he was thinking. I didn't want to know right then. I was certain I would later, though.

"See you in the morning," I whispered, but I knew I wouldn't. I could see it on his face, in his eyes, the sag of his shoulders, and my heart fell.

There was no time to discuss it now. Curfew wasn't far off, and my father would be back if I didn't show up soon, so I had no choice but to turn and walk toward the door.

Still, I couldn't just leave.

With my hand on the doorknob, I looked back over my shoulder to say something, but was struck mute. It hit me then that although I had thought I had it all, I really didn't. That there was a huge part of life missing—someone to share it with.

At the same time, I also realized why I stayed away from men like Lucas—they were my kryptonite.

Or at least he was.

Twelve

INTERCEPTION

Lucas

THE TIME WAS now.

Somehow Coach had gotten pads and helmets sanctioned for one scrimmage before the two week lift.

The practice game was about to start.

It would be the first of the year in full pads. Something I had been looking forward to, and dreading, at the same time.

I'd skipped out on Gillian the past few mornings. I'd seen her throughout the practices, but hadn't acknowledged her.

I was being an asshole, but I didn't know what else to be. I didn't want to ruin her reputation. I didn't want to get caught. The only solution was to stay away from her.

Deep in thought, I was gripping a football with my right hand and standing on a perfectly manicured grass field in my cleats, contemplating what I'd done. This object in my hand was my world. This oval shaped ball made of leather, sewn together by white strings had been my dream since I was ten years old.

There was no way I could let anything get in the way of achieving it.

My entire life I had longed to be better. Faster, rougher, tougher. What I was, what I had become, it was never enough.

I was never enough.

Not enough for my mother to stick around, and not enough for my father to snap out of his depression and participate in my life. If it weren't for my brother, I had no idea where I would have ended up.

In a gutter.

In jail.

In a coffin.

Who the fuck knew.

But being here, right now, in this moment, I felt I was finally enough for the first time in my life.

A million guys would give their nuts to be me, and although I hadn't been thrilled about it at first, I certainly had come around after I thought I might lose it all.

That's why the thought of risking it all for a girl who would be out of my life in five more weeks didn't make much sense. It would be a stupid move.

Right?

A hand hit my shoulder. "Hey, man. How's it going?" the player said as he paused to stand beside me. It was Greg Wilkinson, linebacker and team captain.

That question deserved a sly grin. "Fucking fantastic."

He nodded. "I feel you, man. You ready to do this?"

"Sure, it sounds like fun."

That gave him cause to raise a brow. "Fun," he laughed. "I'm not sure about that. Coach will be on anyone's ass who doesn't know their shit."

I pulled out my playbook, the one I'd flipped through more

than a dozen times, and that was just this morning. "Sounds like even more fun," I joked.

"I hope you still think that when it's over," he laughed, but then turned serious. "Hey man, the first week is the most brutal, and that's behind us, but cuts start today and I'm going to be honest, they suck. Suck for everyone."

I glanced across the field. "Yeah, the mood is pretty somber around here."

Greg clapped me on the shoulder again. "Get used to it, and don't dwell. It will only bring you down."

I nodded. "Appreciate the advice."

"Anytime, man," he called as he ran toward the center of the field with his helmet in his hand.

Cuts were going to suck, no doubt about it. Then again, just about everything sucked in my life right now.

Greg started yelling, "It's fucking go time."

The laugh I had was one I needed, but it was time to get real. I flipped open the playbook in my hand and did some last-minute studying. I didn't want Coach on my ass . . . for any reason.

Kick-off came fast.

There were no warm ups outside of our earlier practice. Coach decided the teams. I was orange. Among those on my team were Thor, Preacher, and Kutch, who I was keeping my eye on since he was keeping his eye on Gillian, who was on the sidelines.

The blue team roster had way more vets than ours, and I wasn't sure if that was good or bad, but I was about to find out.

Coin toss went to blue. They elected to receive. I was on the sidelines, watching. On the third play of the game, our defensive end picked off Swann, blue's quarterback, and returned the ball for a touchdown.

Unfucking believable!

We were ahead.

When it was time for me to hit the field, I was nervous. I called the plays in the huddle, yelled the signals at the line of scrimmage, and then received the ball from the center.

The play was textbook all the way.

When I handed the ball off to the running back, he ran with it until he was tackled. Three plays later I huddled the offense and told them we were going to score. And then we were going to score again. And again. And fucking again.

Hey, I could build confidence.

Scoring didn't happen quite that easy, but sure as shit, by the fifth play, I knew I had it. Dropping back, I was ready to throw the ball, but veteran player Dion Reynolds wasn't in position, and in a matter of seconds, I had to change the game plan.

I looked across the field, but another one of the wide receivers was also covered. I pump-faked to him as I scanned down the middle, but found no one. With only seconds to spare, I looked right, where fuck, I saw Gillian on the sidelines.

After losing focus for a moment, or maybe gained it, I bounced back on my toes and let the ball fly right to Kutch. He caught it in stride and raced to the end zone, where he fucking did a little dance and then looked toward Gillian. I knew he winked at her, even if I couldn't see it.

This made my blood boil. She was fucking mine, and he better stay away.

Wait!

What?

She wasn't mine. I'd decided it was best to end things before they started, hadn't I?

Fueled by this demon inside me, I played the rest of the game like a man on one hell of a mission.

The fourth quarter blew by in a flash. We were up 22–14, and with one minute remaining, all I had to do was run the clock out, and that's what I did.

Game over.

I fist pumped the air and caught Gillian's gaze. She was staring at me, and she had the most genuine happiness over the win written all over her face. That's when I started to second-guess my decision.

She was on my team. My side. And it felt good to have someone in my corner.

Maybe I shouldn't stay away.

Maybe I couldn't.

"Don't start celebrating," Coach yelled, and we gathered for our usual end-of-practice midfield verbal haranguing.

Coach expected mathematic perfection from his players. We'd learned over the past week that most often, whatever the players did wasn't quite right. Looked like today wasn't going to be an exception.

There was always something to improve, even when you got the job done. *Don't make a mistake, and you won't get yelled at . . .* that was the Holy Grail.

Every play of this practice would be watched on film by the whole team tonight after dinner. Whoever made mistakes, they would be pointed out and discussed. And discussed, and discussed even more.

Nothing slipped through the cracks. Depending on the severity of the mistake, and the frequency of the mistake, the reaction from Coach would vary.

Didn't matter, the feeling for the player up front and center was always horrible. Being called out in meetings and having everyone in the room watching you fail in slow motion was demoralizing. Then again, it worked. Most of us never made the same mistake twice.

Coach looked especially pissed off today. "This afternoon was a complete failure," he yelled. "You guys get the opportunity to show me what you got, and you shit all over it. I can't even watch another minute. I'm calling this practice over."

After that he walked away in disgust. Guess a, "Great game, boys," would be too much to ask for.

Whatever.

"That second touchdown should have been mine."

I whipped my head around to see Reynolds marching toward me. Dion Reynolds was probably the biggest name left on the team. *Uncuttable* was how the vets referred to him. Arrogant prick was what I called him. At six-foot four, and two hundred and forty pounds, sure he had some meat on me, I'd give him that. But like I cared. "You weren't in position," I responded, void of any emotion.

"The fuck I wasn't," he yelled.

At first, I was just going to ignore him. It took too much energy to fight, and who the hell had any left.

"You might look like Tom Brady, but you're no Brady, kid, and you better learn that real fast."

Okay, there was no way I was going to let that comment pass. Lean wasn't skinny. Besides, the whole *you're the next Tom* thing was getting old. Already irritated, I leaned in close. "That play was by the book. You might want to open it."

He got up in my face and bared his teeth. "You. Did. It. Wrong. You're the one who needs to study the fucking book."

Deadpan, I repeated. "You weren't in position."

By now, this had become a scene.

"Say it again, rookie, and you won't have to worry about saying another thing," he hissed.

I stood there, looking him straight in the eye, and then folded my arms. "You. Weren't. In. Position."

The look he gave me told me we were about to settle this a different way.

"Cut the shit," Preacher shouted as he shimmied his way between the both of us and pushed Reynolds out of my space.

A few guys started laughing. Others were already stomping off the fields. Some weren't even paying attention.

Surprisingly, Reynolds turned around and stomped off, muttering to himself. "Whatever. You're not worth it. You'll be gone soon enough."

Preacher put a hand on my shoulder. "Want some advice?"

This guy was cool, and I had respect for him, so I said, "Sure."

"Don't fuck with the unfuckable. Reynolds is a diva and we all know it's better to just walk away. He gets off on provoking whoever he can. Don't feed into it."

I kicked my toes in the grass. "Good to know."

He slapped me on the back. "That was the right play."

Okay, so I felt a little full of myself, I'll admit.

Just then two guys started going at it. This time it turned into an actual fist fight. It was Reynolds and Kutch. Fuck, of course it was.

Preacher hauled ass over there. There were a few shoves and a couple of punches, but as soon as Preacher tore them apart, they backed away from each other.

"You catch like a bitch," Reynolds spat at Kutch.

"Reynolds, fucking shut up!" Preacher said, and Reynolds shut the fuck up.

Incredible.

It was noted, Preacher was a good friend to have.

Just as I turned to march off the field myself, I spotted Dallas and Gillian with Swann, my backup, and he was shuffling off the field. He didn't look good. In fact, he looked a little stiff. Injured even? I wasn't sure.

Thor came jogging after me. When he caught up, he pointed toward Swann. "Did you hear?"

I bobbed my chin in his direction. "No. What happened?"

"Groin injury." He winced.

"Shit. How bad?"

He shook his head. "No clue. I guess we'll find out soon. You headed in?"

Under the still-blistering five o'clock sun, I nodded, and we both walked over to the fitness center without saying another word. It was likely Swann was going to be the first to go, and that meant I had no backup.

For some reason, this made it seem like I was invincible, but in fact meant the complete opposite. Whoever replaced him could easily try to vie for first string. Swann just wasn't good enough to surpass me. I knew that from the first day. Whoever was coming up next, could be an entirely different story.

At my locker, I was just about ready to hit the shower when Aiden, the assistant trainer, walked in.

"Hey, Lucas," he called.

"Yeah," I answered, expecting to be blasted after not having shown up this morning for my session with Gillian.

"I really think you should hit the cold tub before you head out."

Okay, that was better than what I had expected, but not much. I nodded. "Yeah, I'll do that."

I knew he wasn't asking.

Gillian had tried to get me to go in it a couple of times. She insisted it would help my muscles repair quicker, but I had refused. Come on, submerging waist-deep in a pool of water set to forty-seven degrees would do more than make your blood vessels constrict, it would make your balls shrivel. Who in the hell would ever volunteer to do that in front of a girl they're into? Not me, but I guessed I was about to go anyway.

Fanfuckingtastic.

"You coming?" I asked Thor who was already headed to the shower, where the rest of the team was.

"Fuck no," he said. "We have ninety minutes of free time today and I have a phone date." He grinned.

"Thanks for the heads up."

"Anytime."

I shook my head at him.

He shrugged. "You know I have to keep my ladies happy."

"Ladies? As in more than one?" I stupidly asked.

With a nod, he said, "Rebecca and Honey."

Now it was making sense why he was on the phone all the fucking time. He had more than one girlfriend.

"Whatever," I said.

"Hey, don't be jelly, man."

I slammed my locker. "Dude, jealous isn't even on my radar. I'm thinking about the shit you're going to be in when they both come here to watch you play next week."

Trace Wentworth went a little blank and I think he might have shit his pants had he been wearing any.

I laughed all the way to the cold tub.

In my gym shorts and T-shirt, I stared down at it.

Through the glass I noticed Swann, and a veteran tight end named Jon Hanover, both lying on training tables, receiving treatment.

Ice, electric stimulation, ultrasound.

And Gillian was there along with the other two interns, whose names I couldn't recall, along with Aiden and Dallas. Liam wasn't around. Then again, he never seemed to be. Not my business.

Gillian caught my stare and stared back at me for a moment too long because Drake noticed and nudged her.

Did he know?

Quickly, I looked away and glared down at the pool of cold water. I really didn't want to do this, but I knew I should. It might be just what I needed. My shoulder was almost back to normal, and I had that girl in the next room to thank for it. The same girl I'd made come the other night. And the same one I wanted to do it to again.

The girl who kissed me like no one ever had.

I peered up, needing to see her, and this time when I did, the team physician was with Swann, who was being put on a gurney. Swann looked grim and by the look on his face, I knew he wasn't coming back.

Fuck me.

I glared down at the water again, and then finally, I poked my toe in. Yep, sure enough it felt like Lake Michigan in March.

Fucking great.

Slowly, I descended a couple of steps and stood there, arms resting on the ledge. "Fuckkkkkkkkkk," I stammered to stifle my screams.

Something had me peering through the glass again, and when I did, I found Gillian, arms crossed, and smirking at me. Aiden was just finishing putting a brace on Hanover, and she was next to him, casually looking toward me.

When I caught her gaze, she covered her mouth to hide her smile, and something strange happened within me. It was a feeling or an emotion I couldn't decipher, or didn't want to, who knew.

What I did know was Aiden catching Gillian would be way worse than getting caught by Drake.

Drake was harmless.

Aiden, not so much.

With that, I turned my back to her for more than just that reason. The tent in my pants was about to become obvious, and unfortunately I knew just how to take care of it.

As I plunged into the cold water, I couldn't help but think how this was new territory for me. Never had I been in this position.

Not to sound insensitive or uncaring, but except for the purpose of pleasing my dick, I never really paid any attention to women. Other than my sister-in-law, Tess, I didn't really even engage in much conversation with the opposite sex.

Being the quarterback of the football team, in both high school and college, had many benefits, and girls at the ready was one of them.

If I wanted a handy, I just had to go to the student center. If I felt like a blowie, the library was always a good choice, and if I wanted to fuck, all I had to do was hang out after a game. The offers were never ending and the strings were unattached.

Shit, I thought the notoriety was crazy then, but now I knew it wasn't even the tip of the iceberg when you entered the NFL.

Between mini-camp and training camp, a couple of vets on the team took me to a club, where we sat in the VIP section. The girls who they had invited were giving hand jobs to every single one of us under the table. They were also all too eager to hook up in the bathroom, the car, or anywhere, for that matter.

For no reason, I replayed the other night with Gillian in my mind. I wasn't in a hurry for her to do any of those things to me. What I was in hurry to do was take care of her.

She was fucking with my head and she didn't even know it.

When my feet and toes began to feel numb, I figured it was time to stop thinking about a chick, since chances were good my dick was at the bottom of the tub anyway, and get out of the water.

After I reached for my towel and wrapped it around my waist, I couldn't resist turning around.

The training room was empty, and if I had thought I was going to get another glimpse of Gillian, or a goodbye, or even a drop dead, I was wrong.

Disappointment surged in my veins. Not a sensation I'd felt in a very long time. I hated the feeling.

Practically shaking from the cold water, I hustled to the locker room, which was now empty. Everyone more than likely taking advantage of the extra free time. I should hurry and catch up with them, but I something was slowing me down.

Not something.

Someone.

Even as I hit the hot shower, I couldn't stop thinking about her. While the warm water sprayed over me, I let my thoughts wander to places they shouldn't.

To her.

In order to force myself to stop, I turned the water all the way to the right.

To cold.

But even the shock of that didn't suppress the image in my mind of her thighs squeezing mine as she hovered above me, looking at me like she couldn't wait for me to take her, possess her, own her.

And fuck, I wanted to.

I really did.

Thirteen

WALK-THROUGH

Lucas

THERE WAS A good chance my arms were going to turn into fins.

If an NFL player typically spent twice as much time in meeting rooms as they did on the field, he must spend three times as much time in water.

Seriously, between hot tubs and cold tubs and showers, I was starting to feel like a fish. The heck of it was there was no denying I was feeling a whole lot better.

Almost normal.

After throwing on a pair of sweats and a T-shirt, I left the locker room and strode down the hall toward the exit.

For some reason, I slowed just before the training room. The lights were still on and I saw movement out of the corner of my eye.

Stopping near the doorway, I poked my head in. I had no idea why I was doing this, but a part of me was hoping . . .

I spotted the Coach's daughter immediately. I think my heart nearly skidded out of my chest when I realized—I missed her.

Missed talking to her.

Being with her.

Her.

Gillian.

She was over at the whirlpools, cleaning them out. Her hair was back in a ponytail and a few strands of red glinted from the glare of the overhead lights shining on it.

I watched as her ponytail swung from the amount of effort she was putting into scrubbing the basin.

I watched as her long lashes brushed her checks when she closed her eyes from the effort she was putting into her work.

I watched her.

"S-s-s-s-s-h-h-h," she muttered, as though wanting to swear but not doing so.

Biting my fist to stop from laughing, I stepped inside. "New curse word I should learn?"

Her head jerked up and when her gaze landed on me, she froze. "Lucas."

With my eyes locked on hers, I found myself walking her way. Normally, I wouldn't bother going after a girl. Not ever. And yet, this was my second time with her. In this case, I wanted to close in before I changed my mind and hightailed it out of this dangerous situation.

"Hi, Gillian," I greeted smoothly.

"What are you doing here?" she asked breathlessly.

I glanced down into the tub and then up at her before shrugging. "Just wondering if s-s-s-h-h-h is another way of saying this part of the job sucks?"

She rolled her eyes at me. Rolled her eyes. And then she shook her head. Shook her head.

"Is it?" I asked.

As if she were planning on ignoring me, she turned the water on and began rinsing the cleanser away.

I reached inside the tub and curled my hand around hers. "Gillian, did you hear me?"

I knew she did.

Yanking her hand away from my mine, she used the sprayer to wash down the sides. "Yes, I did."

"Well, are you going to answer me?"

She sighed. "No, it isn't."

Trying to connect with her some way, I kept on. "If you ask me, it sounded like you were going to say shit."

Her gaze lifted. "Look, Lucas, I've had a crappy week and have a lot to do."

The agitation in her voice hit me hard. She was dismissing me. And although everything in me screamed *fuck it, just turn and walk away*, I couldn't. "Why? What's going on?"

There was a moment I was fairly certain she thought about aiming that water nozzle at me, but then she cocked her head to the side. "Let's see," she said, pulling her bottom lip between her teeth. "Where should I start?"

"At the beginning," I suggested, trying to be funny, however I was certain I sounded more like a smartass.

"Oh right." She gave me the fakest of smiles "That's easy. On Monday I got up extra early to meet this football player who decided to flake on me without so much as a text. He must think he's hot stuff."

Drawing in a breath, I had to interject. "What makes you say that?"

Water splashed her face, but she ignored it. "Well obviously his private training sessions mean nothing to him."

"That's harsh."

She turned the water pressure up. "It's true. I mean even after

I texted him to remind him to show up on Tuesday, he didn't."

I took the nozzle from her to finish the rinsing. "He sounds like an inconsiderate bastard."

Her lips twitched and her eyes flashed. I'd almost gotten a smile out of her. I really wasn't a bastard, but in her defense what I did was pretty rude. "I wouldn't use the word *inconsiderate*. I'm sure he wanted to let me know. Perhaps *scared* would be a better way to describe him."

I shut the water off and moved around the tub to be closer. "Scared? Is that what you think?"

The room looked spotless, but she walked over to the counter and picked up a container of Clorox wipes, yanking one up. "As a matter of fact, I do."

After reaching for some paper towels to dry my hands, I tossed them in the trash and followed her across the room. "This guy's ego is taking quite a beating. I bet he already feels like a big enough ass."

Gillian started furiously wiping down the counters. "Oh, I doubt that. Like I inferred earlier, he's a little full of . . ." She shook off the rest of her thought and didn't finish.

First hot stuff.

Now full of myself.

Is that what she was thinking?

I grabbed her hand to stop her. "If he were here, I'm sure he'd say he was sorry for the way he treated you."

She narrowed her eyes at me, but she couldn't stop the corners of her mouth from tilting upward. "It doesn't really matter, I'm over it. In fact, I've moved on. I have other things to worry about now."

My face fell, and I think my heart did too. "What do you mean by *other things?*" I air quoted the last two words.

There was a desk at the end of the counter and she flopped in the chair. "Just what it sounded like. I have other *things* to worry about."

She was wearing a pair of blue shorts and a white tank top, but it wasn't until she propped her feet up on the desk that I noticed how sunburned her long, lean legs looked. Curious, I leaned back against the counter and stretched my own long, muscular legs out in front of me. "What? Like the sunburn on your legs?"

That comment went ignored, but she did move her head in an exaggerated motion to make sure I saw how she was looking me up and down.

"I'll take that as a no. So what is it?"

This time she shrugged, as if annoyed, and without taking her gaze from mine, she said, "If you must know, the team had a number of injuries today and we were short handed. Liam flew home for undisclosed personal reasons early this morning. The five of us have to pick up the slack, so as it turns out, I don't have the time anymore to dedicate myself to just one player."

That felt like a sucker punch. What was more, I deserved it. "Strawberry Fields," I said with a sigh, "don't be this way."

Those green pools narrowed on me. "My name is Gillian, not Strawberry Fields," she responded. Her tone was clipped, almost pissed off. With a huff, she set her feet on the floor and whirled around to the computer, which was on the other side of her.

"Come on," I pleaded to her back. "You like it when I call you that. I know you do."

Or I thought she did.

Maybe not?

That didn't make her turn around. However, it did seem to stop her from doing any work. She let her fingers hover over the keypad, but she didn't type anything. Then again, she didn't say anything, either.

"Gillian," I groveled, this time a little rougher, a little more raspy. Not only did I not like this silent treatment, I didn't like anything about this current situation.

In less than a heartbeat, she twirled back around and glared in my direction. With a thump, she got to her feet and strode over to me. "Stop whatever this is you're doing."

Understanding the need to get it out, I stood there and gave her time to finish. I knew she wasn't done. I could tell.

She poked my chest with her finger hard enough that I had to lean back. "I'm not going to play games with you, Lucas. I don't like them. I'm sure you're used to getting any girl you want, whenever you want, but I won't be one of them."

I blinked, not expecting this rant. "I don't want you to be."

Now she was waving her finger at me. "Then stop thinking you can come in and out of my life when it suits you because I have news for you—you can't. Do you understand me?"

I stood where I was, an odd ache in my chest.

Her hand dropped to her side. Clearly, she was finished.

"I'm sorry," I said, my voice soft.

With a shrug, she took a step back. "That's great. I feel so much better now. I think this conversation is over. You should go. It's almost time for dinner."

A quick glance at the clock told me I had a few minutes. "Gillian, I'm not trying to hurt you. It's just," I stopped. Ran a hand through my hair, and grouped my thoughts. "It's just I . . . don't know how to say it . . . we can't be together. We just can't."

She sighed and looked away. "You don't want to jeopardize your career. I get it, Lucas, and I don't blame you. I just think you could have talked to me about our situation before you shut me out the way you did. That's all. Now please go."

I shook my head. I hated this. She had it wrong, or at least most of it. I moved a little closer and lifted her chin. "Gillian, listen to me."

Again, she glanced away.

"Please."

Her piercing gaze found mine.

"I'm not good at any of this, and it seemed like letting it go was better than trying to put my feelings into words."

"Well, it wasn't."

"I get that."

"Good," she said. "Now, will you please go?"

I shook my head. "No, I won't. I want you to understand where I'm coming from."

She looked at me, but said nothing. I took that as a green light.

"Sure, my career is part of the reason I know I should stay away from you," I said. "The fact that your father has the power to make it or break it is also most definitely a factor that I have to take into consideration. But there's so much more to us. To the reasons we should stay apart."

"Like what?" she asked.

"Like your reputation," I blurted out. "It's at stake every time you're with me. All it takes is one affair with a player to get out, and then all the guys will think . . . well you know what they'll think."

"No, what will they think? That I'm easy, that I'm loose, that I'm an easy score? Is that what you mean?"

"Yeah," I admitted, "and I won't have that hanging over your head. Whether you're here or not, I don't want that for you."

She crossed her arms. "Is that what *you* think about me?"

"No!" I said adamantly. "Not at all."

"If you're worried about me, you don't have to be. I can take care of myself, and my own reputation. I've been doing it for a long time."

Her words sounded tough, but the quiver of her bottom lip gave away the fact she was upset, and I hated that I was the cause of her sorrow. "Believe me," I said, taking my voice down a notch. "I know you can."

"Then it looks like we have nothing else to discuss." She unwrapped her arms from her body, and then pivoted on her toe in the direction of the open door.

I reached for her and tugged her to me. "I don't want to want you," I breathed, my mouth hovering just centimeters from hers.

She tried to pull away, but not whole heartedly. If she wanted me to let her go, I would have, but I knew she didn't. "Then stop," she sighed.

I took her face in my hands. "I can't. I don't know how to."

And I really wished I did.

"Neither do I," she whispered.

Unable to stop myself, I crashed my lips to hers and drove my tongue into her mouth to retrace every inch that I had explored days ago.

Gillian pushed herself against me and placed her thigh between my legs. I thought I might go out of my mind the minute she nudged upward. In the position she was in there was no doubt she could feel me getting hard, which was fine by me because I wanted her to really understand what she did to me.

Without another thought, I was moving her hand to the bulge in my pants. "Feel this," I muttered into her mouth.

The hoarse, low raspy noise she made was one I knew I would remember for a very long time.

I moved my mouth down her throat. "That's what you do to me every single time you look at me the way you do. Remember how my hard cock feels under your fingertips the next time you question what it is I'm feeling toward you."

Her hand inched up the fabric of my sweats until it settled on the waistband. "I don't think I can ever forget it, even if I wanted to."

I groaned out loud when she pushed her hands inside my sweatpants. There was a really good chance I would get lost in the moment as soon as her fingers found purchase on my more than ready cock, and that wasn't a good idea.

Despite knowing this, somehow our mouths were fused together again. Her tongue slid along mine as her fingers traveled a little further down. She was close, so close to having me in her grasp, and I knew if she did, I would never be able to stop her.

I wouldn't want to.

"Not here," I somehow managed to reason. And then I pulled back and cupped my hands in her hair to lift her face toward me. "I want your touch too much. I have been aching for you. I haven't been able to think about anything else."

"Lucas," she moaned. "I don't want to stop."

"Me either, but here isn't right. Sunday night is our first night off. We'll meet somewhere. It will be just you and me, and no one will know where we are."

Her eyes were wide when she spoke. "But that's three nights away. Come to my room tonight."

I shook my head. "The first time I have you I don't want to have to worry about how much noise we make or who might be outside the door."

Her mouth twisted in thought. "You have a point. But where are we going to go?"

Getting some distance seemed like a good idea, so I stepped back and leaned against the counter, propping one of my Adidas on the lower cabinet. "I know a place," I grinned.

Her eyes glittered with instant interest. "A place?"

"Well, I don't personally know of the place," I confessed. "But I heard my roommate making plans with one of his girls to meet at a historic hotel in the village, or rather I heard him agree to meet her there after he suggested Motel 8."

She lifted a brow. "Your roommate has girls? As in more than one?"

I raised my hands in surrender. "Hey, it's not my business."

"Why do all of the unmarried players have to have harems?"

Seriously, I had to laugh. "Harems? Ummm . . . I honestly have no idea."

Her eyes narrowed on me. "Do you have a harem?"

"Me?" I pointed a finger to myself. "That's pretty funny."

"Why not? Girls don't interest you?"

I straightened. "I think you already know they do."

– "Then why is it funny?"

"Because I don't . . ." Hmmm . . . I wasn't sure how to say it without sounding callous.

She cut me off before I could fully explain. "How many girls do you have on speed dial?"

"None."

She raised her hand, palm up. "Let me see your phone."

I shrugged and pulled it from my pocket. Once I unlocked it, I handed it to her. "Have at it."

Gillian pressed the favorites button and her eyes scanned the short list. "Who's Tess?" she asked with speculation.

"She's my sister-in-law."

She didn't look convinced.

I took my phone and brought up a recent photo and then handed my phone back to her. "That's her with my brother and their kids, Nicky and Sophie."

The smile on her face when she saw the picture made my heart beat a little faster and I wasn't entirely comfortable with that. "They look so happy."

"They are," I said, and I might have sounded a little wistful, but I had no idea why. "And you didn't say anything about the name above hers."

Gillian's smile grew wider. "I saw it."

"Give it to me," I said putting my hand out again. "I can change the name right now from Strawberry Fields to—"

She set the phone on the counter. "Don't do that."

So yeah, I wore an obnoxiously smug smirk. "But you said you didn't want me to call you that."

"I never said that. I said my name is Gillian. Which it is."

"So I can call you that?"

She shrugged, and I took that as a yes.

"Just so you know," I said, "when you asked me if I had a harem and I laughed, it was because I've never found much use for girls, other than sex that is."

"Women," she corrected. "At our age I think the term women is more appropriate, and I'm not exactly sure how to take that comment, or what it even means."

"It means football has been my life, and since girls, women, whatever, don't play, I've never been inclined to stick around."

"I play," she said, sounding offended.

My lips twitched in amusement. "Yes, I'm sure you do, and I'm also certain you're pretty good at it. But if you'd let me finish, what I'm trying to say is other than my sister-in-law, I've never really had a meaningful conversation with a woman . . . until you."

Those green eyes glittered with an emotion I couldn't quite define, and for a moment the sassy, full of fire woman standing in front of me was speechless.

Admitting that should have made me look arrogant and uncaring, but hell, I was, so I didn't let it bother me. It felt good to say it out loud. Confess something I had never realized about myself until her.

All of this taking place right now though meant I was going to move forward. That I was Adam and I would be giving into Eve's temptation.

That I would take a bite of the forbidden fruit standing in front me. And God help me, I hoped I wasn't going to burn in hell because of it.

Or in the context of my world . . . lose my position on the team.

I glanced back up at the clock. "Shit, I have to go."

Her head twisted to look at the time. "You better hurry," she said, swatting my ass as I rushed passed her.

Oh, no, that was not going unaddressed. I whirled around and took her in my arms. "Extra-low fives are for the field, between players. A girl should kiss a guy properly when saying goodbye," I breathed really close to her mouth.

When she brought her lips to mine, I pulled away, and strutted backwards. "Meet me in our spot on the bridge at ten."

Gillian's mouth was hanging wide open in protest. "But you just said you wanted to wait until Sunday?"

"I do, to be inside you, but that doesn't mean we can't start the foreplay early."

That made her smile and blush.

"Oh, and have those lips ready," I winked. "I want that proper kiss."

She smiled even wider. "You really are too much, Carrington."

She had no idea how much I was, but then again . . . *neither did I.*

Fourteen

Bump and Run

Gillian

THIS WAS A day I had dreaded for as long as I could remember, but this year I didn't dislike it as much as I usually did.

No, this year, for the first time, I had a reason not to dislike it.

I had Lucas.

The end of the first two weeks of training camp marked the last of the private field time. Tomorrow practices would be open to the public.

Fans in the stands weren't the bad part—the bad part was that opening practices to the public meant the cheerleaders had arrived to put some pep in everyone's step.

And I mean everyone's step.

The single players were already foaming at the mouth, and the girls were only just unloading their stuff from the bus.

Like the players, the cheerleaders surrendered their car keys at Soldier Field and took a bus down here.

My father lived in a very calibrated world. One where each second of every day had a purpose. Therefore, no one under his watch needed his or her own set of wheels. There were very few exceptions to this rule.

Since it was Sunday, and there had been another scrimmage my father wasn't too pleased with, he'd called practice early.

In truth, the game was unbelievable, but that was my father for you, always striving for something better. I didn't blame him, of course. This was his life, after all. Every day was the same—get up at five and go for a run, eat breakfast, watch some film, lead the eight a.m. meeting, more coaching, practice, workouts. His schedule was just as grueling as the players' schedule.

He also had a sixth sense about when to pull back, and today was the day. It was the first full round of cuts, and every player was on edge.

While my father took care of that, the guys were left with a little more free time before Sunday meal. And then after Sunday meal, they got the night off, with curfew being extended to two a.m.

And tonight I would be meeting Lucas, and we would be doing more than we had been the past few nights.

Lucas and I had met on the bridge each night since deciding we were going to be together. However, during the day it was a bit risky to meet up, and neither of us suggested it, which was why we weren't together right now.

The past few nights when we met, I felt like I was sitting on a glitter-covered cloud. On that rickety old bridge, the world around us faded away, and it was just the two of us, talking, laughing, kissing.

Lucas and I talked about everything. We had so much in common, more than just football. Our views about life, the universe, and the world. Our favorite basketball teams, foods, and even our mutual love of chocolate ice cream.

We shared our favorite movies, of which his was *Rocky*, whereas mine would always be *Jerry McGuire*.

He told me how he thought he would end up playing for the Patriots, and the emotional wall he put up when he ended up playing for the Bears.

We'd also talked about past lovers, his list was much longer than mine, and he left it at that. So did I.

I got off the elevator and looked around.

Since the cheerleaders were arriving today, most of the single guys were hanging out in the common area.

Of course they were.

Kutch was sitting on one of the sofas when I walked by. I had just showered in preparation for Sunday meal and thrown on a dress. This one was a long maxi-dress I had gotten at Top Shop. It had a different black floral pattern on each side and was a wrap. Again, living in Florida had made my wardrobe not only heat tolerant, but easy to wear. Hence the black flip flops I'd chosen for my feet.

My plan was to go to the library and read some trashy magazines to kill the next two hours until dinner.

Kutch was hopelessly trying to tape his own ankle. I'd heard Dallas say that during any single season, an athletic trainer would tape more than three thousand ankles.

As I looked at Kutch struggling, I figured I might as well add his to my count. Besides, somehow over the course of the past couple of years, I had become a master at taping. Massage, not so much—that I was still working on.

"Need some help?" I asked over his shoulder.

He glanced up. "Wow," he said. "Girl, you gotta date or what?"

"Funny," I answered. "Do you want help or not?"

He nodded. "You're my saving grace. Hit me."

With a shake of my head, I circled the couch and sat down. "Let me see," I said, directing him to move his leg from the coffee table to the sofa.

I set the materials next to me and began to undo what he had tried to do. While I was unwrapping his ankle, a rookie named Sean Juggerson, flopped down next to Kutch with his laptop in his hands.

"Juggs, my man," Kutch greeted.

The guys called him Juggs because of his last name, or maybe for a different reason, I had no idea.

"Hey," Juggs said to Kutch, "so this girl on Tinder says her three favorite things are whiskey, beer, and nachos. What should I tell her are my three favorite things?"

"Blowing the barn," one of the guys yelled from the chair across from us.

"No, I got, it," said the other guy in the seat beside him. "Porn, playboy, and jerking the turkey."

Everyone was laughing.

I didn't really know either guy, but I think they were from the practice squad.

Kutch shook his head in laughter. "No, Juggs, they got it all wrong. You should say balls, balls, balls." And then he cracked up even more.

I was used to this kind of talk, just like I was used to being treated like I wasn't even in the room. As the coach's daughter, the players preferred to interact with me as little as possible. I got it. Most of the time they censored what they said, but sometimes they forgot I was even around.

Like now.

"Fuck all of you," Juggs said. "This is serious shit here! What if she turns out to the be *the one*?"

As I started wrapping, I glanced over toward Sean and saw that he was furiously typing away.

I wondered what he'd decided to tell her. I wanted to offer my opinion, and I was about to, when I caught sight of Lucas entering the room. He was over at the Ping Pong table across the room. And just like that, my heart started to do that pitter-patter thing it always seemed to do when he was in the same room as me.

His expression was hard though, and he didn't look happy to see me. His gaze flickered between me and Kutch, me and Kutch, me and Kutch.

I sighed inwardly. That territorial *she's mine* thing, the alpha male in him, was emerging. I could tell by the look on his face. I only hoped he knew how to keep a lid on it. He was going to have to learn how to temper it, especially since he knew being around these guys was my job.

Out of nowhere, one of the squad guys shouted, "Yo, Carrington, you ever try Tinder? Or are you a Match.com kind of guy?"

Lucas slammed the ball down and swatted it with his paddle as hard as he could. Thor returned it, and this time when Lucas swung his paddle, he blitzed the ball, nailing Thor right in the forehead.

That at least averted the conversation from dating and Lucas, to Thor. While the guys ripped on Thor, Lucas's gaze slid over me in the laziest way. This time it was warm and inviting, and I found myself getting hot despite the air conditioning that was blasting all around us.

While the Ping Pong game continued, the squad guys started to talk low, but loud enough that I could hear them, even over Juggs and Kutch's Tinder conversation.

One of them said, "That Carrington dude is wound way too tight. He needs to get laid."

The other guy responded with, "No shit. I've never even heard him crack a single joke about chicks. Everything is all business to him. He needs to lighten up."

"Dude can't. He's an arrogant prick, that's all there is to it."

"Right, I know. He never jokes, never laughs, never even swears."

At that one I had to suppress my own laughter. He swore all the time.

Even though I hated what they were saying. Even though they had no idea who Lucas really was or what he was about, at the same time I loved hearing he never talked about women.

Over the past three nights, Lucas and I had talked about so much. We'd also kissed so much my lips still tingled when I laid my head down at night. And I couldn't help myself, but I'd begun to think of him as mine.

Dangerous thought.

Very dangerous thought.

The conversation between the two squad players wasn't over. One said, "All starting quarterbacks are dull as rocks and completely humorless."

"Yeah, but I bet it works for him. Just watch him when he's out tonight. I bet he doesn't even have to try to score and a girl will be in his lap within minutes from the second he walks into the bar."

The snarl I wanted to unleash was only tempered by the cackle I'd hoped to avoid. Here they came, the beauty brigade, thirty-five of them with their manicured nails and perfectly highlighted hair. And let's not forget their boob jobs.

It might sound like I was jealous, but I wasn't. The thing about cheerleaders was that for all of their eight counts and high kicks, most of them were only here for the pseudo-celebrity status that came with their pom-poms. And of course their hopes of landing a player.

Mallory Harlow, who was their coach, was waiting for them to enter. She was an attractive woman in her early fifties, and she had arrived days ago to prepare. I actually liked her.

As the girls filed in wearing their big smiles, short shorts, and cropped tops, all of the guys' heads turned in their direction.

I finished up with Kutch, who was paying no attention to me, and stood. Frozen in place, I was almost afraid to look over at Lucas. Afraid that when I did he too would be gawking as much as the rest of the players at the cheerleaders.

My heart stopped, that's how nervous I was.

When I finally forced myself to look over at him, my pulse started to beat erratically. His gaze wasn't over at the door, but rather, it was on me. And it was filled with an emotion I hadn't seen before. He nodded his head toward a counter where a water container sat and I started walking toward it.

It was halfway between us, and with each step closer I took toward him, the air seemed thicker, and it was harder to breathe.

He poured a glass of water. I stood beside him. My knees were a little weak, and my breath grew tight and ragged while I pretended to be waiting for a turn at the pitcher. Slyly, he handed me the paper cup and then started to fill another. "You look beautiful," he whispered.

Beautiful was not anything anyone had ever called me, except him. Cute. Pretty. Freckled. Sure. But the way he said it made me feel beautiful. I flushed from head to toe. "Beautiful is in the other direction," I quipped, trying to be funny.

He set the pitcher down. "No, it's standing beside me."

I sipped my water and hated that my hands were trembling. "Thank you," I said, and it sounded bashful, something I had never been.

Those blue eyes simmered when he glanced toward me. "I can't wait until tonight."

I was just opening my mouth to tell him I couldn't either, when two short blondes with big boobs started rushing for him. "Oh my God, you must be the new quarterback."

To his benefit, he didn't turn right away. Instead he allowed his gaze to linger on me a moment longer. "I'll text you," he whispered.

I nodded, and then tossed my cup in the trash before heading toward the door. I didn't turn back as I left. I couldn't. Jealously was roaring in my ears and I knew the best thing I could do was walk straight ahead.

Yeah, so I guess Lucas wasn't the only one who had to learn to temper the green-eyed monster.

I hated that this thing between us was so hard. It felt so right when it was just the two of us that being together should have been the easiest thing in the world.

Too bad it was anything but.

Fifteen
Touchdown

Gillian

I'D BEEN ON my share of dates.

Ranging from disastrous, to sweet, to not really memorable, there wasn't a single one I would ever want to repeat.

Gatorland was my least favorite. That date was with an animal science bio major. Then there was the completely unexpected Soduko tournament, which turned out to be more fun than the guy I was with. That date was with an accounting major. I'd also gone on a date with an art history major, and he took me to a museum, which I found really boring.

The thing all those dates had in common was that I had nothing in common with the guys.

Lucas and I had everything in common. And yet, as I got out of the Uber and stood across the street from the hotel, I couldn't help but think having to get a room to have sex was a bit sleazy. I almost felt like I should have worn a raincoat with nothing under it.

He'd left with the guys on the bus to go to the village around seven. The plan was that he'd hang out with some of them and then disappear and go to the hotel.

The plan must have worked without him getting sidetracked by girls sitting on his lap because he'd sent me the address and room number thirty minutes ago. I'd replied immediately and told him I'd be there soon.

The both of us had called this a date, but it didn't feel like one. It felt like what it was, an arrangement to have sex.

Of course there was the cover-up lie I was still concocting in my head should my father ask me tomorrow where I'd gone, which didn't help ease my feelings about the situation.

The night off was for the players, of course, but the staff always took advantage as well. While most of the players headed to the bars in the village, the staff did things like go to the movies or do some shopping or go out to dinner.

I usually went to the yoga studio, and my father knew this. He also knew I liked the coffee shop next door to it and hung out there whenever I could.

At twenty-three, I shouldn't have to lie about meeting a guy, but in this case I did.

I was such a bad daughter.

All of a sudden that engineering major I had turned down for a date last semester was looking more appealing. Although I do think I was about three inches taller than he was, and if I remembered correctly, his hair was longer than mine.

Okay, so maybe not so appealing, after all.

Besides, Lucas was all I had been thinking about for the past two weeks. And although I had never been obsessed with a guy before, I was pretty certain that since I was, that meant if I wanted to get him out of my head, I wouldn't be able to.

I straightened my shoulders and looked at myself in the glass as I entered the building. I hadn't changed my clothes because I liked the way Lucas had looked at me earlier.

As I strode quickly into the building, I kept my head down. The light breeze of the closing door behind me caused my dress to flap open and expose my legs. It was a bit chillier tonight than most nights, and I felt a little cold.

In the elevator, I let out the breath I'd been holding, and suddenly felt nervous. Lucas and I weren't strangers anymore. We had kissed and touched and explored each other's bodies, but we hadn't gotten naked. Hadn't had sex. That was about to change, and I wasn't sure what else would change along with it.

The hotel room door was propped open and I knocked lightly before pushing in. The room was decorated in reds and golds with dark wood and antique furniture. The lights were dimmed and the curtains drawn. Neither of us drank alcohol, so when I saw the bottle of sparkling juice on the dresser with two wine glasses beside it, I knew Lucas had brought it.

Romantic.

He had been sitting on the end of the bed, but jumped to his feet as soon as I walked in. He looked as nervous as me, and instantly I felt at ease. Suddenly this didn't seem sleazy or unnatural at all . . . it felt right.

"Hey," he smiled. He'd changed since dinner and was no longer in his dress shirt and black slacks, but was now wearing a pair of worn jeans that hung low on his hips. He was wearing a Bears T-shirt, and it molded to his muscles like a second skin.

Unable to resist, I devoured the sight of him and when my mouth went dry, I licked my lips. "Hi," I replied, dropping my purse to the floor.

His gaze drifted over me, warming every inch of my skin, which only moments ago had felt chilled. When his eyes reached mine, he held out his hand for me to join him. That warmed me too. With his head, he indicated the bottle of sparkling juice. "Do you want some?"

I shook my head no. "Not yet, thank you." What I wanted was to run to him, but I settled for walking as I closed the distance between us. When I was close enough, I slipped my palm over his.

He circled my fingers to squeeze them, pulling me toward him. "God, you're so fucking beautiful," he said as he stared down at me.

"You're the beautiful one," I responded squeezing our locked hands.

He shook his head. "Don't say that. It's way too much for my ego to stand. And besides, you are the beautiful one. I don't get why you don't see it. You're a thousand times better looking than any of those cheerleaders."

How had he known what I was thinking earlier?

Could he read me that easily?

"You're just saying that so you can get in my pants," I joked, trying to make light of my insecurity.

His face grew serious and his stare was fierce. "I'm telling you that because it's the truth. Do you believe me?"

"I do now," I said, feeling slightly intoxicated by him. Feeling beautiful just because he was looking at me the way he was.

His mouth descended in a fiery rush over mine and his hands came up to touch my face where strong fingers stroked my cheeks.

I closed my eyes and surrendered all of my doubts as I melted into his strong arms. Our desire for each other was turning into a living, breathing thing that was swallowing us up whole. It was so strong that I swore the air crackled around us as it rose.

When his tongue pushed into my mouth, it was soft and slick and warm over mine, and I melted a little more into his embrace. Passion ignited and we lit up the room. His hands skimmed down my neck, my shoulders, my arms, gripping me tighter and pulling me closer as the heated sounds of our kisses erupted to fill the space between us.

In that moment, we both burst out in laughter. It was hard not to considering all the noise we were making.

With the heart-stopping kiss broken, my mouth tingled from his rough possession in the sweetest way. I touched my fingers to his lips. "Sorry," I said at the same time he did.

"It's strange not to have to worry about being quiet or sneak around, isn't it?" he asked.

I nodded and giggled until his gaze turned dark and scorching hot. Lucas had this way of looking at me that made my breath catch and hold at the same time it made my chest tighten in anticipation. This time was certainly no different than any other.

"I want you," he whispered even though he didn't have to.

Little wings that felt like butterflies hit the inside of my belly, and I closed my eyes. "I want you, too, so much."

He slid a hand to one of my breasts and started caressing it. He was softer and gentler than he normally was. It was surprising. "Do you like this?" he breathed, hot in my ear.

I opened my eyes then and looked into his. "Yes."

Something flickered in his gaze. It got hard and then his hand slid up to cup the back of my neck, where his fingers threaded through my hair. He pulled it, tilting my head back and exposing my throat. "And this?" he asked as his lips skimmed down my neck.

I nodded. "Uh-huh."

He pressed his lips harder and began biting as his mouth slid down, down, down. His fingers tightened in my hair, and I gasped when he tugged on it again.

I wanted to touch him, to strip him naked and stare at him before I explored every single inch of him. But when I tried to move, I was rendered motionless. He was sucking my skin between his teeth, and then circling his tongue against it to sooth the pain. As if the sensations flooding my body weren't already causing havoc, his hand began to thumb my nipple, and soon it was turning into a stiff peak even through the fabric of my dress.

Through all of that, I still somehow managed to run my fingers up his muscled chest, over his broad shoulders, and down his strong back. I stopped touching him the moment his other hand slid between my legs.

"And this," he said, no longer asking.

"Yes, I like it," I cried out. There was no reason to deny any of it. *I liked it all.*

I wanted it all.

I wanted him.

"What do you say we put that big bed to use," he said as he brought his mouth back up to mine. Again, it was not a question.

"This one? I asked, letting my head fall toward it.

"Yeah, that one," he grinned trying to capture my mouth even at the awkward angle I was at.

It happened so fast. Both of us a little off balance, we fell to the mattress in a tangle of arms and legs. I burst out into laughter, covering my face with my hand before peeking through my fingers at him. "God, I'm so sorry."

Lucas was laughing too, and then he pulled me into his arms and stroked a hand over my hair. "Don't be, it was my fault."

I shivered under his touch and turned my head to kiss his palm. "It kind of was, wasn't it?"

He stared at me in silence for a moment and then pulled me even closer. "I've never had anything like this with anyone."

I pressed my cheek to his chest and closed my eyes. I knew exactly what he meant. "I haven't either."

"I have to be honest, Gillian, it scares me," he whispered.

Opening my eyes, I pulled away to tip my face to his. "It scares me, too, Lucas. I thought my life was perfect until I met you, and now I feel like I don't know anything anymore."

He stroked his thumb along my lower lip, urging me to open for him. "You know this," he said, kissing me, hot and wet. "And this," he whispered as he pushed his tongue inside my mouth.

It sent an electric thrill all through me.

I did know that.

Boy, did I know that.

His hands moved down my body to slide beneath me, lifting me in a way that caused me to let out a startled gasp. With a chuckle, he moved a little, or he rolled, and somehow I ended up on top of him.

Straddling him, I pressed my knees to his hips and pushed his shirt up to reveal every ridge, ripple, dip and hollow of his abs.

God, he had strength.

And God, he was so hard.

I felt like a kid in a candy store as I traced the lines of his body, discovering nothing but sculpted muscle with each stroke. I was careful not to press too hard near the bruises, which served to remind me what he did with his days. Soon I found myself needing more, so I bent to nuzzle him, to taste him, to do more to him.

Fast as sin, he had me on my back and he held both my wrists above my head with one hand. Like this, he settled between my thighs and stared down at me through the dark fringe of his lashes. Those eyes of his were summer-sky blue, and I found myself lost in them.

In a heartbeat, he lowered his mouth very close to mine, but didn't kiss me. I craned my neck, seeking to meet his lips, but Lucas kept them a breath away. Control. We were fighting for it.

We were always fighting for it.

But when I felt heat and hardness on my hip, I made a disgruntled noise. I yearned to touch him, taste him, have him, and I couldn't. Shouldn't? I blinked that thought away. Here, it was the two of us, and no one would know.

Still, I knew I was the bad daughter.

"I'm first," he said, and his grin tipped the corners of his mouth. I let everything go and looked at him. Smug-like. Annoying. Really annoying. And really, really cute.

"Why are you first?" I asked, impatiently.

His free hand inched up the hem of my dress and found my bare thigh. "Because I am."

I thrust my body upward and huffed. "Haven't you heard of ladies before gentlemen?"

"I have," he chuckled. "And that is exactly what I plan on happening here, if you would stop wiggling."

Feeling like a caged animal, I used my instincts and pressed my teeth to his neck, since it was all I could reach.

He arched at the pressure of my lips on his skin and made a slight gasping sound.

I was surprised. It wasn't meant for pleasure. It was meant for him to let go of my arms, not that I really wanted him to. I just liked the challenge of it. "You like it when I bite?"

"Yeah . . ." Lucas breathed out with a small groan. "I like it when you bite."

Awareness simmered low in my belly. I had this. I so had this. He was under my control and he didn't even know it. "Will you do something for me?" I asked.

"Sure, what is it?" He let go of my arms and shifted to hold himself above me.

Power coiled tautly through his arms when he did. I found myself staring at them like I had his stomach, and almost forgetting what it was I wanted. When I said nothing, he started to reach for my arms again, but then I blinked out of my lustful haze. "Stand up and take your clothes off. I want to see you naked." It wasn't that I was some crazy perverted kind of girl. It was just that I had been dying to see his body.

"Girl . . ." he said with a smirk as he got off the bed. "That's not a problem."

"Girl?" I laughed.

He shrugged. "There's no way I'm letting Kutch be the only one to call you that."

All I could do was shake my head.

The amusement in our stares disappeared the moment he pulled his shirt off. Riveted by what I was looking at, I sat up as soon as he began to unfasten his jeans. I sucked in my breath when his pants hit the floor and he stood in front of me in only a pair of white boxer briefs. They were tight. So tight. And they not only encased his muscular thighs, but they very clearly outlined the rigid length of his erection.

He was beautiful, exquisite, a god in his own right. The Adonis that was mine for the night devoured me with his gaze as he reached for the waistband of his briefs. In that moment, I forgot to breathe. Forgot who I was. Forgot about everything except him and me and what we were about to do.

And then I gasped when his cock surged from his underwear. It strained upward, thick and pulsing, and I think I might have drooled. I know I licked my lips.

Lucas stepped forward, leaned down, hauling me off the bed and into his arms. "Your turn, Strawberry Fields."

That was much better than Girl.

Those butterflies took flight in my belly, and lower still, until I had to squeeze my thighs together in an effort to stop the ache. Once I felt I could stand on my own, I released my hold on his biceps and took a step back.

Without hesitation, my hands went to the tie that held my wrap dress together and with trembling fingers I undid it. Lucas was watching me, and when I let the fabric fall to the ground in a way I never had, he hissed a breath at the sight of me.

Flushing, I could feel heat creeping up my throat and covering my cheeks in pink. I'd never blushed this much in my life until I met him.

I was wearing black lace and satin garments beneath. They were new. I'd gone to the village a few days ago at lunch to get them. My bra was the push up type and my panties were the skimpy thong-style that made my legs look even longer.

His chest rose and fell as he stared at me. "The rest. Take those off, too." His voice had grown thicker, full of desire. Two weeks of wanting each other wasn't that long, but in the high-adrenaline environment we were in, it seemed like a lifetime.

While looking at him, at the size of his cock, I almost lost my footing, but then I found it and reached behind my back to unhook my bra. I watched him watch me and allowed the straps to fall down my shoulders. As I let the cups fall away to reveal my tiny swells, I noticed I wasn't the only one flushing. Pink tinged his cheeks, too, and he licked his lips as he watched me.

"The panties," he rasped.

Hooking my thumbs in the sides of the lace, I eased them over my hips. I did it slowly, enjoying the look on his face as he focused on me like I was the only thing that mattered. I let them fall to my ankles, where I stepped out of them. And then I was completely naked—just like him.

"Fuck," he muttered and ran a hand through his hair. "Turn around."

I did, one time only, and wished I had thought to ask him to do the same earlier.

"You're perfect," he breathed, reaching for me and splaying his hand over my ass to draw me close. "I can't wait to fuck you."

"I can't wait, either." My breasts were crushed against the hard wall of his chest and my entire body was on fire.

Lucas lowered me to the bed, and I thought he was going to fuck my brains out, but instead he slid his hands lower over my body, caressing and touching along the way as if he couldn't help himself. His palms glided over my breasts and then to my belly and finally to my hips. Then he pulled me down the mattress and positioned me so my ass was right on the edge of the bed with my legs dangling over it.

To my utter shock, he knelt on the carpeted floor between my thighs. My breath hiccupped and tore violently from my throat as he lowered his mouth to my sensitive flesh and licked up the center of it. "You're so wet for me, Gillian.

"Oh, God," I moaned.

"I'm going to fuck you right after I taste your sweet pussy," he breathed out.

"Oh, God," I moaned again.

When his tongue touched my clit and circled it, my entire body spasmed and I made a noise I had never heard before.

Using his fingers to spread me open, he licked me again and again and again, using the flat of his tongue to drive me higher and higher. I shuddered as pleasure began to roll through my body.

"Lucas," I called out as I felt myself tipping over the edge so hard and fast. I wasn't expecting it to happen so quickly.

Going up on my elbows, I stared down at his wicked, beautiful mouth and tongue.

He glanced up. "I can't get enough of the noises you make when you get turned on."

There was no shame on my part because the orgasm was now flooding my body and all I could do was shout out his name again and give him what he liked.

His breath blew hot against my sensitive flesh. "That's it, Gillian. Come for me."

Sweet tension curled inside my stomach, and each beat of my climax pulled another low moan from my throat. Unable to control myself, my fingers curled in the sheets and my body shook as I rode his tongue, shuddering and jerking and pulsing.

When I could see again, breathe again, function again, I looked down and saw his eyes burning brightly with lust. I extended my hand. "I want you inside me."

He licked his lips, as if liking the taste of me. "Fuck, I want that too. Just let me grab a condom."

I nodded and scooted up to the top of the bed.

Even though I laid there dizzy with exhilaration from the aftermath of my release, I watched every move he made.

The sexy way he bent to pull out his wallet from his back pocket, the strong way he stood to flip it open, how quickly he retrieved the foil packet, and then the hot way he slipped the condom on, stroking the latex down to the base.

The gasp I made wasn't on purpose, but if I knew I would be rewarded with the lustful gaze he sent my way, it would have been.

My body was already humming in anticipation when he positioned himself on top of me. His palms were on either side of my head and he leaned to kiss me, just once, soft and light.

Using his arms to keep from crushing me, his cock nudged me, and I parted for him, tilting my hips to allow him entrance. Moving above me, he rubbed the tip of his cock along my folds, pushing in a little before reaching between us to guide himself all the way in.

I moaned when he entered me, and he not only did the same, but he also shivered. There was something about that shiver that made my heart beat even faster. Something that made this all the more right—it was the fact that we both craved this, needed this, couldn't not have it.

Still, I was very aware of how wrong it was.

It was instinctive to reach for him, put my hands on his face, to brush his hair from his eyes. His face looked a little pained when I did, but then it softened. I wondered then if he ever allowed anyone to touch him, I mean really touch him, the way I was, not just on the surface.

He'd told me about his mother leaving when he was a baby and his brother raising him. Like me, he'd had no female figure around as a child to show him warmth and tenderness. Perhaps unlike me, he was never even aware he had missed it.

"Gillian," he breathed.

"Lucas," I breathed back.

With our gazes so full of intensity, he started to move—in, out, in, out—in slow, even strokes. I slid my hands over his shoulders down to his biceps and when I did, I felt him trembling.

It was the same vibration I felt in my own body.

It was raw, real, and undeniable.

It was a feeling fueled with such intensity, neither of us could ignore it.

His eyes closed for a moment, and he put his forehead against mine before he opened them again. Without taking his gaze from mine, he began to move faster, harder, and I mimicked his rhythm.

He'd said he wanted to fuck me, but that one word could mean so much. This felt like more than that, though. Like he wanted to be a part of me. Like he wanted me to be a part of him. Like he wanted us to become one.

My pulse accelerated, nearly exploding when he started to pound into me. It was then that I put my arms around his neck to bring his mouth down to my neck. Happy to oblige, he kissed me there. I tilted my head to offer more, and he took it. He pressed his teeth to my skin like I had done to him and like me, he bit a little and then used his tongue to smooth the spot.

I closed my eyes, clamping my teeth together to hold back the cry that threatened to burst free.

In.

Out.

In.

Out.

When he slid his hands beneath my rear to tilt me against him,

I snapped my eyes open. He withdrew and then surged again. Almost instinctively, I wrapped my legs around his waist as he hammered into me.

Now his expression was fierce, the strain of what he was doing evident in the clench of his jaw.

I let out a sharp cry, my arousal taking over.

"Are you close?" he asked.

"Yes," I cried out. "Are you?"

"Fuck, yes," he hissed as he drove into me. He was deep. Impossibly deep, and when I felt the pulsating hardness of his cock as he took me, I couldn't hold back any longer.

An orgasm quaked through me like an erupting volcano. It was hot, explosive, and so intense that I shook with the magnitude of it. I arched, giving myself up to him, going wild beneath him, and then I screamed his name. "Lucas!"

His eyes glittered as he slowed his thrusts. Then he closed them, his cock stroking deep and then shallow, deep and then shallow before going deep one last time and remaining there.

I knew he was coming when his entire body went taut. I pushed through my limpness to keep my eyes open and watch him.

All the muscles in his arms and chest were straining before they coiled tightly. "Gillian," he gritted out as he pulsed into me. "Fuck, Gillian."

The way he said my name almost made me come again.

His release seemed to go on and on, and I relished the look on his face. The *I'm coming* look on him looked way too good.

It was something I could get used to.

Slowly lowering his body onto mine, he covered me completely for a moment before rising on his elbows and pushing the hair from my eyes. His chest heaved and his breath was hot against my skin as he placed feather-like kisses all over me.

I made a noise, or two, arching slightly and pressing my breasts upward.

He was still inside me, and as I continued to wiggle beneath him, I started to feel him getting hard again.

Astonished, I slid my hands over his shoulders and laughed a little. "How are you—?" I stopped, more than dumbfounded that he could actually be ready to go again so quickly.

"You can ask how I'm already getting hard again, it's okay," he grinned.

I raised a brow. "Obviously, I don't have to."

Believe it or not he looked just as surprised as me. "No, you don't because you know it's because of you."

Confusion creased my brow.

"There's just something about you," he whispered in my ear. "You do crazy things to me."

My hands were roaming over his body in that way I had dreamt of, but when he spoke, I paused for a moment. "There's something about you," I repeated, and then I squeezed the muscles in his biceps. "Here," I said, and moved up to his shoulders, "and here." I pressed my fingers into his skin as I slid them down his back. "And here that does crazy things to me."

Although he made a sound of satisfaction, he didn't laugh. Instead, he placed his palms on the mattress and pushed up to look at me. "I'm serious, Gillian," he said. "Not only am I unable to stay away, but I don't think I can get enough of you."

In that moment I knew he was serious, and my heart nearly pounded out of my chest, because like him, I felt the same way.

And like him, I had no idea why.

Or maybe I did.

Sixteen

Holding

Lucas

FOOTBALL SPEAK WAS a language.

Any player not fluent in it would be lost, both on and off the field. Luckily for me, our offense at Notre Dame used the same terminology as the Bears.

But *after-sex speak* was not a language I was well-versed in, or fluent in, and I hated to admit I felt out of my element.

I stared at her as I stroked my hand down her back, but when she tried to lay her head on my chest, I didn't know what to do, so I kissed her and covered her body with mine. I didn't want to upset her, but the bottom line was I was *not* a cuddler.

Never had been.

In fact, the only time I ever actually slept in the same bed with anyone was during my high school years, and that night was not on purpose.

Sometime during the summer following my sophomore year, I got involved with this group of guys who liked to indulge. Drugs and alcohol had started to become my focus, and football had taken a back seat. Partying was at an all-time high.

My behavior was out of control, and I was headed down a road that would lead me nowhere good.

It was three weeks before my junior year was about to begin that my brother scared me straight.

The guys and I were cruising around town when we got pulled over. Turned out the car we were in didn't belong to any of them. It was stolen. The cops hauled us all down to the station. When I called my brother, he told me he wasn't going to bail me out unless I promised to get my shit back on track.

At first, I hung up on him. Who the hell was he to tell me what to do? But as the hours passed between those four walls with the smell of puke and piss all around me, I started to think about what he'd said.

When my bed creaked and one of the guys laid down at the other end because there wasn't enough room for all of us to sleep, I knew I never wanted to end up in a place like this ever again.

In the morning, after I shoved out of the small bed and climbed over the dude who was dead to the world, I was called into holding, where my brother was waiting for me, and as soon as I saw him, I agreed to his terms.

Shortly after that incident, Nick moved the two of us out of the house we had both lived in since birth, the one in the ghetto. The new place was small, but in a much better school district. By then he had graduated college and started to invest in real estate. He was doing pretty good. Good enough that we didn't have to worry about if we were going to have enough money to eat that week and pay rent, at least.

It was the first time in our lives money wasn't our primary concern.

Ever since that summer I hadn't drank or done drugs or slept in the same bed with anyone.

With my brother beside me, I found my focus, and knew what I wanted. Together, we went after it.

It was after I'd had Gillian for the third time that she tried to lay on top of me and nestle against me.

To cuddle.

Again, I didn't say anything, but when I went to get up, she pulled me back to the bed. "Where are you going?" she asked.

I was uncomfortable.

I must have looked pathetic.

And she saw it.

Always thinking everything I did, felt, or said had a reason, she prodded me for information. Although I couldn't believe it, I found myself not only telling her about the sleepover, but about my *no cuddling* thing.

"You're afraid of intimacy." She said it so matter-of-factly she could have been telling me I was next in line.

"You're crazy," I told her. "Stop overthinking everything."

It might have turned into an argument, but she diffused it quickly. "Then prove it to me."

When the gauntlet was thrown down, there was no backing away. And before I knew it, I ended up lying beside her—cuddling.

Cuddling.

Even the word bothered me.

So why did I do it?

Because she just had this way about her.

With her head on my chest, I was stroking her hair and listening to her tell me about what it was like to grow up the daughter of one of the most famous quarterbacks in NFL history.

Whenever Gillian told a story, she had my attention. Tonight though, I listened to every word, to every detail with astute awareness. So much so, that she rose up on her elbows to make sure I was paying attention.

Didn't she know she didn't have to?

Didn't she know she captivated me?

Once satisfied that I was all in, she fell back down and continued to trace my body with her fingers.

She had a thing about that.

And I kind of liked it.

In fact, I kind of liked all of this. The sparkling juice we'd drank together and toasted to the upcoming season, the exploration she'd taken over my entire body, the way she looked at me when she did, and how I felt with her in my arms.

Like a million dollars.

Damn it. I could not let this thing between Gillian and me get complicated. Get away from me.

Shit, my brother used to be a lot like me when it came to women . . . until one day he just wasn't. It happened that fast. One minute he was single, the next he was married and becoming a father.

It was crazy.

This thing between Gillian and me, though, was complicated and short-term. It would end when she went to college to finish her doctorate and I started the regular season, both of which would happen at the end of training camp.

That was one thing we had both agreed upon.

Abruptly she sat up and her expression looked troubled.

"What's wrong?" I asked, frowning.

"You never answered that guy's question earlier."

Drawing a blank, I asked, "What guy and which question?"

"The player from the practice squad. He asked you if you preferred to use Tinder or Match.com?"

I shook my head and pulled her down onto the bed where I let my hand travel up her thigh, over her hip, and to her breast. "That's because I didn't have to."

She started to push herself up. "Why not?"

The hell she was going anywhere, and I used a little force to keep her in place, not enough to hurt her, of course. "Because it was a stupid question."

Her frown deepened. "Stupid because it should be obvious or stupid because you—"

I should have let her go on, dig herself into that grave she was carving out so nicely, but time was short and I didn't want to waste it. "Gillian, come on, you have to know I've never been on any dating sites."

She gave me a doubtful look.

I loosened my hold on her. "I swear. In fact, until tonight, I've never even been on a real date."

"You've never picked a girl up and taken her out?"

I shook my head. "Never."

"What about prom?"

"Didn't go. Anything else you have to know right now?"

She stayed where she was, but did turn to glance at the clock. When she did, she sighed. "No. Well . . . yes. When do you think we'll see each other again?"

Taking the chance to be a smart-ass, I answered with, "Tomorrow on the field."

Then she did try to shove me back. "You know what I mean," she said, sounding a little wistful.

"We don't have time off for twelve more days," I sighed, not moving an inch, "but it's an overnight," I added, a little more upbeat, pulling her closer.

Her expression lightened. "Something to look forward to." She didn't sound convincing.

Not that we had the time, but I sat up and spread her gorgeous thighs to bare that pretty pussy of hers. "I want to make you come again."

Her smile turned heated, but she shook her head no. "We really should get going. You can't miss the bus back to campus or my father will serve your ass on a dinner platter tomorrow night."

Seriously, she was right. "It would be worth tasting you one more time."

Her chest rose with the forceful inhalation of her breath, as if she was waging a war to decide, but then she sat up and threw her legs over the side of the bed. "Tempting, but we really should get going."

I got up too, and like her, started to dress.

As she pulled her panties up, I stared at her, watched her, and memorized everything I could about her.

"Will you touch yourself this week and think of me?" she asked bluntly.

Most of the time she amused me and I found myself wanting to laugh at the things she simply blurted out.

I liked that about her.

A lot.

But this time I didn't laugh at her straightforwardness. This time I answered seriously. "Every night," I admitted.

Her eyebrows went up and there was a mischievous twinkle in her eye. "You could call me."

The thought was like receiving an electrical charge. "How about as soon as we get back?"

She was tying her dress when she looked up with a flush that made me realize just how sweet she really was. "Ummm . . . sure."

I pulled my shirt over my head. "Why do you sound uncertain?"

While she slipped her sandals on, she said, "I've never had phone sex."

How could I not chuckle? "Me either, but how hard can it be? No pun intended."

At that she laughed. "Call me, and let's find out."

The statement was simple, but it made my body roar with the need to have her. Our time was up though, so I settled on crossing the room and kissing her for the few minutes we had left.

This kiss turned soft and tender. It was a direct contradiction to the raging out-of-control kisses we had shared up until now.

When she pulled back, she said a little breathlessly, "I had a really good time on our *date.*"

I waggled my brows. "Girl, if I knew dating was this much fun, I would have done it a lot sooner."

She fixed me with a stare that was a lot like her father's when he was pissed.

I raised my palms. "Kidding, just kidding."

"It wasn't funny."

"No, it wasn't," I confessed.

She grinned at me. "Come on, smart-ass, we have to go."

With a shake of my head I took her hand and headed for the door. In a hurry, I never slowed until we reached the lobby. Once there, I disentangled our hands just in case anyone knew us, which I was certain no one would, or else I would have been worried.

Neither of us said a word, but we both felt the implication of what we were embarking on.

This private affair.

It was not without consequences.

It was off-limits.

Forbidden.

Outside the hotel, I bent down so that I could see inside the back of the Uber car. With my hand grasping the door, I said, "Later, Strawberry Fields."

She gave me a wave, and then I closed the door.

I didn't like ending the night this way. It felt wrong, but all I could do was stand on the curb and watch the car pull away.

"Hey, Carrington."

I turned to see Thor with his arm around a girl and his mouth hanging open. I knew he would be at the hotel, but never thought I'd run into him. I mean come on, the chances of coming and going at the same time were small, and yet they were still there.

I should have been smarter.

"Was that Coach's daughter you were with?" he asked, a shocked expression on his face.

Unnerved, I ran a hand through my hair. "Thor, this stays between us."

"Coach's daughter," he said again, as if he still couldn't believe it.

"Thor," I hissed.

He patted his girl on the ass and kissed her. "Bye, baby," he said, and then set his attention on me. "You don't have to tell me twice."

"Thanks."

"No problem. Now, come on, roommate, we need to hustle if want to catch that bus."

He knew about Gillian and me, but at least I knew he'd keep quiet.

What I didn't know then was that was only the start of the dominos I couldn't stop from falling.

Seventeen

The Grind

Lucas

TODAY WAS FAN day.

Although practices had been opened to the public for the past week, it was the first time the players were required to interact with them.

Since days in NFL training camp were beginning to seem infinite, I wasn't as opposed to what was coming as the vets were. They'd started bitching about it days ago. Guess they knew what to expect.

Waking up before six, breakfast seemed like nothing but a chore. Today, I was so sore from the day before that I decided to skip it and just sleep in.

The drops of water I felt splashing me had me jerking upright. "What the fuck?"

Thor was standing over me shaking his wet head. "Hey honey, wakey, wakey, eggs and bakey."

With my glare, I told him to back the fuck off.

Fresh from the shower, he was naked. I swore the dude never had his fucking pants on. "Seriously, Carrington, time to get up."

"Relax, man, I'm skipping breakfast," I said.

All of a sudden the covers were jerked off me. "No fucking way. Whitney will eat me for breakfast if I show up in the cafeteria without you."

I rolled over and punched my pillow. "Then skip."

The mattress dipped. "Dude, you know I'm all for booty calls, right?"

Not wanting to hear his wisdom, I put the pillow over my head.

Thor laid his body right beside mine.

I wasn't having that, and I shoved him off the edge.

Unaffected, he sat up. "What I'm saying my friend is you might want to get some sleep tonight."

I glared at him, but I knew he wasn't exactly wrong. For the first few nights after our date, Gillian and I met at the bridge and then went to our own rooms before curfew, where we spent another hour or so on the phone. But then somehow the phone thing started to seem ridiculous. I mean she was just a few floors away. That's how I ended up sneaking down to her room and slipping out later.

It wasn't smart, but then again I wasn't thinking with that head, was I?

"You listening to me?"

"Yeah," I answered.

"Then get the fuck up. I have to get over there and chow."

There was an edge in his voice that sounded like concern. I avoided looking down. "Why? What's going on?"

The dude didn't know when to cool it and got back on the bed. He pressed his head into my pillow like we were about to cuddle. "Yesterday, after the second practice, I weighed two hundred and sixty-two pounds," he sighed.

No wonder the bed hadn't collapsed when he got on it. "Man,

you're eight pounds under your magic number. Isn't that a fail for you?"

The bed did wobble when he stood. "Fuck you very much for finally getting it. Now, get your horny ass out of bed and let's go."

Not wanting to be a dick, I got out of bed and threw some clothes on. I figured I'd better eat too. If I went down on the field because I'd skipped breakfast, Coach would have me up on that podium tonight for his daily roasting, and trust me, fun was fun, but that didn't look too fun.

In truth, as quarterback I didn't have to adhere to the same weight standards as the positions. Some guys were too heavy, some too light, either way they were cut on the spot at weigh in time if they didn't hit their magic number.

Not being accountable for that rule was a good thing for me because I had always been on the lean side. No matter how much I ate or worked out, my weight stayed the same. I was built like my father and my brother.

Lean, mean, fighting machines was what Nick called us.

So yeah, I got Thor's issue. Felt it. And the kicker was I knew he had a reason to be worried. Right now the team was sitting at seventy guys, twenty had already been let go, and it seemed lately each day another one dropped due to injury or because they broke one of Coach's rules.

To make matters worse, the team trainers had started keeping tabs on every bruise, strain, or ailment reported. If an injury was reported, that player became obligated to attend treatment sessions during the few windows of downtime that existed throughout the day. This was quickly becoming a great incentive for the players to *not* report any injuries that were otherwise manageable.

Thor was unusually quiet as we walked along the pathway to the cafeteria, not a word about his girls or Gillian.

It was so unlike him, I knew he must really be worried. I had to try to ease his mind. "Hey, dude you've been killing it in practice lately. I'm sure even if you're under weight, your performance will be taken into account."

He was wearing his baseball cap so low that if I was trying to read him, I wouldn't have been able to. "You hear about Robson yesterday?"

I shook my head. "Just saw him bagging his stuff, but I don't know why. Do you?"

Some of the dew from the trees dripped down onto his hat, and when he took it off, he glared over at me with an entirely too pissed off look. "Yeah, I do. And so would you if you weren't so preoccupied."

"Just tell me," I snapped.

"His goal weight was two hundred and fifty-nine pounds. He weighed in at two hundred and fifty pounds."

"Shit," I muttered.

"Yeah, it happened just like that." He snapped his fingers. "His weigh in was before practice started. And not even an hour later, he was carrying his shit out to the van, which, by the way, was waiting to take him and three others back to Soldier Field. Things are getting serious around here, Lucas, and you might want to remember that the next time you head downstairs after curfew, or any other time for that matter."

Seriously, that comment was uncool, and I glared right back at him. "Don't take your shit out on me, and keep your mouth shut about her."

He shook his head. "Whatever, dude."

The mood altered, I kept my own mouth shut the rest of the walk and so did he. Wouldn't you know it though, as soon as we opened the big double doors, the first person the both of us see, was Coach.

And our mood once again altered. No longer angry, but now

nervous, anxious, anything but ready to face him.

Of course I had a shit ton of guilt to deal with, and Thor had the reaper hanging over his head, so being pissed at each other was no longer on top of the list. We both turned our heads toward each other and started talking, and walking faster. It was a great avoidance strategy, and it usually worked with Coach.

Just not this time.

"Carrington," Coach yelled, almost as if he were waiting for me to arrive.

A cold sweat poured from my brow, as I nodded my head toward him in acknowledgement.

"Grab your tray and take a seat over here."

Did he know where I was last night?

That I was with Gillian.

With his daughter.

"Yes, Coach. I'll be right there," I told him as I passed by him, and then hustled as fast as I could to escape his appraising glance.

"You're on your own," Thor muttered.

While I grabbed oatmeal, eggs, and two glasses of juice, Thor went for whole-grain pancakes. Stacks and stacks and stacks of them. When he covered them in syrup and brown sugar, I seriously thought I might puke.

"How the hell are you going to scoff down all that food and keep it down during practice?" I asked.

He grabbed some silverware. "I don't care about keeping it down during practice. Just until after weigh in."

"Good luck." I patted him on the shoulder.

At the end of the line, he veered to the right.

I had no choice but to go left. "Thor," I called.

He turned his head.

"See you at practice. You got this."

With a nod, he mouthed, "Thanks."

I took a deep breath, and headed toward Coach. I wasn't headed toward his office, but it felt that way.

There was a roil in my gut that more than likely was going to prevent me from eating anything. But with Coach watching me, I knew I would be doing what Thor was going to do, force it down.

Over the past few days Coach had been relentless. His end-of-practice lectures had grown more scolding. His ire raged when players dropped balls, missed blocks, or showed a lack of concentration.

I got it.

It wasn't the individual he was after. As a team, we weren't connecting, and he could see it. We were running every play four to five to six times, and we were still making the same mistakes.

Something had to change, and it was up to him to make that change.

Was I going to be it?

The cafeteria was almost full, but the seat across from Coach was wide open. Guess it was my lucky day.

Hardly.

It wasn't like I hadn't been spending enough time with him. *Only a minimum of two and one-half hours a day.* He was the quarterback coach, after all.

And it wasn't like each and every time I had to look him in the eye, I didn't want to confess that I was banging his daughter.

Not using those words exactly.

Of course, I also wanted to let him know I had the upmost respect for his daughter.

Which I did.

And it wasn't like every time I stepped foot out on the field I thought it could be my last.

I did.

This time would be no different. Worry plagued me. Did he know? Did someone see? Did he see? Was I out?

By the time I got to the table, I seriously thought I was going to puke.

Turned out Coach had finished his breakfast and was studying a playbook that he had in front of him.

He was using his pen to draw lines. Coach was a fanatic when it came to pace. Always wanting us to move faster, think faster, act faster, and I was certain he was coming up with something to make that happen.

This was about football.

Thank fuck!

"New plays?" I asked as I set my tray down, relief rushing through me.

With a glance in my direction, he pushed his reading glasses up on his nose. "Yeah. After yesterday's practice it's became pretty damn obvious the offensive line needs some help in learning how to move together."

Not that I would ever disagree with him to his face, but I didn't think they were that bad. The problem wasn't the line, but rather a single person on that line. "You think?" I asked.

He nodded.

I said nothing more, and shoved a forkful of eggs in my mouth.

The book had his new play ideas mapped out to the letter. He pointed. "The offensive line's priority is to work together. They are a moving, thinking, adapting wall that is *supposed* to be protecting you, and at the same time, creating space for the running back to run. The problem is there are way too many Goddamn cracks in the wall."

Okay, so I nodded, which I hated doing because I felt like I was selling the team out. But he was right. And he was looking right at me for affirmation. As I gulped my juice, I had to force myself to relax my throat or it was coming back up. And with my luck, more than likely landing right on Coach's playbook. That would not go over well.

There was a red pen in his hand and he used it to demonstrate as he spoke. "If one guy, just one, misses a block or goes in the wrong direction, then the entire wall comes tumbling down. That's what I'm going to change."

Whether he knew it or not yet, the issue was the starting center. Walton was a three hundred and five pound rookie who needed some help. Execution wasn't his problem. He could snap the ball to me like it was no one's business. He just couldn't call the plays to the line fast enough or loud enough.

That was for the Offensive Coordinator to work out, not me, but he hadn't addressed it yet. I guess Coach must have noticed it though, or he wouldn't be working on new strategies.

After walking me through several different eighteen-second plays, all meant to prevent me from getting crushed nose-deep in the turf, I had to admit I was thankful for the time he was taking to work on the situation. The days were proving to be pretty grueling.

When he looked up to tell me about another idea, his gaze went over my shoulder and he called out, "Gillian."

Shit.

Shit.

Shit.

I wanted to get up and excuse myself before she came over. I wanted to run hard and fast. I wanted to—.

Just as I jerked my head around, I knocked over that second glass of juice I'd taken—all over the playbook. His playbook.

Yeah, me, the big tough guy was nervous. But come on, who wouldn't be. The girl I was . . . screwing . . . for lack of a more politically correct way to put it, was being summoned over to the table I was sitting at . . . across from her father . . . who didn't know about us . . . who also happened to be my coach.

So yeah, I was nervous.

Coach glared at me as I popped to my feet and started wiping up the mess with the few napkins I had on my tray. He didn't help though. Instead he got to his feet and waved his daughter to sit beside him.

This wasn't happening.

Why hadn't I just stayed in bed?

"Hi, Dad," she said as she circled the table.

"Sweetheart, I feel like I haven't seen you in days. Where have you been hiding?" he asked.

"Oh, in Lucas's pants," I imagined her saying, and cringed even at the thought.

"You're the one who hasn't been around," she answered, setting her tray down and giving him a quick hug. "Where have you been?" she asked. She was smart, I had to give her that.

Me, I was the dumbass wiping up the head coach's playbook.

Coach actually looked a little sheepish. "Nowhere," he said, and quickly directed his attention to me. "Let's hope you didn't ruin it," he muttered.

With the most amused grin on her face, Gillian followed his gaze. "Lucas, are you okay there? Here, it looks like you could use some help," she giggled, setting a wad of napkins from her own tray beside me, and taking one to assist.

Smooth, Gillian.

I would have glared at her, but then I'd have to explain to her father why I was being rude to his daughter, which would lead to a whole other conversation that was not going to take place.

When our hands touched, I tried to keep my face neutral. "I got it," I replied, as I started to wipe even faster.

She and her father both sat as I shoved the soggy napkins onto my tray right beside what was left of my scrambled eggs, and then picked up a dry one to finish cleaning up.

"I think that should just about do it, Lucas," Coach said to me.

Being dense was never a problem I had. I knew that was his way of dismissing me, but all of a sudden I wanted to stay. I picked it up. "I don't think it's ruined. It should dry fine. I'm really looking forward to executing those plays later," I said, and then boldly sat back down, where I promptly started shoveling the cold eggs in my mouth.

The fierce look he gave me should have sent me packing, but I wasn't going anywhere. His daughter had started something I was all too happy to help her finish.

Completely ignoring me, Coach turned in her direction. "Did you ever take your car in for that recall I told you I read on the manufacturer's website?"

She shook her head. "Not yet, but I will. I just haven't had time."

He narrowed his gaze at her and started explaining the importance of whatever the issue was.

Now she was rolling her eyes.

I had to fight hard not to laugh.

Seeing them together put Coach in a different light. My father would never have taken the time to look up recall notices on my vehicle. Hell, he'd have to know what I was driving, which happened to be my brother's hand-me-down Range Rover at the moment.

Yeah, I was still dirt poor. No money had been deposited in my account yet since I wasn't officially on the team until camp was over and my contract was signed. If I wasn't tossed out on my ass, that was.

Then the signing bonus would be all I would get.

While Coach and Gillian went back and forth about the car, the best thing I could have done was avoid looking at her. But since when did I ever do what was best? While her father talked to her about something or other, I stole a long glance across the table.

She really was beautiful, and not in that fake way, like the cheerleaders who seemed to be everywhere lately. Gillian had a natural beauty.

Today she wasn't wearing athletic wear. Instead she wore a navy skirt that stopped just below her knees with a white Bears tank top. Her hair was upswept into a messy bun like she sometimes wore it, secured with a clip that I always undid whenever we were alone.

That would not be right now, I reminded myself.

Gillian was slight, even at five feet and ten inches, she still appeared small and fragile. It was her frame, her high, prominent cheekbones, her narrow hips, and her tiny breasts, that lent to that. But trust me, she was anything but.

She was fire and ice, and it really turned me on.

She really turned me on.

The hell of it was, this was so unlike me. In the past, I had never given a girl more than a single thought, but I couldn't stop thinking about her.

Nick said that's what happened to him with Tess when I talked to him last night about her. He said watch out, bro, or before you know it you won't be able to take the bull by the horns because they'll have you. *Whatever the hell that meant.* Shit, was this what he meant. That being around her would turn me into mush.

The eggs stuck in my throat and I had nothing to wash them down with. I started coughing uncontrollably.

Coach glanced over me. "You okay, son?"

I nodded, pounding my chest.

"Here, drink this," Gillian offered, handing me her half glass of juice. I took it and gulped it. "Thanks," I said as I set the empty glass down. "I'll grab you another one."

She shook her head. "No thank you, I'm done."

Shit, I'd sat across from them the entire time she'd eaten her breakfast and had no idea where the time went.

Was that what Nick meant?

That I'd get so lost in her, I'd lose track of time.

No, what he meant was that she'd own me.

The thought didn't sit well.

It was really time for me to leave. I started to gather up my items just as Coach said, "Don't you agree, Lucas?"

I blinked at him while he wrote something in the playbook that was still partially wet. I had no idea what the hell he'd even asked, but I nodded my head anyway. "Yes, Coach, I do."

"You do?" He glanced up in surprise with the first grin I'd ever seen him crack, but then went back to writing his play with a shake of his head. For all I knew I could have just told him I wore girl's underwear out on the field. Gillian started cracking up, and this time there was no way I could stop myself from narrowing my eyes at her. All she did in response was shrug.

This was about to get interesting.

Just then Thor walked by, and with Coach's back to him, his mouth formed a silent O as he pretended to hightail it out of there with animated arms, or maybe he really was.

"Hold up, Thor," I stood and called out. "Sorry, I have to run," I said to Coach, who just grunted back. I gave Strawberry Fields one last look, and fuck she was too much with that smirk on her face.

Thor slowed his pace.

"Gillian," I said with a tip of my head having no idea how I should be saying goodbye to Coach's daughter. I knew how I'd be saying goodbye to her if we were alone though, and that would be with a swat on the ass.

"Bye, Lucas," she said with a small wave.

I wanted to kiss her right here in front of everyone, but in absolutely no universe, or galaxy for that matter, was that happening.

Football.

The scale would not be tipped. Absolutely could not be tipped. I was here for football, not fucking. Football. Football. Football.

Playing was my dream.

When I caught up with Thor, all he could do was stare at me. "I can't believe you just did that."

I walked faster, wanting to get outside, out of earshot of everyone. "It wasn't like I had much of a choice. And keep it down, will you. People are around."

"Fine, did you tell him about Walton?"

I sighed. "Not really."

"Why the fuck not?"

"It didn't feel right."

"Fuck," he muttered, and caught my pace.

Outside the sun was hot. It was going to be another scorcher. It hadn't rained once since we got here. Christ, I was thinking about doing a rain dance just to shake up the gross humidity. A little mud sounded really good.

Thor sped up and started walking backwards in front of me. "Can I talk now?" he barked sarcastically.

The air was still a little cool, and I breathed it in. "Do I have a choice?"

He shoved his hands in his pockets. "Look man, guy to guy, you're getting in way too deep. Nothing but trouble is going to come out of what you're doing, and you know that."

Annoyed, I glared at him. "You're seriously going to lecture me? Wasn't it just last night that you called Rebecca, Honey? Good thing Rebecca thought you meant it in fondness because if she knew you were calling her by your other girlfriend's name, you might have had one pissed off chick pounding at our door."

It was no surprise that shut him up all the way to the training center, which, when we opened the door, was already jammed packed with players.

Mandatory treatment on all reported ailments and injuries looked like it was applying to practically the entire team. Since I had sustained an injury early on, I had to report in as well.

This was where Thor and I parted ways. He went his way, and I bid him luck again, and then I went to find Dallas.

This part of the day always worried me. Sure, the injury I had suffered was much better now. No lingering signs of shoulder trauma, but there was always the chance of a flair up, and since I was on the radar, I felt like Dallas was scrutinizing me during every exam.

Before my injury, I wanted to be anywhere but here. Now, I couldn't imagine being anywhere else. Gillian was a part of that, but only a small part. There was something else, a feeling of belonging that felt right.

I belonged here.

Not in the training center, but with the team.

This team.

After my exam, it was time to head over to the gym for an hour of weightlifting. Lifting weights was becoming more and more difficult. My body was feeling like it had been in a car accident, and between the long days and the long nights, I was incredibly worn out.

As torturous as this felt in the moment, once I got my body going, I could feel the benefits of the lifting session instantly.

Dallas had told me the weights were being used to refortify my body's natural layers of protection.

Probably not far off the mark.

With lifting out of the way, it was off to the team meeting. I'd received a text that our schedule for today had changed—that we would be skipping position meetings, and instead we would be attending a team meeting.

I took a seat next to Thor. I already knew he'd passed his weigh in because he'd texted me, but still I was happy to see him. I punched him in the arm. "I told you not to worry."

Full of himself, he said, "You only want me around to watch your back."

"Whatever, dude." I grinned.

Coach called for our attention and we all shut up. "Today is Fan Day. And for all of you ponytail swinging girls who haven't figured it out yet, Fan Day has a completely different meaning than *open to the public.*"

All of us kept our mouths shut.

"Today," he yelled from the podium, "you will be expected to take every single photo asked of you, sign every single autograph asked of you, and you will not leave the field until every single fan is satisfied. Do you understand me?"

"Yes, Coach," we all said in unison, like we were in the military. Hey, we were learning.

The rest of the meeting was spent with Coach instructing us how to interact properly with the fans and still have a decent practice. Practice first, he insisted, fans after. With each word he spoke, it became obvious the circus out there wasn't something he looked forward to.

With the position meetings canceled, we were shuffling through the football field's iron gates, flanked on either side by the cheerleaders, in record time.

Music was already blasting, the media was everywhere, and there were so many people I wasn't sure where to look.

The sun was hot by now, and the humidity even hotter. And since it was Fan Day, today we were wearing full on gear—helmets and pads. We were also on the actual college football field, not the practice field.

The whistle blew and the clock started. We were on. Drills first, of course, and then another scrimmage.

During the first play of the game, Walton snapped the ball, and the line went in the completely wrong direction.

Fuck.

Fuck.

Fuck.

The play wasn't dead yet, but it was close to dying a quick death. The guys were scrambling when Thor grabbed Walton by the jersey and said something to him.

Walton looked at him like he was fucking crazy. I was seriously about to lose my shit and go over there and pound them both for not paying attention to the field.

Suddenly the whistle blew, and now the fucking play was dead.

Coach marched out on the field with a look of fury on his face. "What the fuck was that?" He was pointing at Thor.

"I was trying to help him out. No one can hear him. He needs to talk louder," Thor responded. It was a bold move.

"You don't correct him. I do. I watch the playback, and *I* correct him!"

"That's not until tonight, and by then it's too late."

Coach stared at Thor.

He stared back.

Walton said absolutely nothing.

When Coach started to turn around, I had no idea why the hell I opened my Goddamn mouth, but I did. "He screwed up the whole play. He keeps screwing up the plays over and over. Someone has to do something."

Coming to an immediate halt, Coach reeled around and stared right at me with the coldest eyes I'd ever seen. "I. Watch. The. Tape. And. I. Correct. Do. You. Understand. Me?"

Every word was said like I was a fucking idiot. I wanted to roll my eyes, but refrained. Still I said nothing further. He knew I was fucking right.

"Burns, you're in. Carrington, you're out," he shouted to the sidelines.

Jeb Burns was Swann's replacement. He was a cool guy, and extremely motivated, which had been keeping me on my toes. Then there was Harper, the third string who had finally been appointed. He was quarterbacking for the other team.

"Fuck," I muttered and strode off the field pissed as hell. When I removed my helmet, I wanted to throw it, but I knew Coach was watching.

Two plays later, I was back on the field. I guess Coach just had to make a point. Whatever. *What the fuck ever.*

When the scrimmage finally ended, no one was in the mood to stick around, but we had to.

It was Fan Day.

And we got mobbed. Absolutely mobbed by kids, women, babies, guys, adults, senior citizens, and everyone else in the world. Before I knew it I was knee-deep in signing shirts, programs, banners. Shit, one girl wanted me to sign her tit. I didn't of course. We weren't supposed to touch the fans inappropriately. Team rules were team rules.

After I'd smiled at least a million times for pictures, I pushed through the crowd to grab a bottle of Gatorade. That's when I saw Gillian with her sunglasses on, leaning against the water cart and watching me with a smile on her face that lit me up from the inside. Despite the shitty practice and Coach removing me from my position for a few plays, the dire mood I was in instantly lifted.

There were so many people around, and I felt that made it safe to walk over to her. No one was watching us or paying attention. The place was a zoo. The music had been turned off so the video screen could replay the practice that we'd just fucked up.

Her eyes widen when she figured out what I was doing. "Gillian," I grinned.

She reached behind her and grabbed a water bottle. "Hello, Lucas," she said a little shakily. "Tough game, huh?"

I wiped my brow with my forearm. "Shitty is a better way of putting it."

She nodded in agreement and then handed me the bottle in her hand. It made a good rouse. I cracked open the lid and drank before asking, "What exactly was so funny at breakfast this morning?"

The crowd was thickening and we were lost behind them. It was loud. No one could hear us. Even so, she waved a hand. "I'll tell you tonight when we meet at the bridge."

With a scowl, I said, "No, I want to know now."

Not that she had any reason to feel bad. It was my blunder, whatever it was, but still she didn't seem to want to say anything.

I smiled then, a predatory smile that slid over her like she was my mark, and she knew it because she shivered.

With a dismissive wave of her hand, she sighed. "Fine, but really it was no big deal. My father just said you have no idea how difficult it is to be the coach sometimes."

There was nothing about that which wasn't a big deal. "And I said, *yes, I do*, like I fucking know what it's like to be the coach. Fuckkkkkkk!"

She reached for me, but as soon as she touched me, I jerked back and looked around. "Lucas, he thought it was funny. Stop worrying about it."

It wasn't that easy. "Seriously," I sighed, "I need to pay more attention and shut my big mouth."

"Or find something else to do with it," she joked.

I turned my gaze back on her, and I saw the blaze in her eyes. "Gillian," I warned.

"What?" She batted her long lashes innocently.

I took another sip of water. "Stop looking at me that way."

Her head tilted to the side. "What way is that, Lucas?"

Despite where we were, I took a step closer and whispered, "The one that screams you want to introduce me to your father, as your boyfriend."

She narrowed her gaze at me. "That is so not one of my looks."

The music started up again and the field was getting louder. "Are you sure?" I whispered.

She frowned at me. "Yes, I'm sure. In fact," she bit out, "I've never introduced anyone to my father as my boyfriend. Therefore, I couldn't possibly have a look like that. And not that it matters, but if I wanted to introduce you that way, he might be fine with it. I think he likes you."

"Yeah, he picked me, to play for *him*, not with *you*, remember?"

Her gaze grew piercing. "I know that, smartass I meant he likes you as a person, not just a player."

I shook my head. "What gave you that idea—the way he glared at me when I looked at you, or the way he all but told me to get lost in your presence? It was so obvious he didn't want me anywhere near you."

"No, it wasn't."

"Yes, Gillian, it was."

She bit her lip. "Well, he laughed at you. That's something."

"Yeah, he laughed at *me*."

"He never laughs at anyone but me."

"Gillian," I said, making sure she was looking at me, "this thing between us ends when you leave because it has to, for both of us, remember? And your father will never know. He can't know."

She was silent for a moment. "Yes, I remember what we discussed, but you don't have to be such an asshole about it," she scowled, irritation clear in her voice. And then she turned, and using her key, opened the door behind her. She walked inside the old locker room that was no longer used, leaving me right where I stood without so much as a goodbye.

Furious, I grabbed the door before it closed on my face, but didn't go in, not right away, anyway. Instead I stood stunned in the doorway and tried to figure out what the hell had just happened.

Days ago she'd said she was onboard with our agreement. Now, I wasn't so sure she was.

Then again, I wasn't sure I was either.

Eighteen

END ZONE

Gillian

HE HAD A million dollar smile.

When that full on, teeth-flashing grin was directed at you, there was no way to stop your knees from buckling or your heart from pounding out of your chest. But he could also turn that charm off in the blink of an eye, and make your heart stop in an instant.

I hated the emotions he was evoking in me. I didn't like the mood swings. I wasn't like him. I didn't know how to turn it on and turn it off just because—

Every thought I had vanished as soon as I opened the stall door in the women's old locker room because Lucas was standing right across from me.

Waiting for me.

With his hands in his pockets, he was leaning one shoulder against the wall of the beat up purple lockers and his head was down.

The moment I stepped into his line of sight, his gaze lifted and found mine, and although I really hated that it did, heat spread through me like a wildfire in my veins. "Lucas," I said, surprised.

How did he get in here?

His jaw bulged and anger glinted in his blue eyes. "What are you so fucking pissed about?"

I took three steps closer to him and stopped just before the battered wooden bench that separated us. This locker room facility wasn't used anymore, except for storage, and I had been given the key in case I needed to replenish any of the merchandise that was stocked in here for fan day. "What am I so pissed about?"

Confusion wrinkled his brow. "Yeah, that's what I asked."

I surged forward and practically jumped over the bench to waggle my finger at him. "Because you're callous and uncaring, Lucas Carrington."

"What?" he bit out.

I pressed my finger into his chest. "You don't think I don't know what we agreed upon? Well, here's a newsflash, buddy, I do! You don't think I know you have a lot at stake? Well, again, guess what buddy, stop the presses, I do! But for you to stand out there and make me feel like some bimbo who's trying to make herself your girlfriend, now that, that—I can't even talk to you right now I'm so mad."

One minute he looked completely startled by my vehemence, and then the next minute he was throwing his head back in laughter, which only served to piss me off even more.

I gaped at him. "This isn't funny."

With his shoulders still shaking, he said, "I know, but you're so adorable when you're pissed off."

"What. The. Hell. Lucas?!"

Now he was the one gaping. "Shit, you look a lot like your father when you do that."

Sucking in a deep breath, I closed my eyes. I considered laughing because I knew I probably did just do the *Do-You-Not-Understand-English?* thing my dad does all the time. I also considered bolting. Just leaving him here to contemplate his rude behavior all by himself.

But then his mouth was on mine in a deep punishing kiss, and it ignited the hunger I had for him that seemed to be incapable of ever being satisfied lately.

As our kiss intensified, I noticed it seemed to be different than any other. It was all consuming. Devouring. Passionate. Like he didn't just want me, he needed me.

Oh my God. He was going to fuck me right now. Here!

"Gillian, I'm sorry," he breathed, pausing his lips for only the short time it took to speak. "I wasn't trying to be a dick. I would never intentionally hurt you. I just needed to make sure we were on the same page . . . for the both of us."

Of course I knew this.

I knew him.

I did.

"I know," I said, nipping at his lip and pressing my body against his. "It's just really hard to hear, and I don't want to talk about it anymore, okay?"

"Yeah." It came out of his mouth as a breathless whisper, but I heard it.

The whole Romeo and Juliet, star-crossed lovers thing was unbearable, and I hated to think about this thing between us ending, but I wasn't stupid. I knew it had to.

Lucas surged the two of us forward. I should have been worried we would get caught together, but I knew the door was locked, and I knew only a few people had the key. Not that any of that mattered because no one ever came in here.

Besides, he moved so fast that he had me down on the bench tugging down my panties before I had time to react. To tell him I was still mad at him. To tell him this wasn't a good idea.

I was about to speak up, but then his mouth found my breast, and through the thin fabric of my top he tugged and sucked on my nipple with his lips. After that, I was completely lost to him. His mouth moved up my neck as he yanked his football pants down, freeing his raging erection.

Flutters rose deep in my belly at the sight. Oh God, he was so hard.

There was something savage in his features. He moved fast, spreading my legs wide and positioning himself at my entrance in mere seconds. I was unable to help him in any way because I was too busy holding onto the bench for stability. This was going to be over so quickly, but then all of a sudden he froze.

An uncontrollable shiver worked its way up my spine. "What?" I asked in alarm.

He stared down at me with grave intensity. "I don't have anything," he breathed.

A long silence filled what was left of the space between us while I considered this. "I don't care," I finally breathed back, more than breathless. "I'm on the pill and I know you're clean, I've seen your record."

Those blue eyes glittered. "You've looked at my medical record?"

I gave him a *no dah* look. "Yes, of course."

With a shake of his head, he said nothing more.

It wasn't like it was a HIPAA violation; I was a trainer and had automatic access to the players' medical records. I had to look, for his shoulder injury, but I didn't want to explain that now. Later would be just fine.

The blunt head of his cock pressed against my opening. He pushed, forcing his way inside. As soon as I pushed back, he shuddered. His expression in that moment took my breath away. It was so very masculine and so filled with undeniable pleasure. And I was doing this to him. Me.

A soft moan rose in the air and I knew it was from me but I was helpless to silence myself.

"Touch yourself," he said in a strained voice. "Use your fingers, Gillian. It will make it easier for me to take you all the way."

I reached down, sliding my fingers over my clit. God, it felt so good.

"That's it," he growled. "You're getting so wet. Fuck, so wet. Keep touching yourself. Don't stop."

He pressed halfway in and then thrust forward, forcing himself the rest of the way in. I nearly came off the bench and a cry lodged in my throat. I took my hand away then because I was going to come before he even got started.

This was down and dirty. A quick fuck in the locker room that we never should have been in. Things were getting out of control. *We* were getting out of control. Lucas fucked me so fast and hard that I was nearly gasping for air.

Each time he withdrew and thrust back into me, my body shook, and so did his. I wrapped one arm around his neck to keep me on the bench, but I knew he wouldn't let me fall. His hands were everywhere, all over my body, keeping me right where I needed to be.

His mouth met mine in a heated clash that left me gasping for breath. Then he hoisted me up, and in one swift movement, he turned and pressed me against the lockers. "Wrap your legs around me," he growled.

The fierce command had my belly clenching and butterflies took flight in my chest. As soon as I hooked my ankles at the small of his back, he plunged again, deeper, so much deeper. His hands held onto me as he pounded into me with so much strength and ferocity, my body felt like it had started to coil into a tight knot.

When he made a noise that was so erotically charged, he looked down at me. "I'm close, fuck, I'm so close."

I'd gotten so caught up in my thoughts I wasn't quite there yet, so I started circling the taut bundle of nerves between my legs again. This time faster, harder, and God, I was there. I was so there. "Oh God, oh God," I chanted as I hurdled over the edge, exploding around his cock in an earth-shattering rush that had my ears roaring.

This was us. Who we were together. It was raw, fierce, explosive, and it would never be allowed to last.

Exertion showed on his face as he came inside me, his cum leaking from my pussy.

Marking me.

For a long moment he stood there with his eyes closed and his chest heaving from exertion. When he opened those baby blues, he looked down between us. "Jesus, Gillian, I don't know what's happening. I can't control myself around you."

Feeling the same way, I looked down too. My thighs were shaking and my entire body was still quaking from the force in which he'd taken me. "It's not like it's a hardship or anything," I joked.

His grin broadened. "Good to know."

Despite knowing I should, I didn't want to move. I wanted to stay like this. Just him and me, but I knew I couldn't. I got to my feet and when I did, his semen dripped down my legs. Unsteady, I gained my footing and then looked into his blue eyes once again.

With an amused grin, he tugged me to him for a kiss that left us both breathless. When he pulled back, he said, "I'll go first. Wait a few minutes before you follow and let me get lost in the crowd."

I reached up to kiss his jaw. "You're good at this."

"Not really," he said, disentangling himself from me as he spoke.

Right then the door opened and closed. We were hidden behind a block of lockers, but still I jumped away from him, pushing my skirt down into place as I did. He grabbed my panties from the floor and yanked his pants up. Tucking my panties in his waistband, he motioned toward the stall. He was just about to lunge for it when the door opened and closed again. Whoever it was had left.

It was in that thirty seconds of terror that we both knew if we didn't do a better job of watching ourselves, we were going to get caught.

In hindsight, maybe that was what we both wanted.

To out ourselves to the world.

Nineteen

Extra Point

Lucas

AND THAT MADE fifty-three.

The final round of cuts had come. Four weeks into training camp, and our team was finally assembled. Walton had been cut on Fan Day, along with five other players. The rest were notified this morning.

Those of us in this room were the new Chicago Bears. No one would ever know just how worn out and tired we were because of the energy buzzing all around us.

Coach was telling us to quiet down, and once we had, he smiled. "Trace Wentworth, front and center," he ordered.

It was the end of the day team meeting, and not a single player was considering this assembly one of the grind because after it was over, we were off—for the night. The entire night. A Friday night besides, and the guys were raring to go.

And so was I.

This would be only our second day off since arriving, and the clock couldn't tick by fast enough for any of us.

"Who are you?" Coach screamed as Thor took the podium.

"Trace Wentworth."

"No! Who are *you*?"

"Thor," he bellowed into the microphone. The room exploded as testosterone blazed and adrenaline soared.

Let the hazing begin.

"Tell the team how you got the nick name, Thor." Out of all people, Coach was adopting the standard rookie hazing.

I couldn't fucking believe it.

And who knew there was a story behind Thor's nickname. Here I thought people called him that because he looked like Chris Hemsworth with his chin length blonde hair. Maybe it was because he had a fetish for hammers, instead.

I couldn't wait to hear this.

Here was the thing, he either told the story or he was going to get his body shaved, head to toe, or painted in red paint, or God knew what. I had to try to control my laughter because I didn't want the tables to turn on me, although my moment would come, I was sure of that.

Up in the front, he dimmed the wattage of that pretty boy personality of his as he circled the question. The comments from the peanut gallery were flying, rude, crude, and sexist, but he continued to sidetrack the topic of how he got his name.

Finally, after way too many insults, he broke down. "Okay, here it is, you pussies. When I was in college, I got really plastered one night and told everyone that the Nine Realms really did exist, and then I insisted I could take a spaceship and go to Asgard."

The team roared, throwing out words like warrior and Norse god in the most mocking way. The dude had a thing for Thor? Who knew? He was never going to live that down.

And as he strode away, all I could do was picture him in the movie wielding a hammer and donning a red cape. The image would be ingrained in my mind for the rest of eternity, I was certain.

One by one, players were called up.

Called out.

Teased.

Taunted.

I waited for my turn. What would they say? Nothing about Gillian, at least I knew that. Or I hoped I did.

But I knew I didn't have to worry anymore when at exactly nine p.m., Coach glanced at the clock and then casually strode up to take the podium.

Showing once again that he actually had a sense of humor, he did a little drum roll that had all of our eyes bugging out of our head. Then, finally, he gave us his trademark goodbye. "Now get the fuck out of here!"

Everyone stood and started to hustle, worried Coach might call us back, change his mind, order another practice, we practically ran.

Before the door opened though, Coach blew his whistle and we all froze. It was all a hoax. Shit. We weren't going anywhere. "And girls," he said, "I almost forgot to tell you—don't come back until Sunday morning at nine."

What?

Had I heard him right?

Wails of joy erupted and I knew I had.

Thirty-six hours off?

Thirty-six hours off!

Holy fucking shit.

"Going to the hotel?" Thor asked, his voice low as we exited the room.

I shook my head. "Nope. You?"

He nodded. "You know it."

"Bringing your cape and battle armor?" I couldn't resist.

"Fuck you."

I grinned. "Come on man, I had to, and you know it."

Getting right back on track, he asked, "Aren't you going to see Gillian?"

I kept my mouth screwed tight until we got to our room, and then I told him just what I had planned.

"You did that?" he asked in shock. "I'm impressed."

"No, not exactly," I admitted.

"Gillian did it?"

I shook my head. "No. She doesn't have a clue," I told him, and then grabbed my phone to text her and let her know what was up.

I had to admit . . . what I had planned was fucking great!

Twenty

TIME OUT

Lucas

MY CONTRACT WITH the Bears was now official.

As a first round drafted rookie, I received a four-year contract, with a fifth year option. My projected salary over those five years was somewhere around thirty million, including my signing bonus.

It was surreal.

Every time I thought about that much money, it blew my mind. I could still remember times when Nick and I didn't even have thirty dollars.

The signing bonus was due to be deposited in my bank account first thing Monday morning. Although this wasn't the first time in my life I didn't have to worry about money, it was the first time I could spend money and not feel guilty about it.

When you grow up with nothing and then suddenly everything changes, your world turns a little upside down. After Nick started earning a decent salary, he gave me whatever I needed without hesitation.

The thing was, I wasn't his responsibility and I hated taking from him, so I only took what I absolutely needed. Which wasn't much. Only what I needed to play football.

Whatever I could do for him now, whatever I could buy him, it would never be enough to pay him back.

Light reflected on the water from the headlights of a car coming down the driveway. As I turned around to see if it was her, my bare toes sank into the sand. When the truck drove past me, I drew in a thick, soggy breath.

I was both nervous and excited to see her. I don't think I ever felt this way before, and I wasn't sure I cared for the feeling.

Lifting my face to the stars, I thought about how far I'd come, and took another deep breath.

Even as the eleventh hour approached, the night air still held the heavy humidity of the day, but I didn't give a fuck how hot it was.

I was outside, and not playing ball.

And I needed this.

I drew in another breath. Blew it out. Let my toes sink even further into the sand as the water rippled around my ankles. Unfortunately, the cold river water wasn't nearly enough to cool my heated body.

The sound and smell, the pull and push of the waves, it was so much like that of Lake Michigan, and yet so incredibly different.

Here at the inlet, the surroundings were much more quiet and peaceful. The scent that surrounded me was the same though, the feel of the water on my skin was the same, and the air identical. I loved being around the water.

Don't get me wrong, I knew it wasn't the warm waters of the Bahamas, or the rippling tides of the Gulf of Mexico, nor was it the blue depths of the Pacific, that was for sure. Still, it was a patch of water with a small sandy beach, which was far enough away from training camp that Gillian and I could be together without worry.

This small indentation of land in the shoreline led to what was more than likely a pond, but called a lagoon by the bed and breakfast owner. Five small cottages plus one large house surrounded this lagoon. The one all the way on the far side would be Gillian's and mine for the weekend.

Tess had found this place online and taken care to reserve it for me, along with making sure it was stocked with what was needed.

That woman was the only one I had ever let in my life . . . until Gillian . . . and she spoiled me rotten. We'd forged a relationship over the past few years that I found invaluable. My sister-in-law had become someone for me to confide in, seek advice from, talk to, and discuss the few things I couldn't talk about with my brother.

I found myself doing those very same things with Gillian more and more with each passing day.

Two more weeks was all we had left together. I wasn't going to lie, it was going to be strange not seeing her every day. At the same time, I knew once the season started, I'd be busy with games and she'd be busy with school, and it wouldn't be long for all to be forgotten.

Wasn't that the way it worked?

I threw a stone into the water and watched how it skipped across the surface. I'd turned a few of the lights on in the cottage across the way, but now I wondered if I shouldn't have lit the candles I'd seen scattered throughout the place.

Perhaps I'd go back.

The rumble of tires on gravel alerted me to the arrival of another vehicle. This time when I turned, I knew the candle lighting would have to wait.

Gillian was here.

Barefoot, I ran to the top of the grassy hill and waited near the edge of the circular driveway for the Uber to come to a stop. The main house was the first to come into view. The owners must have already been in bed because the house was dark.

Opening the car door, I extended my hand to first take her bag, and then settling the strap over my shoulder, I took her hand. "Hey, you made it," I grinned.

Her eyes were wide as she glanced around. "What is this place? It looks amazing."

After greeting the driver, I closed the door and then slipped an arm around her waist. "Don't laugh, but it's called the Blue Lagoon."

She wrapped her arm around my waist, and together we started walking down the path that led to the cottage. "I'm not laughing. I love it. It's . . . magical," she sighed, her eyes darting around everywhere.

"Good, because we're staying over there." I pointed to the yellow cottage with the deck. All we could see from here was the back of it, but it was enough for Gillian to understand we would have privacy.

"It's perfect. More than perfect. How did you ever find this place?" she asked.

My eyes were on her. On the thin white top she wore with something lacey covering her breasts beneath it. On the gray knee-length skirt she had on, which slit up the side to expose the soft skin of her thigh. On her.

She stopped for a moment and looked up at me.

I glanced down, mesmerized by her features in the moonlight. I licked my lips at the sight of her. "Can't give away all of my secrets."

She started to walk again, and as she took her first step, her fingers pinched my side. It was meant as a punishment for not answering her question, but it was anything but. I wanted to feel that again, but next time under the fabric of my shirt instead of over it, with her nails digging into me. "Seriously, when did you have time to do this?"

That magnetic pull between us was so strong and I felt it more than ever when I leaned in to whisper," I already told you, I can't give away all of my secrets. Besides, if I did that it would take all the fun out of seeing that brain of yours working in overdrive. And I'd hate to ruin my fun."

"No, I wouldn't want to do that to you, Lucas," she said in a husky voice that sent shivers down my spine. That voice alone could seduce me in a matter of seconds.

And there it was. My name on her lips. It hit me deep, filling me with inexplicable satisfaction. Despite my euphoria, I still raised a brow at her. "Are you mocking me?"

Both her brows popped and her shoulders lifted. "I don't know. You tell me."

I narrowed my stare. "I think you are, and I also think it's time you learned there are consequences for teasing. I hope you don't mind a little midnight dip," I taunted.

Just as I was about to scoop her up and toss her over my shoulder, she took off, running as fast as she could in her flip-flops.

I tore after her. She was fast though and because I wasn't wearing shoes, I had to stay on the grass. I also had her bag on my shoulder, which wasn't exactly light. She, on the other hand, veered onto the more direct path, which was covered in gravel. It looped around to the front of the cottage, and I lost sight of her.

There were two rocking chairs on the porch, and she was sitting in one rocking away when I circled the cottage from the back. "Took you long enough." She smiled as I climbed the steps.

Dropping the bag near the door, I stalked over to her and put my hands on either side of the chair as I leaned in. "Paybacks are a bitch, Strawberry Fields, just remember that."

She gave me a perfect, puppy-like look.

I shook my head and leaned even closer. "Not going to work, baby, you're so going in."

This time she bit her lip and let the tip of her pink tongue sneak out. "What if I make it up to you instead?"

The pulse at the base of my throat leapt in excitement. "Depends on what exactly it is you have in mind."

She reached for the button of my jeans. "I could suck your dick. You'd like that, wouldn't you?"

"You on your knees in front of me. Hell, yes, I'd like that."

Her eyes flared with heat. "How about you ask nice."

"How about I don't," I growled.

She pulled her mouth to the side in contemplation, but her fingers remained still. "You could beg."

I roared with laughter. "I don't beg."

"Okay, your choice," she said and started to undo my pants.

With that settled, I scooped her out of the chair. She melted against me, wrapping her legs around my waist and burying her face in my neck as I carried her inside. I dimmed the lights, and it was strange, but everything around us was so quiet.

We were alone.

Really alone.

And it felt fucking good.

Slamming the door shut behind me with my bare foot, I set her down on her feet. But I wasn't going to give her time to admire the surroundings. There would be time for that later.

Those green eyes of hers twinkled when she looked up at me.

I smirked at her and then whispered in her ear, "I want to fuck that smart mouth of yours so bad."

Her lips parted on a huge sigh. "Is that all you want?"

The grin I wore was for a dozen different reasons. Her smart mouth, her wicked ways, the inexplicable urge that came over me whenever I was near her, and then there was the electrifying spark I felt every time she touched me.

Something this volatile, this consuming was going to be hard to extinguish. It was going to sting like hell, I thought. Or more than likely burn.

When she took me by my shirt and forcefully pushed me against the wall, I let all of that go.

Focusing on this moment, I was determined not to look past the present, which was pretty damn easy considering how turned on I was.

As soon as my back hit the paneling, I pulled her top up and over her head. I had to see what she was teasing me with beneath it. Before I could even focus on the skimpy lace, she was on her knees in front of me.

Holy fuck.

Without fumbling she yanked my zipper down to expose my straining cock, which had pushed out the front of my boxer briefs. I was in her fist before I even had a chance to make a sound.

Gillian used one knee to nudge my legs farther apart as she pulled my jeans down to my thighs. My boxer briefs, too. I was mostly naked for her in half a minute.

My cock pulsed against her palm as she skimmed her hand upward. She was barely brushing my head, but it was enough that my hips jerked forward in excitement. As soon as they did, she gripped my shaft, keeping me in place.

Oh, fuck.

I flattened my palms against the wall and held on. I had never been at a woman's mercy like this. Sure, I'd been blown a million times, but never had I not been the one in control. And never had I wanted it as much as I did right now.

I looked down at her, my gaze darkening with an unbelievable amount of lust. When her eyes drifted up, I saw in them the same need and want. The same maddening desire. And in that single moment that our stares locked, she opened her mouth and let her hot breath seep over my hotter flesh.

It made me shiver.

With a smile on her face, she brushed my cock against her cheek, close, so close, and yet my tip was not quite close enough to be inside her mouth.

Lower.

Lower.

A little lower.

Not low enough.

Shit.

Teasing me, she breathed against my cock as her hand worked me.

I smoothed a hand down the side of her hair, staring down into her eyes awash with eagerness.

When she nipped at the skin of my thigh, I cried out. I wanted to reach down and push her head so her mouth was right there, right on my cock, but I didn't.

I was giving her this.

Letting her control this.

She ran her tongue along the underside of my cock, stopping just before she reached the tip. Arousal splintered hard and fierce through my body until I could feel my dick swelling even bigger, threatening to burst if she didn't hurry up. I closed my eyes and forced my head to drop back. "You drive me crazy," I blurted out.

"I'm okay with that," she said as she flicked out her tongue, circling my broad head and teasing the sensitive underside.

The long, tortured cry that escaped my throat when she did wasn't a sound I'd ever made. Oh, fuck, she was using her teeth and my body was shaking in a way that I couldn't stop. "Jesus," I breathed. "I've never felt anything better than your mouth wrapped around my cock."

And it was the truth.

She shivered and I knew it was because of what I'd said. Soon her hands were moving up and down, up and down, and then a little higher to graze my cock head—that's when I couldn't wait another minute and pumped my hips, needing to be in her mouth, needing to fuck her mouth.

"I've spent the day imagining you in so many ways," I said in a strained voice. "Under me, on top of me. Me eating your sweet pussy while you suck my dick. You name it, I imagined it."

She tore her mouth away from my cock. I opened my eyes and looked down. Her body had gone still. "I can't believe you think about me that way," she said, almost astonished.

"Gillian, I think about you in every way." Perhaps it was an admission that shouldn't have been said, but in the throes of passion, I couldn't stop what was coming out of my mouth. I also wanted more of her mouth on me, so I thrust forward. "And right now all I can think about is how good your mouth feels around my dick."

Nothing more was said because she was back at it. With quick flicks of her tongue, she slid it up my cock from my base to just below my head, and then up a little higher to let the wet, hot abyss of her mouth hover over my tip.

I looked down.

Again she had gone still.

I licked my lips.

Blinked.

Waited.

Waited some more.

Still, she did nothing, but then she smirked, and I got it.

Holy fuck, she wanted me to beg.

No way. No way. No way.

But I couldn't take it.

So I begged. "Please, Gillian, please."

At last she engulfed me, took me down the back of her throat. Tasted me. Sucked me. Devoured me.

That's it.

Oh, fuck.

That's it.

Greedy, she sucked me hard, concentrating on my head, while her hand, slick with her saliva, stroked up my shaft. Unable to control myself, I slid my fingers into the back of her hair and anchored her there. When I gave a little tug, she gasped.

This made her fuck me with her mouth faster, harder. She was all mouth and teeth and tongue.

Shards of pleasure spiked in my every nerve as I sank deeper into her mouth. I twitched at the back of her throat before sliding out, enjoying the rasp of her tongue over the sensitive underside of my dick with the withdrawal.

Pleasure coiled tight and hard, low in my belly and balls. I fucked her mouth harder, faster, and I groaned, or maybe roared, it was that loud. I couldn't stop myself. I fucked her mouth with an urgency I'd never felt before.

My fingers twisted and tangled in her hair. "Gillian," I groaned. She smiled around my cock.

"Shit," I said, "oh, shit, this feels so good . . . I'm going to come, Gillian, I'm going to come."

She didn't pull away.

I prepared myself to pull out of the blissful cavern that was her mouth, but she didn't let me.

"Fuck. Yes."

My thighs shook as my body started to surge toward an explosion. Muscles tensing and nerves rapid-fire releasing, getting ready to come.

And then it happened.

I groaned.

Wordless.

Desperate.

And I was coming. Coming. Coming so hard.

Gillian took everything I gave her, sucking until I was spent and softening in her mouth. Even then she wasn't done. She placed small, tender kisses in the most sensitive places. And then her mouth was on my balls, licking, touching, driving me crazy and sending bolts of energy racing through me.

Never wanting this feeling to end, I watched her take everything I had, and I knew I had never felt like this before.

Not ever.

Moved in a way so unlike me, I tugged her to her feet so I could tell her something I never should have. But like always, I spoke before thinking. "Fuck, Gillian," I muttered, "I think I could fall in love with you."

She swallowed. Stared at me, but only long enough to gauge my sincerity. *I got it.* It was the barrier that we needed to keep up. "I feel the same way," she finally said, quiet, as if someone might here. "But—"

I hushed her with my finger over her lips. "No buts, and no more talking about it, okay?"

She nodded knowing it was for the best.

My hair was damp with sweat, my body ablaze like it had never been before, and the fire in my eyes was the only thing she needed to see to know that what was said was a secret we had to keep.

I slumped back against the wall. What were we doing? How was this going to end? Not well, was all I knew.

She leaned closer and our bodies were touching.

That's when I figured since I couldn't go back and undo what had been said, the only thing I could do was move forward.

I swooped her into my arms and found her mouth. When I tasted myself on her lips, I smiled. "Just so we're clear," I started "that is the one and only time I will *ever* beg."

Eyes half-lidded and super sexy, she looked at me. "Don't count on it."

And fuck, she was probably right.

If she kept looking at me like she was right now, I might be begging—a lot—this weekend.

And what the hell did it matter . . . time was running out.

Twenty-One

BACKFIELD

Gillian

HE LOOKED LIKE ten different kinds of sin.

Wearing the brightest pair of swim trunks I'd ever seen, he walked down the grassy hill with a glass of fresh squeezed lemonade in one hand and a protein shake in the other.

That hard body of his should have come with a warning label. Something like *once you touch me, you'll never want to touch anyone else—ever again*—because that was how I felt.

But I couldn't allow what was going to happen in the weeks to come bring me down. I wanted this time alone with him too much to let anything bring me down.

Those finely sculpted abs of his came into view and I licked my lips, recalling how I traced over every inch of them last night, first with my finger, and then my tongue.

We'd stayed up way too late doing all the things he had imagined during the day, and more.

It was around one in the afternoon now and we'd just eaten breakfast or lunch or whatever you wanted to call it at a diner down the road.

We were alone, and I loved it.

No one knew we were here, and we had nothing to worry about. My father had gone up to Lake Forest for the weekend. He never even asked me if I wanted to go. Just asked me if I would be okay. Of course I told him I had things to keep me busy, and not to worry. It wasn't like him, but maybe he was trying to let me go in his own way.

Very comfortable where I was, I watched him from behind the lenses of my new red plastic sunglasses. They had a strawberry on each corner, and Lucas had purchased them for me at the tourist shop attached to the restaurant, along with two rafts for us to float in the lagoon.

I paddled toward him when he started to stride into the water, watching as the muscles in his legs disappeared beneath the surface of the water.

"Here you go," he said, handing me the plastic cup, letting his fingertips linger a moment before letting go.

Flipping up my sunglasses, I took a sip. "Mmmm . . . that's so good. Such service," I said squinting against the sun. "I could get used to this."

He leaned on his blue plastic raft and let his tongue sneak out. "I could interpret that statement a few different ways."

I splashed him with some water before quickly using one hand to paddle away. "I meant being waited on . . . perv."

His enigmatic grin told me he liked when I called him that. "You could hire a houseboy once you start working."

"You know, that isn't a bad idea."

"He could serve you lemonade, but I bet he couldn't *do you* the way I do," he quipped, and then plunged under, leaving his hand above water so the cup didn't spill.

Floating away, I giggled and wiggled my toes against the sun-warmed plastic. When he came up, he shook himself the way a dog does when coming out of the water and I laughed even harder.

My skin was already warm from the sun, but suddenly I felt really hot. I sucked down the lemonade in a few huge gulps. When I looked back up, Lucas was on his raft, propelling toward me. Gone from his hand was his cup. I saw it lying in the sand.

He came close and anchored his raft to mine by throwing his leg over it. "So tell me more about this houseboy job. What exactly would he do for you?"

I flipped my sunglasses back down and closed my eyes as I imagined all the things Lucas had done to me. "Well," I said, opening my eyes and looking over at him. "He would do the laundry, and mop, and maybe even wash my car, and then when he was done, he could strip out of his clothes and get on his knees to wait for me to decide if he should be rewarded for his efforts or not."

Lucas snorted under his breath. "Sounds like you're a dominatrix who's been hiding in the closet."

I waited a moment before going on. I could say all kinds of dirty things under this guise, but when I looked into those languid blue eyes, what came out of my mouth instead was, "No, not at all. I was just kidding. I kind of like it when the guy takes control. I think it's hot."

The look he flashed me told me to watch out.

I gripped the sides of my raft, but it was too late. He'd already lunged for me, and together we went under. I screamed and took in water.

Strong hands grabbed me around the waist and pulled me upward. "What was that for?" I spurted, trying not to laugh.

"Payback for earlier."

"Payback?"

"Yes, now stop the teasing, Gillian."

I flung my arms around his neck and kissed his mouth. "Oh, come on, you know I can't stop, it's way too fun."

He nipped at my lip. "For you, maybe. Do it again and I might just have to spank you," he practically growled when he spoke, and then he gave me a warning smack on my butt.

Arousal hummed through my veins. Need, a craving for him that felt stronger than ever, seemed to possess my soul, and I had to get it in check. "I'll keep that in mind," I murmured, and then swam back to my raft, where I climbed back on.

The cup I had been holding was floating away and he grabbed it, tossing it to the sand beside his before climbing back on his raft.

We floated in silence for a while. The sun warmed me, and as it did, I couldn't stop thinking about him, how much I loved being with him. How much I—I refused to think about that. We'd both said we'd let that word go.

The fact that Lucas and I got to sleep beside each other for one more night gave me the strength to stay like this and not ask him to go inside and fuck me.

I wanted this time to just be. To take advantage of the short time we had left. Then again, there was more to us now than just sex. I wasn't sure how that happened, but it had.

When he floated close to me again, I took hold of his raft this time. "We don't do much of this," I murmured.

He glanced at me over his Raybans. "Much of what?"

"This . . . nothing."

A hand on my thigh followed the soft chuckle. "You mean when we're alone we've usually got our hands all over each other."

I smiled over at him, and then pushed away to float further out. "Yes, I guess that's what I mean."

He paddled in my direction. "I'm happy to oblige right now."

Pulling his raft close to mine again, he said, "If that's what you want."

There was no denying the tingle that zapped through my body or my instant reaction to the idea of going back inside. I smiled slowly. "I'm not saying I don't want that too, I just mean other than meeting at the bridge, we never have time to just be."

Lucas leaned over and kissed my mouth, then said against my lips, "I know what you mean."

He did know, and there was nothing more to say about it.

I closed my eyes and left it that way because if I went on, I had no idea what I'd say, but I knew it wouldn't be anything he wanted to hear.

Then again, did it really matter what I said when this thing between us would be ending so soon?

Twenty-Two

CALLING THE PLAY

Gillian

TAKING NAPS HAD never been my thing, but right now I didn't mind them one bit.

A hard male body was wrapped solidly around me as I came awake, and it belonged to the man who'd said he didn't do cuddling. Perhaps he and I had a different definition of the word, or perhaps he did do cuddling, he just hadn't realized it.

Between staying up late last night and being out in the sun most of the afternoon, I had felt worn out. So when Lucas asked me if I wanted to go for a run, I had declined and while he was gone I decided to lie down. I meant to just close my eyes for a few minutes, but I guess I had fallen asleep.

When I fluttered my eyelids open, I saw that at least it was still light outside. I twisted around to see him.

His eyes were on me.

He was watching me.

I smiled at him.

Having changed out of my bathing suit, I'd slipped into his T-shirt after I'd come inside. I smelled like suntan oil and the sun. He, on the other hand, smelled of soap from a fresh shower, and was completely naked.

"I'm sorry I fell asleep on you," I said, stretching and pushing my body back against his.

He pushed aside the length of my hair so he could press his mouth to the back of my neck. "I know how you can make it up to me," he whispered as his hand curled over my hip.

I didn't say anything right away. I didn't have to. I wiggled against him in a way that was definitely going to cause a reaction, and then I finally spoke. "What did you have in mind?"

He slipped his hand lower, over the softness of my belly.

"Mmmm."

His hand moved lower still to the heat between my legs. It only took one small, inquiring stroke of his finger to see just how ready for him I was.

"You didn't answer me." My voice was husky and low.

When he didn't answer, I twisted around. With a gleam in his eye, he crooked a finger at me and then scooted down the bed a bit. "Crawl up and put your knees on either side of my head," he instructed.

"Are you sure?"

He pressed his thumb to my clit in a way that sent a tendril of desire curling through me.

"Sure. If you insist."

Not only could I lose myself in the sound of his throaty chuckle, but the feel of his skin against mine drove me wild. Bold and ready, I climbed up his hard body and rocked up on my knees.

Just as I was about to lower myself to his mouth, he put a hand on my waist to stop me. "Use your hand and spread your pussy for me," he said huskily. "I want my tongue over every inch of you."

When I spoke, my voice was ragged. "Lucas, I can't do that."

"Gillian."

That one word sounded more like an order and it cut right to my core. I lifted the shirt over my head and then slid my hand slowly down my belly.

"You're so fucking sexy," he growled, his eyes glued on me.

Sexy.

No one had ever called me that, either. Athletic, fit, tone, cute even, but never sexy. He had a way about him that made me feel special, and I didn't even think he knew what he was doing.

Wanting to give him whatever I could of myself, I parted myself for him. As soon as I did, he grabbed my hips with both his hands. His grip was hard and he slammed me down onto his mouth with a force I would never have done on my own.

He ate me like he was a starving man. Licking, feasting, sucking, sliding his tongue inside me and all over me.

Devouring me like this, he very quickly worked me into a mindless frenzy. Before I knew what I was doing, I was riding his face like it was his cock. When he pressed a finger to my clit, I bucked and writhed as waves of pleasure rushed through me.

Exploding into his mouth, I came all over his face.

There was nothing I wouldn't do with him. I trusted him. I loved him. As I thought it, I knew I shouldn't, but it was hard not to. I sagged downward trying to expel that feeling and then rolled to the side so I didn't smother him.

His lips glistened with the evidence of my arousal and he ran his tongue over them, tasting me once more. "Get back up on your knees," he murmured, pulling me on top of him. "I want you to do that again, but this time on my cock."

I smiled down at him. "I'm not sure I can move right now."

He gave me that easy smile that first caught my eye and slid one finger inside and then pulled it back out. "I think you can manage, but I'll help you if I need to."

A thrill began low in my belly and fanned throughout my chest. I already knew how easy it was to lose myself in him, what I didn't know was how easy it was to imagine I belonged to him.

His cock surged upward and he reached down to grasp it with one hand and took hold of my waist with the other. He was ready. I lowered myself down, giving him the very heart of my being.

I leaned forward to kiss him and my tongue darted into his mouth, stroking tentatively and then harder when he did the same.

The help he provided was in the way of positioning both of his hands at my waist and thrusting upward. Like that he held me in place as he arched and withdrew. Faster. Harder. Rougher.

Back in sitting position, I arched back, changing the angle.

His hips lifted, thrusting into me harder, as sweet pleasure caused my thighs to squeeze around him.

I couldn't believe it when pleasure started to sweep through me. I was coming again, and this time in a hurried, frenzied rush. Everything became Lucas. Every breath, every pulse, every second. Images of him flashed through my mind as I shook with my orgasm. "Oh, God," I cried.

He groaned. "Gillian."

At the sound of my name I sat straight up and stared down at him. With pleasure still sweeping though me, I ran my nails up his chest to hold onto his shoulders. He groaned again, calling out my name over and over as he erupted inside me. Hot, spurting deep into my body, he pulled me even closer onto his cock until there was no space between us.

Lucas laid there a long moment, his cock still pulsing and twitching inside me. I loved how it felt. A moment later he cupped my face and then kissed me softly, a direct contradiction to the way he'd just fucked me. "I should probably feed you," he panted.

That was the first time since waking up I glanced at the clock. It was almost seven. I rolled off him and sat on the mattress, my toes sneaking under the covers. I hated that I'd slept some of our few precious hours away. "You mean I should probably feed you," I smirked. "With all this sex, you have to keep your strength for tomorrow or you won't make it through the day."

He pushed himself onto one elbow and stifled a yawn. "You don't see me complaining."

I untangled myself and slipped on his shirt, then padded over to the kitchen where I opened the refrigerator. "Do you want to go out or stay in? But if we stay in, it has to be breakfast for dinner."

The sound of bare feet on wood alerted me that he'd gotten out of bed. "Let's go outside before it gets dark and throw the ball around. And then I'm happy to stay in or go out. Your choice."

By the time I turned around, he'd pulled on his jeans and thrown a baseball cap on his head. "You want to play football with me?"

Taking a football out of his bag, he started for the door. "Sure, unless everything you told me about how good you are was just hot air."

"It was not hot air!" I said, scurrying to pull a pair of shorts out of my bag.

He was already out the door before I'd gotten myself decent.

Hurrying outside, I found him sitting on the lawn, staring down at the ball gripped tightly in his hand. I flopped beside him. "Penny for your thoughts."

Those blue eyes darted in my direction. "Do you think it will be easier for us if we start the process of letting this thing go between us when we get back to camp tomorrow morning?"

The words were unexpected and I sucked in a breath, unable to answer him. I'd never been blindsided, but I felt like I had just then.

His eyes were still on the ball. "I mean I feel like the more time we spend together, the harder it's going to be."

Exhaling, I fought to stop from screaming at him. Did he really think we were something he could just turn on and off?

"Don't you think?" he asked flipping the ball around in his palms. Silence.

He glanced over at me.

More silence.

"Gillian."

I was at a disadvantage because I hadn't been thinking like that at all. In fact, I was thinking the very polar opposite. I swallowed, and then swallowed one more time before I spoke. "I think it's going to be hard either way."

This time he was silent.

"What if things don't end?"

His head snapped in my direction and for the first time since I sat beside him he made full eye contact. "You know they have to."

"Why do they have to?" I bit out my words.

His features drew together in a hard, chiseled way. "Because your father will more than likely freak the fuck out, and I'll be left in a situation I don't want to be in come this fall. Because you have school to get back to and a job to start after, and neither includes the Bears. And because, Gillian, that isn't the plan."

I wanted to be dignified about this, but I also wanted to scream, *"Fuck the plan."*

His expression softened, but he was still guarded. "And a thousand other reasons why," he tacked on.

I nodded stiffly, wondering what those thousand reasons were, but not wanting to ask. "Well," I said, my voice a little weak, "if I have a say in the way things are going to end, I'd like to spend as much time with you as I can before they do."

He nodded. "Okay, but I think we need to start the process of letting go."

"What does that mean?"

"I don't know. Maybe not see each other for a while."

"A while?"

"Yeah, a while."

What did that mean? We only had two weeks left. My throat burned with unshed tears. "If that's what you want."

Standing up, he offered his hand. "It's not what I want, but I think it's for the best."

Up on my own two feet, the ground felt shaky beneath me. "I understand."

The conversation was left open-ended, and it was probably for the best. There was a forced smile on his face when he raised the ball. "Now show me your stuff."

I forced a smile too and backed up so he could throw me the ball. We played a mock game for almost thirty minutes, and the whole time Lucas pretended to be the announcer. I think he was trying to lighten up the mood, but there was no way to do that.

We had less than twelve hours left together, and then we'd be back at training camp and starting the process of letting go.

Was that even possible?

"Whitney thinks she can make this touchdown. Let's see if she can," his voice boomed as I ran with the ball.

Sucking up my despair, I pretended too. When he had the ball, I yelled, "That's Hot Stuff over there, he thinks he can recover his fumble and score, let's see if he can."

Pretending.

I'd be doing a lot of that.

Holding it together, I played along, but the more I thought about the ticking of the clock, the more my mind started to shatter.

The next time he threw me the ball, I missed it and it went rolling down the hill. While I ran what seemed like miles to retrieve it, Lucas started to practice his throw.

I stopped and watched him. The way he moved. The way he

carried himself. The way he was.

His shoulder arced with a precision that screamed of years of hard work. This man was born to be a quarterback.

And it was in this moment I realized that no matter how much I'd hoped we'd dissolve our pact to end things when training camp was over, it could never be that way.

This game was his life, and he was right, my father was a wild card. Like him, I honestly had no idea what he'd do if he found out.

Although, I'd like to think he'd be happy for me, he had this whole thing about my life being normal, and being with Lucas would not be normal, or at least not his normal. There was also the fact that Lucas was *his* player. *His* quarterback. *His* Hail Mary.

And I couldn't compromise that.

Despite the feelings I had for Lucas, I would never do anything to put my father or him in jeopardy because football was their life.

And it was mine too . . . *or at least it had been.*

Twenty-Three

Intentional Grounding

Lucas

ORGANIZED TEAM ACTIVITIES, otherwise known as OTA's were more than beginning to suck.

Time off had long since passed and like clockwork, just past midweek, we were right back to the level of exhaustion and misery we had been at before the thirty-six hour reprieve.

It was only the beginning of practice, but Coach was already in rare form. His temper was explosive. Someone had started a rumor that he had taken up with the cheerleading coach, and he was taking it out on us.

At least I knew his mood had nothing to do with Gillian and me. He'd gone up to Lake Forest over the weekend and didn't even know she hadn't stayed on campus. And I hadn't seen Gillian in anything except a professional capacity since getting back, so it wasn't like he could suspect anything.

We'd both agreed long ago this thing between us would end

when training camp was over. The letting go early part had hit her harder than I thought it would, and to be honest it hadn't been that easy on me either.

Sure, ending things after our weekend had seemed like the right choice at the time. Our time had been amazing, and ending on a good note was how I wanted to remember us.

But relationships were new to me, and I had no idea what to expect from a breakup. Getting attached to someone and then trying to unattach yourself was way more complicated than I could ever have imagined.

In fact, it was pretty fucking hard. I'd even started to second-guess myself, which was never a good thing.

The whistle blew, and I had to get my mind on football, not her.

Drills.

Drills.

And more drills.

Doing basic moves I could maneuver in my sleep, I still had to maximize my concentration so I would hear exactly what Coach wanted done.

I'd been sucking ass this week.

The worst part was this stuff I was doing, I'd done a million times, and I was still fucking it up. I needed to make sure to do it right today in order to minimize the chance of being the target of Coach's ire.

It was another hot day, and the sweat was pouring off my brow as I ran the cones in a twist and turn motion. Then I moved on to plays. The defense showed a blitz to the safety, and I knew I should call an audible at the line of scrimmage, but fuck me if I could remember which one.

Burns swooped in and saved the day.

Motherfucker.

Two-a-days were wearing on me, and when we broke for the

morning, the only thing I wanted to do was crash.

After showering, I walked past the training room. It wasn't on accident, so of course I looked in. Gillian was in there, I knew she was, and she was taping Kutch's ankle. The two of them were alone.

What the fuck—did he get taped twenty-four seven or what?

She wasn't into him, I knew this, but still it infuriated me. I paced, waiting for him to clear the room. It took more than ten minutes with all his bullshit talking until he finally walked out the door.

As soon as he did, I was standing in the doorway. I knew I should have just gone to my room, but I couldn't. I needed to hear her voice. It was Thursday and we hadn't talked since Sunday morning. It had been a long week.

"Hey," I said, staying where I was.

Her head jerked around at the sound of my voice. "Lucas."

I took a step toward her. "Meet me tonight?"

She shook her head. "I don't think that's a good idea."

"Why not?"

"Because," she sighed. "The days have been hard, and the night's harder. Meeting you tonight will only make tomorrow that much worse."

I was inches from her before I could stop myself. "Please. I need you. I can't do this the way we are. It's too hard."

Her bottom lip quivered as she spoke. "But it was your idea to start the letting go process now."

I traced her lip with my finger, hoping to ease her pain. "And I was wrong."

She stared at me, contemplating my words.

The sound of Dallas's voice coming down the hallway had me jumping back.

"You should go," she whispered.

"Not until you say yes, Gillian. Agree to meet me tonight."

"No." Her voice was soft and raspy. I knew she was going to cry.

I had to leave before Dallas got here.

"If you change your mind, I'll be there tonight, at ten," I said, and then I was gone.

During afternoon practice, I couldn't stop thinking about her and our situation. I threw a couple of terrible balls and made more than a few obvious mental miscalculations.

"Carrington, over here, now!"

Coach was calling me aside.

Great!

I ran over to where he stood. "Yeah, Coach."

"Do you think you can take your head out of your ass this week?"

"Sorry, Coach. I don't know what's going on with me."

"Well you better figure it out. And fast. Burns is scoring, and you, I don't know what you are doing. Are you pulling this shit because you want me to put him in your spot?"

The words *fuck you* were on the tip of my tongue, but if I let them fly, I'd be out, and I knew it. "No, Coach, I don't."

He practically spit as he spoke. "Then show me you deserve to be the starter."

The pressure was demonic, and as I ran back onto the field, I tried to figure out where this rotten streak I was in had come from.

It wasn't like I had to think too hard.

Before I picked up the ball, I pulled the football shaped rock from my pocket and stared down at it. If this was my good luck charm, it better start fucking working right now.

By the time practice ended I knew the fucking rock wasn't my good luck charm. Damn it, she was. She was my good luck charm. I almost threw the rock across the field, but then at the last minute, I couldn't let it go.

She was a part of it.

And I'd pushed her away.

I had done that.

In the locker room, I avoided conversation with anyone, opting to be alone in my own head space. When I could, I grabbed for my phone and sent Gillian a text. It was short and to the point.

Me: Meet me tonight. I'm begging.

The hours passed slowly until it was time to head to the bridge—and she still hadn't responded to my message.

At ten past ten I sat on the bridge alone. I thought for sure she wasn't coming, but then I heard the snap of twigs and an odd relief washed through me.

Holding onto the rope rail, she walked slowly toward me across the old rickety bridge. I stood up. Waited for her to reach me.

As soon as she did, I reached for her. Pulled her down to sit on the edge of the bridge. Her touch was what I needed. Words were for later. Right now I needed to feel her against me.

All of her.

And I was going to start with her mouth, right here, right now. I kissed her until my face was numb. Until my lips ached. And even then, that wasn't enough. I wanted to reacquaint myself with every inch of her from her head to her toes. "Let's go back and I'll come to your room after curfew," I breathed.

Her roaming hands stopped their movement, but only to pull me closer and hold me tighter. "Lucas, no, we can't."

"Yes, we can," I insisted, and kissed her again, a little harder, a little rougher, and with a lot more need.

She broke away. "What are you doing? You ended things between us."

"I don't know what I want, but I know ending things with you isn't it. What I do know is I can't go another night without touching you, talking to you, being with you. In you."

If I sounded more desperate than I ever had, that was because I was.

With her arms around my neck, she murmured, "Okay," and then rested her head on my shoulder and held onto me even tighter.

I did the same.

Our hold was fierce.

Forgiving.

Indefinable.

I tried to unwrap myself from her hold, so we could head back. "Come on," I managed.

She didn't move. Just held me tighter.

Beneath my fingertips, I could feel her body tense. "Gillian, what is it?" I asked.

Finally, after a few moments, she pulled back, and I nervously watched as she stood up. "You were right to end things. You know this is only going to get harder as the days pass and our time comes closer to ending."

I stood and took her hand. "I wasn't right, Gillian. That's just it. Nothing about this is right. I'm not right, not without you. I don't know how it happened, but I need you."

Tears filled her eyes. "What are you saying?"

I cupped her face in my hands. "I'm saying I don't want to say goodbye."

She was shaking. "But what about my father and—"

I cut her off. "Let's worry about that tomorrow, please," I begged.

"One night isn't going to change anything, Lucas."

"I know, but I just can't worry about it right now. I want you. I need you. I really need you."

With a smile, she nodded. "Okay, but tomorrow we have to figure things out."

Tomorrow came, but we didn't figure things out, nor did we the next day, or the day after that.

Figuring things out meant facing the fact that there was no way we could really tell her father about us.

We both knew he would never accept it.

I was his star player.

She was his daughter.

And although I might not be able to explain why, I just knew in my heart he would never allow the two of us to be together.

Besides everyone knew the unwritten rule in football when it came to any coach's daughter—don't touch.

You.

Did.

Not.

Touch.

This meant after training camp there was never going to be an *us*.

And facing that wasn't anything either of us were willing to do.

Twenty-Four

SCRAMBLING

Lucas

IT WAS THE fastest photo ever taken.

All fifty-three players stood in a giant pack, row by row by row, one set of massive shoulders next to the other.

"Say cheese," Coach yelled.

I plastered a giant smile on my face, but the only thing I could think about was *we were done*.

Training camp was over.

"Come on you big bunch of pansies, you can do better than that." Coach was never going to let up.

The thing was, we didn't give a fuck. I mean come on, after tomorrow morning's short team meeting, training camp would be over. We'd be out of the dorms and come Monday we'd be practicing at Soldier field, and not living together.

Oh, and no more two-a-day practices didn't hurt the grins we wore.

Sure, starting Monday there would be meetings in the morning, practices in the afternoon, weight lifting sessions and more meetings after practice, but then we would be dismissed.

"Okay, get the fuck out of here," Coach said, lowering his camera.

The farewell party was almost over. Friends of the owner, retired players, fans, press. They were all here. This was Fan Day all over again but times ten. I'd spent the night signing autographs, smiling, talking, and taking photos. I was ready to bail.

"I'm going to Vegas," Thor said as we stepped off the platform.

My head jerked in his direction. "Are you getting hitched?"

He practically choked. "Fuck no. Rebecca and Honey both broke up with me. I'm going with the guys to drink our asses off and whatever else happens to come along. You should come."

I shook my head. "Can't."

He shook his head back. "Don't tell me, I don't want to know."

I glanced around. "Great, because I wasn't about to."

"Dick," he muttered with a smirk. "Hey, did you figure out your living situation yet?"

He was renting an apartment in Chicago since he wasn't from there. "Yeah, shit I meant to tell you earlier that if you're still looking for a roommate, I'm in."

Nick would soon have three kids and the last thing he needed was me coming in and out, and besides, I was a grown-up now. Wasn't I?

Thor clapped me on the back. "Looks like we'll be roomies for a while longer."

"Yeah, but I'll have my own room so I don't have to listen to your calls of passion at all hours of the night."

"Dude, don't be jelly. It doesn't suit you."

I was laughing so hard that I couldn't even talk.

"There you are." It was Coach and he had someone beside him.

"See you, man," Thor said, and slipped away.

"This is Jason Builder. He's interested in interviewing you for an article in next month's Inside Sports."

Holy shit. This was Jason Builder, the award-winning journalist. Normally, as a rule, I wasn't interested in the press, but Jason was renowned, and my brother Nick read every article he ever wrote. I shoved my hand out. "Nice to meet you."

His grip was firm. "Same here. Got a few minutes?"

"Yeah, yeah, of course," I said. Gillian was waiting for me but I knew she'd understand.

The interview took nearly an hour, and even still the party lingered on. Jason left and I was just headed out when Coach found me again.

"Good, you're still here," he said.

"Did you need something?" I asked.

He looked at me for a moment, and in that moment before he spoke, I thought, shit, he knows. "I wanted to tell you, Lucas, that you've surpassed my expectations over these six weeks, and that I just know this season is going to be a winner with you on board."

Surprised as hell, all I could do was stare at him. Did he just tell me in his own way that I was good at this quarterback gig?

I was pretty sure he did.

Maybe, just maybe, things were actually looking up for me.

And that was a big fucking maybe.

Twenty-Five

Extra Point

Gillian

THIS WAS THE polar opposite of letting go.

Frantic to be alone for the last few precious days we had left, Lucas and I were taking risks we shouldn't have been taking.

Sneaking around.

Hiding in places that weren't that hidden just to press our bodies together.

Being careless.

It had been almost a week since we'd gotten back together after our *break up*, for lack of any other word, and time was running out—quickly.

Earlier in the week, I had even gone to back wondering if telling my father was really that bad of an idea. He might just be okay with it. He might just embrace the idea.

Then again, he might not.

His star quarterback had looked phenomenal on the field all

week and he was actually smiling at him whenever they passed each other. I'd witnessed it numerous times.

Lucas was his Hail Mary.

And because of that, because I knew how important Lucas was to my father, I wouldn't tell him. Couldn't tell him. The risk was too great.

It might just ruin everything.

For everyone.

Tonight might be our last night on the Olivet campus, but it wouldn't be Lucas and my last night together. We were going to be spending the next two nights together in Chicago before I had to leave for Florida.

I'd already told my father I was going to be staying at my favorite hotel in Chicago until my early morning flight on Saturday so that I could catch up on some rest and attend a yoga seminar that was being held close by.

He never questioned it. In fact, he wasn't even going to Lake Forest right away, but instead to some golf resort for a few days before heading home.

This was so unlike him, and when I asked him about it, he just told me he wanted to catch up on some rest, too.

Made sense.

Time was passing so slowly. I laid on my bed wide awake. Waiting. Usually I fell asleep and then woke when Lucas came to me, but tonight I found myself unable to do so. It was midnight by the time I heard him slipping into my room.

A few things had changed between us. A few things had been figured out. A few things hadn't.

We'd discussed *us*, and decided once I left we'd talk on the phone when we could and then, when I finished school, well, we'd take it from there. The season would almost be over by then and neither of us knew what would happen afterwards.

Would he still be playing for the Bears?

What city would I get a job in?

Could we manage a long-distance relationship?

Neither of us had answers to any of those questions. It wasn't the most upbeat situation, but it wasn't the worst, and I could live with that.

As soon as he locked the door, we stared at each other for the longest time without saying a word. Knowing this was our last night in this room was part of it. The other part was the unknown that was coming so fast.

Discussing this with him seemed like something I should do, but I was still trying to figure out exactly what to say when I forgot about everything.

I don't know who moved first, him or me. I only knew that his lips were on mine and they felt so good I wasn't going to deny the moment just so we could talk about something that suddenly seemed to have been talked to death.

I opened for him—my mouth, my arms, my legs, and my heart.

His hand curled against the back of my neck, possessively, drawing me nearer. Need so big, so large it was like an ocean, a mountain, the world, was consuming us.

My pulse was pounding.

Still without words, he pulled away and unbuttoned. Unzipped. I tugged my shirt off, my leggings, my panties. Eyes only on each other, both naked, our bodies found one another as if we were two magnets.

Frantic for each other, we kissed. We touched. We tangled ourselves together.

His hands roamed.

Mine did the same.

He kissed my mouth, my jaw, my chin, my neck, and then lower.

Only one light in the room was on, but I could see everything.

All of him. The leanness of his body. The tanned, smooth skin that covered his ribs, his stomach, the jut of his hipbones, and his beautiful, long, fully erect cock. I reached for it, and the feel of him in the palm of my hand made my clit pulse with so much dizzying need that I had to close my eyes.

"Fuck me." The words slipped from my mouth.

He made a noise and for a second I thought he wanted to say something, but then he rolled us over and before I knew it, I was staring down at his handsome face, straddling him.

I wanted to lick every inch of him, to kiss him from his head to his toes, and to tell him everything was going to be okay, but I didn't want to talk. I didn't want to ruin the moment with words. Instead, I shifted a little, raised myself the smallest amount, and then he was inside of me. Ecstasy. With a shudder, I squeezed my knees against his sides and absorbed the pleasure.

After a few moments, he started to move. Slow. Easy. Up and down. In and out. My hands flattened on his chest. His body continued to lift and fall, his hands now possessively gripping my hips.

"I love you." This time there was no "I think I could." This was the real thing. The words just came out in a hushed whisper, and there was no taking them back now that they'd been said. And I didn't want to.

"I love you, too," he whispered back.

Those words were spoken between us like a secret, but that was all that had to be said.

It was all that could be said.

Declarations couldn't change the fact that the end was near. I accepted this. These last few nights would be what we had together—for now, *and maybe for always.*

So I lowered my mouth to his, and I kissed him with everything I had. Gasps of pleasure escaping through open-mouthed kisses filled the room. And then all that was left was he and I, and absolutely no sadness.

It became hard to concentrate on kissing him when with every slide of his cock there was a glorious press against my clit.

Our need for each other kept building.

Higher and higher.

On the edge, I wanted more. I had to have more. I pushed upright and rode him. Faster. Harder. Eyes locked, he fucked upward and I rolled my hips.

My heart beat faster.

My breath rushed out.

And then I was coming.

He was coming.

It was fast.

Intense.

My body quaking in perfect spasms of ecstasy, I looked down at him. He stilled, groaned, and I could feel his cock pulse inside me as he rode out his own release.

Once our breathing slowed, he pulled me to his chest and held me tightly. He kissed my head. Once, twice, three times. I never wanted this night to end. I wanted to stay awake until he had to leave, but soon exhaustion won out and sleep pulled me under.

Early in the morning, too early, I awoke in my bed—on top of him. "Lucas," I whisper yelled.

At first he didn't move.

"Lucas, it's morning."

That statement made his eyes fly open.

"We fell asleep. You have to get out of here."

Like a bat out of hell, he flew out of bed and got dressed as fast as he could. He started for the door, but then hurried back to me. Slipping down the sheet, he stared at my naked body, and then with a wicked grin, he kissed me once and said, "I'll see you tonight in Chicago."

I smiled up at him. "Tonight," I whispered.

Everything that happened after that happened so fast.

Like he always did, he cracked open the door to make sure the coast was clear. But it wasn't the middle of the night. It was the early morning. And as soon as he slammed the door closed, my heart stopped, because I knew. I knew we'd gotten caught. I just didn't know by whom.

"Who's out there?" I asked, my voice failing in alarm.

Before Lucas could answer, the door flew open and practically bounced off the wall. My entire body went taut when I saw my father looming in the opening.

A dark cloud seemed to shadow the room as he took in the scene. Me naked on the bed. Lucas tiptoeing out in the early hours of the morning. It wasn't like I could make up an excuse. It wasn't like I could do anything. *It wasn't like it was hard to figure out that we'd screwed.*

I snatched the blankets up to cover myself fully, but it was too late. *Too late to do anything.*

"What are you doing in my daughter's room?" my father roared as his gaze shifted from me to Lucas.

"I can explain," Lucas bit out.

Fury blazed in my father's eyes.

"Lucas, leave, let me talk to my father," I cried out.

Lucas's body coiled tightly and I could see he wasn't going to back down.

My father stepped toward Lucas. Neither of them looked at me. I worried my father was going to punch Lucas. I worried Lucas was going to punch my father. "What exactly is there to explain?" my father spat. "It's pretty clear to me you took advantage of my daughter."

"No, Daddy, that's not true," I shouted.

They moved toward one another, both sets of their fists balled at their sides. It was like I wasn't even in the room.

Hot tears pricked my eyelids as I scurried off of bed. Wrapping the blanket around myself, I lunged forward and stood between the two of them before either of them could say or do anything else that would destroy all of us. I placed a palm on each of their chests when I spoke. "Daddy, stop! This isn't what you think it is. Not at all. I love him."

My father cringed at my words. Then again, there was no way for him to understand any of it. "Love?" He practically spat the word.

I forced myself to breathe deeply. "Yes, I love him," I said, my voice quivering despite my best efforts to steady it. "And he loves me."

My father's expression grew dark. "Carrington, in my office, now! Gillian, you and I will discuss this later."

There was an edge in his voice that told me just how angry he was, and I knew better than to challenge him. All of my fears had been realized. I wasn't worried for me, but I was terrified for Lucas.

I didn't know what my father would do and I didn't think I could fix this.

When he yanked my hand as if to separate me from his quarterback, I frowned and turned to fully face Lucas. "Lucas, you have to go," I implored.

His gaze was distant even as he spoke. "I'll be okay," he told me, as if that would convince me.

I shook my head.

"Carrington!" My father's voice boomed. "My office now."

I twisted back toward my father. "Let me explain first," I pleaded.

He ignored me. "Now, Carrington! Or you're off the team."

Dread filled my chest and my heart squeezed the breath right out of me. I opened my mouth to speak again. To try to calm him down.

"Don't," Lucas whispered, warning me to keep quiet.

I ignored him. I had to. "Daddy, please let me explain." I was practically begging.

It didn't matter.

He wasn't listening, and Lucas was already leaving with my father hot on his heels, and slamming the door behind him.

I clutched the material tighter around my body and my lips quivered as I stared at the door. I wanted to go after them both, but I knew my efforts would only make things harder for Lucas.

There was nothing I could do . . . but wait.

Twenty-Six

AUDIBLE

Lucas

THERE WAS NO disputing the importance of the quarterback position.

As the team's biggest decision maker, my ability to perform timely plays and efficiently manage the game was of key importance.

And yet, as I stood in the office of Head Coach Jack Whitney, I couldn't help but feel none of that was going to matter to him in the next few minutes. He was going to bounce me out on my ass. I wished I could say I'd fucked up, but I couldn't.

What I had with Gillian was real, and I wasn't going to downplay it, not even to save my position.

He stormed in right behind me, and flying past me, he sat in his chair. "Sit down!" he ordered in a terse voice.

I planted my palms on his desk, leaned over and leveled my stare at him. "I have something to say to you before you fire me."

"I said sit down!" he bit out.

"Not until I tell you what I have to tell you," I responded bluntly.

Surprise flashed in his eyes and he sat back, staring harder at me. "Go on."

The challenge didn't bother me. I was gone either way, so I might as well fight for what I wanted. "I love your daughter, and I want to be with her. I also love this team, and I want to keep my job. I will do whatever it takes to keep them both."

He slammed his fist on his desk. "Sit down!"

I pushed off the desk and took a seat.

Coach shook his head. "Do you even know what love is?"

"I didn't," I said, "not until Gillian, but I do now, and I know I've never felt this way about anyone."

He almost laughed. "If she's your first, you can't possibly know what love is."

"That's not true. I don't have to ever have been in love before to know we share a connection."

Standing up, he paced a tight line behind his desk. "You do understand your life is football now, don't you?"

I nodded. "Yes, I do."

"And that means football always comes first."

I said nothing. I didn't like where this was going.

He stopped pacing and pulled his wallet from his pocket. Opening it, he pulled out a worn piece of paper. "I have a story I want to tell you about love."

There was something in his voice that told me this wasn't going to be good.

Leaning forward on the back of his chair, he looked at me, but I didn't feel like he was seeing me. "Three days before Gillian was born I was at home with my wife. She was a schoolteacher and had decided to start her maternity leave early. I'd asked her to come with me to so many games, but she'd always said no, so I didn't bother to ask for the next one. It was close to eight at night, I think, and she wanted me to take her out for fish tacos."

My gut roiled. The fish tacos I saw him eating so many weeks ago.

He was lost to the past as he spoke. "I was tired, and had a game, so I told her no. That we would do it another time. She got angry with me and stormed off to bed. We'd been arguing a lot by the time she'd gotten pregnant with Gillian, so it was nothing out of the ordinary. I knew to leave her alone. She had a temper and needed to cool down."

I drew in a breath, not wanting to hear the rest. I could already tell the version of the story Gillian had told me was very different.

Slowly, he unfolded only one part of the folded paper that had been curled between his fist and the chair. "So I got up the next morning, said goodbye, and left to meet the bus without bothering to try to make things right. I figured when I got back, I would bring her some flowers and she'd forgive me like she always had because by then she would have calmed down."

A cold sweat broke out across my forehead.

Carefully, he unfolded another square. "She still had six more weeks before she was due, so I wasn't worried about the baby. The game was in Indianapolis and when I got the call mere hours before kick-off that she'd been in a car accident just outside of Lafayette, I assumed she'd changed her mind, and had been driving down to watch me play."

That was the story Gillian had told me.

Another piece of that paper unfolded in his hands. "My wife had died by the time I got to the hospital, but somehow Gillian had survived the accident. She's a fighter, you know," he said, and I thought for a moment he was going to cry his voice was so hoarse. "Anyway, when I got home with her days later, I found this note." He held his hand up.

Feeling like I wanted to crawl out of my own skin, I shifted in my chair.

Grabbing his reading glasses from his desk, he opened it up completely. "My Dearest Jack, I am writing this letter with so many regrets, but I can't go on like this," he read, and then stopped, took a deep breath, and looked at me.

I shook my head. "You don't have to read it to me, Coach."

"Yeah, well I wasn't going to. I think you get the idea. She was leaving me. She wasn't headed to Indianapolis like I had thought, but rather Louisville, where she was from. In this note," he waved it in the air, "she told me she wanted a normal life for herself and our daughter, and that the life I was living in the NFL was anything but normal. She went on to tell me she needed someone who would put her and our daughter first, and that wasn't me. She wrote that she wanted someone who would take her out for fish tacos whenever she wanted them." His voice broke then and his hands shook as he set the letter down on the desk.

"Coach, I'm sorry." It was all I could say.

Standing tall, he came around the desk and glared down at me. "Gillian is the most important thing in the world to me, and I've spent my whole life trying to honor her mother's wishes. I didn't do the greatest job in making her life normal. Football was all I knew, but Gillian is so close to having what her mother wanted for her. Don't ruin it for her, Lucas. Don't fool yourself into thinking you can have her and have your career, because, son, ask anyone around you, it doesn't work that way."

"Coach," I said, "I think you have your daughter all wrong. She doesn't want a normal life. She loves this life."

His eyes went wide. "She's twenty-three. She doesn't know what she wants. She only knows what she's had," he bellowed. "Of course that's what she'd think she wants, don't you understand that?"

I swallowed hard. "Yes, I do."

His voice softened. "I am not going to take your position from you, Lucas, or threaten you, but I am going to ask you to listen to me."

I nodded, not feeling an ounce of relief.

He sat in the chair beside me. "If you love Gillian like you say you do, you won't drag her into this life. She deserves a chance at experiencing normalcy. A husband who's home every night, a house with a white picket fence, a station wagon, a dog, a couple of kids, and fish tacos every night if she Goddamn wants them."

That last part got me. I glanced over toward the desk and when my gaze landed on that worn piece of paper, the words, *fish tacos* jumped out at me.

It was then I knew he wasn't wrong. I might not fully agree with him, but Gillian at least deserved the chance to find out for herself what it was she really wanted.

To discover if normal was for her.

And with me in her life she never would.

I knew I had to let her go.

After all, if you loved someone you set them free.

Twenty-Seven

PASS PROTECTION

Gillian

ONE OF THE reasons I loved this room was the view of the planes.

Feeling nervous, I looked out the window at the lights on the runway that seemed to jut out for miles. One jet landed, taxiing toward the terminal, while another took off, slowly disappearing in the distance.

The sun was setting and the colors in the sky were mesmerizing. When I was a kid and we stayed here, I stared out this window for hours and thought of nothing.

It didn't work anymore.

My thoughts were still there.

Alone at the Chicago O'Hare Airport hotel, I was feeling uneasy. Lucas had yet to respond to a single one of my text messages and my father refused to talk to me about anything that happened. All he did was look at me like I'd disappointed him.

Like I'd disappointed him!

Well, he'd disappointed me.

It wasn't the most mature thing I'd ever done, but I stormed out on him and after saying goodbye to Dallas and Aiden, I'd left. We both needed time to cool off or we'd say things to each other we shouldn't.

This wasn't anything new. We'd battled before, but never over a guy, never over one of his players, never over someone I loved.

I swiped my tears away. I was crying over a guy. I never cried over a guy. I hated that I didn't know what happened.

And now I was here alone, so I cried.

What had happened to me? Just six weeks ago I felt like my life was perfect, and now it couldn't have felt further from perfect.

I walked out onto the field, I think, and he was there, that's what happened.

I checked my phone.

He'd be here.

Nothing.

Nothing.

Nothing.

Another hour ticked by, and still nothing. I tried to call him and it went straight to voicemail.

Two hours passed and I was no longer crying. I did however feel like I'd been stabbed in the heart, and I hated that feeling even more.

Back to staring out the window, I couldn't stop thinking about him. I was that freshman roommate again.

I got that he might not show up, that his position on the team came first, I did. But I wanted what I couldn't get, what I would never get, was how he could let me just wait for him without even a call.

The light rapping on the door startled me. It was almost ten and I'd been standing at this window for hours.

Maybe things would work out after all.

The steps I took were hesitant and then when I got to the door, I even opened it slowly. As soon as I saw his face, I knew we were over, but then I knew that hours ago.

Didn't I?

Every part of me tensed.

It was in the way he stood, the way his shoulders weren't as square as they usually were. It was in his eyes. And as he stepped inside the room, he knew I knew.

"Gillian," he said, closing the door behind him. The act itself was so familiar, but that was the only thing that was right now.

I drew in a breath. Then another. I wanted to kiss him, but even though he was only a few steps away there was so much distance between us. He stepped forward as if realizing this and pulled me into his arms. I tucked myself against him, my hand covering his heart.

"I wasn't sure you were going to come."

He covered my hand with his, curling his fingers tight around mine. When he looked down at me, the darkness in his pupils had nearly swallowed up his blue eyes. "I know I should have called, but I had a lot to take care of before exit interviews and then well, shit, Gillian—"

I shook my head. "You don't have to say it. I already know." My voice cracked and I had to look away. "At least tell me you still have a position on the team. Tell me you're still the quarterback for the Bears."

Gently, Lucas lifted my chin. "Your father didn't threaten to take my position from me."

"Then what did he do?"

Lucas stepped back. "Gillian, we said from the start this would be over when you left for school, but then we allowed ourselves to get carried away. We shouldn't have. You have college and a new job to worry about, and I have the team. We'll both be so busy we won't have time for anything else, especially not each other."

My knees felt weak, so I went over to the bed and sat down. "You know as well as I do that isn't true. You can pretend you believe it, but I know you don't, Lucas. I know!"

He came over to me and knelt down, placing his palms on my knees. "You're wrong. I do believe that. Just like I believe you will be okay, and so will I."

"What did he say to you?" I screamed.

Lucas pushed my hair from my eyes. "Like I said, he didn't threaten my position, and that's all you need to know."

I shook my head. "Don't do this!"

"Close your eyes, Strawberry Fields," he said, his voice hoarse.

I did. And when I did, I waited for him to kiss me. I waited for his touch. I waited for him to throw me down on the bed and take me, even if it was for the last time.

But then I heard the soft click of the door, and when I opened my eyes . . . he was gone.

And I was not okay.

I would never be okay.

Twenty-Eight

Hut, Hut, Hike

Lucas

THE FIRST NFL game I would ever play in was going to be at Soldier Field.

It was bitter fucking sweet.

The love/hate relationship I had with the Bears had nothing to do with the team or this city and everything to do with my father.

The Bears had been his favorite team, and during the times in his life that he decided to be a part of mine, he shared that love with me.

Wanting his attention so badly, I learned everything I could about his favorite team. By the time I was eight, I knew every stat, every player, every detail of that team. I knew McMahon was his favorite player and that he wore jersey #9. I knew Ditka was one of the best coaches that ever walked this earth. And I knew no one ever questioned the toughness of Jim McMahon.

Shit, I had wanted to be just like him.

The goalposts stood like fluorescent yellow glow sticks in the dark of the night. I still couldn't believe I was here wearing jersey #9.

I'd grown up coming here my entire life. Sometimes with my old man, sometimes with my brother, sometimes alone. There were times I couldn't get in because I didn't have enough money to buy a ticket. There were times I snuck in. And then there were times I flat out refused to even watch the game, and those times were when my father was manic.

You see, my brother refused to admit my father suffered from something very close to being bi-polar. He blamed my father's mood swings on our mother leaving him, but what my brother didn't know was that I'd found our mother and discovered the truth.

The woman who looked like me, had the same color hair and eyes as me, told me what I needed to hear. And other than the resemblance, I'd found no connection worth pursuing.

That one time I met with her she told me why she'd left us. It wasn't because she was in love with someone else, like my brother had thought. Although she was, and it had made leaving easier. Still the truth was she'd left because of him.

My father.

He was unstable.

Crazy, she'd said, and she couldn't take it.

She had to get out of there. She'd wanted to take my brother and me with her, or so she'd said, but my father had threatened to kill us all if she did. And she truly believed he would. I had to admit, she probably wasn't wrong.

The last thing she said to me before I left was what stuck in my head. She told me that *if you loved someone, you set them free.* And since my father refused, she ran away.

Sure, I had a person I could call Mom and one I could call Dad, but neither was my parent. No, my parent had been my brother, who was only ten years older than me. It was Nick who took care of me, made sure I was fed and bathed and went to school. And because of that I would never tell him I'd found our mother. He believed what he believed, and that was how he'd made it through life.

Who the fuck was I to rock his foundation?

He was here tonight up in the box seats reserved for him, as they would be for every game. With him were Tess and their three kids, as well as his two best friends and their families.

Tess had given birth to their second daughter. Celia was tiny and had the bluest eyes just like my brother. Just like me. Just like our mother.

When I held her for the first time, I thought of Gillian and what our kids might have looked like had we been able to stay together. Would they have had her strawberry blond hair or my brown strands? Her green eyes or my blue ones? Would they be tall like us?

That was the one and only time since saying goodbye to her I'd allowed myself to wonder about what might have been.

The lights flicked on and the stadium lit up. I was nervous. So fucking nervous. My stomach wasn't feeling that great earlier, so for dinner I'd passed on the meal and ate two Power bars and two bananas.

Not sure if that was the best choice.

On the sidelines of the field, I stretched and then picked up a ball to start rotating my arm like a windmill.

When the whistle blew, it was time to gather as a team.

"This is our time," Coach said.

We all nodded.

"Today, Pittsburg is going down."

Again, we all nodded.

Coach blew the whistle again, and we all took to the field to warm-up.

Soon, we were headed back to the locker room.

Thor walked up to me near the lockers. "Did you hear?"

"Hear what?"

"Over seventy thousand people are estimated to be in the stadium tonight. It will be the largest football crowd in Soldier Field history."

I stared at him. "Seriously?"

"Yeah, the Bears haven't come this far in so long, I guess all the fans that have died off over the years must have decided to show up."

For some reason this news made me feel even sicker. I ran to the bathroom stall to kneel over the toilet. Suddenly my dinner came up.

The rap on the door annoyed me. Couldn't a guy have a case of nerves in private?

"Lucas, it's me, Nick."

"Nick?" I yanked the door open in disbelief.

"Hey, you okay?" he asked, taking a step back.

I smiled and strode out. "Yeah, just nervous. What are you doing in here?"

He gave me a shrug. "Couldn't let you take the field for the first time without saying good luck to your face."

I washed my hands and then turned to lean against the counter. "Big brother," I said.

He leaned against the counter beside me. "Yeah, little brother?"

"I don't think I've told you this, but I owe you everything."

His eyes filled with emotion.

I turned and pulled him to me, hugging him like I never had. "Thank you."

He slapped my back and then whispered, "You never have to thank me. I owe you everything too. Without you, what the hell would I have done with my life?"

I'd never looked at the two of us as needing each other, but maybe he was right, we were who we were because of one another.

Just then Coach called everybody in.

Nick gave me one final squeeze and then headed for the door, tossing over his shoulder, "Make Chicago proud, brother, make

Chicago proud."

I choked down every single emotion I felt as I headed toward my team.

The locker room was packed as we all took a knee.

The veins were pulsing in Coach's neck and forehead when he spoke. "We are going to win tonight!" he shouted.

All fifty-three of us responded with primal yells. "Hell, yeah."

After giving us some time to chant, he led us in reciting the Lord's Prayer, and then it was time.

As I put my helmet on, my brother's words were still fresh in my mind.

The moment I looked through my facemask though, I let everything go. This was my time to shine. As Gillian would say, it was time to show my stuff.

It was her voice I heard as I propelled through the cramped locker room doorway into the tunnel. "You think you're hot stuff."

Yeah, I did, and I wished I could tell her so.

Condensation dripped from the low ceiling above my head. The click clack of cleats was loud in my ears as it echoed in the tunnel, but the rumble of fans was even louder.

Together as a team we stopped at the end of the tunnel and waited.

I took it all in.

When the announcer thundered, "Lucas Carrington!" I stepped to the ledge and darted out.

Jogging under the goalposts and through the gauntlet of teammates, I looked around in awe. Ushers in yellow jackets surrounded the entrances to the field. The cheerleaders were lined up, high-kicking and shaking their pom-poms. Gillian would be rolling her eyes right now if she could see them. And the Chicago fans were screaming loudly.

Although I'd wanted to abandon this city once, Chicago was my city, and in this moment I knew I wanted to take it back. Make it mine again. More than anything I hoped I could give these people what they wanted, what they needed to believe again—a win.

Maybe it was what I needed too.

Pittsburg won the coin toss and elected to receive. On the fourth play of the game, one of ours picked off their quarterback and returned the ball for a touchdown. We were ahead 7–0.

It was a great start.

Except by half time we were down, and in the locker room Coach focused on what we'd done right, not wrong. It was so unlike him.

During the third quarter we made a comeback and by the near end of the fourth we were tied 24–24.

"Don't let up!" Coach was loud in my ear.

I wasn't about to.

It was my time to shine. To show Coach he'd made the right choice in choosing me. To win this game.

On the snap, I took three quick steps back to pass, but then Thor came like a lunatic around one end and created a brief opening for me.

Taking advantage, with the ball tucked under my arm, I headed for the end zone.

I was almost there when a linebacker hit my legs. I bounced off him, but he wrapped up my feet as another linebacker went for my head.

Fuck them. Fuck them all.

I ducked just in time to land hard inside the end zone.

Touchdown!

The crowd loved it. My teammates loved it. Coach loved it. I loved it! And I knew if Gillian were watching, first she'd be worried I'd been injured and insist she check me out, but then once she knew I was fine, she'd love it, too.

As we celebrated our very first victory of the season, I couldn't help but wonder whether Gillian had been watching. And then I let myself do something I vowed not to.

I wished she were here to celebrate with us . . . with *our* team.

Twenty-Nine

Gillian

I WAS OKAY.

Or I would be okay soon. That was what I told myself every day over the past four and half months as I went through the motions of finishing school and job hunting, both of which were now complete.

The Mayo Clinic Sports Center in Minneapolis had offered me a job three days ago, and I had two weeks to give them a decision. I was going to take it, of course. I just hadn't told them yet.

I would, soon.

Things with my father were better. He had come to Gainesville for my graduation in December. It was the first time I'd seen him since that morning in the dorm. Sure, we'd spoken on the phone, but the conversations had been bland, and we'd never spoken of Lucas again.

I was no longer upset with my father. I knew from the start how he'd react when he found out, if he found out, so what happened shouldn't have shocked me like it did. The thing about it was he didn't care about the feelings I had for Lucas, or I should say, didn't want to hear about them, and I think that was what still bothered me.

Was it easier that way for him?

In the end, did it really matter? It was Lucas's decision to end things. He was the one who told me he loved me and then left me without saying goodbye.

It was the final game of the regular season. I hadn't flown up for a single one all year, and my father hadn't asked me to either. But this was one I couldn't stay away from. This game meant everything to the Bears, and despite the tension between my father and me, and despite my complete break with Lucas, I loved this team and wanted them to succeed.

With three minutes and twenty-two seconds left in the fourth quarter, the Bears had taken over at their own eight-yard line. The Packers were up 27–21. They'd scored three touchdowns and kicked two field goals, and we'd scored three times.

The Green Bay Packers had already sealed a playoff spot, so you would have thought they would have rested their starters to avoid an unnecessary injury, but that was not the case. Chicago versus Green Bay was one of the league's most storied rivalries.

It seemed that back in the nineteen twenties, Chicago pounded the Packers 20–0, and for extra measure, one of their guards threw a sucker punch that broke the nose of one of the Packer's tackles. And ever since then the two teams shared a love / hate relationship, which is why they weren't about to back down now, even with their own spot secured.

At eleven wins and four losses for the season, the Bears were a far cry from last year's complete reverse. But their position in the playoffs rested on this one game.

Snowflakes fell over Soldier Field, but the cold drizzle did nothing to dampen the mood of the Bears fans. They wanted this for Chicago. The team wanted this for Chicago. I wanted this for Chicago, for my father, *and for Lucas*.

The clock was ticking and I found myself biting my nails. I'd opted against being on the sidelines with the trainers like I always had been at every game before, because . . . well, just because.

On the first and ten, Lucas handed the ball off to the running back, who ran it for one-yard. Running it all the way wasn't going to be easy. The Packers defense was one of the best in the league.

On the second down, Lucas changed strategies and passed it to Preacher, but the play was incomplete.

Tick-tock.

Time was running out. Finally, after getting a clean snap, Lucas dropped back. With his feet firmly planted beneath him, he had just pulled the ball back to throw it for a pass when a Packer's tackle blitzed him, and he fumbled the ball.

The ball was on the ground, but it was live at least, and when Lucas stood and dove for it, I held my breath. This wasn't a dropped snap though. He couldn't fall on the ball and cover it. No, he had to reach for it. With several three hundred pound tackles converging on him, he extended his right arm.

Oh, my God, I felt like I couldn't breathe.

Was he hurt?

But then he recovered the ball and I finally exhaled.

The crowd around me roared, and I swiped a stray tear away. It was nothing. It didn't mean anything. I had not allowed myself to cry for all this time, and I wasn't about to start now. I would force myself to laugh when this was over and I knew he was okay before I cried.

Moments before Lucas hit the ground, he threw the ball to Kutch. There were only twenty seconds left on the clock. The ball was safe, but Lucas was not. With the play already in motion, Kutch caught the ball. At the same time, the Packer's defensive tackle did what every defensive tackle would do in that situation; he took a legal shot at the quarterback—at Lucas.

The force of the collision was ferocious, and I gasped, "Lucas."

The team box was filled with people, but it was only then I noticed a man off to my left that looked so much like Lucas, only he was a bit older. He had to be Nick, and he was holding his hands over his face in distress.

That hit that Lucas took hadn't come alone. It came with the weight of the other tackles that were now piled on top of each other, on top of Lucas.

With the Packers going after Lucas, Kutch was more than able to run the ball all the way. It was unbelievable, but somehow he managed to score a touchdown before the whistle blew.

Everyone cheered, except for Lucas's brother, and me. We were both holding our breath. Yet after the immediate roar of the crowd, there was a stunned silence throughout the stadium as the fans, and me, and Nick, waited for the bodies to lift and for Lucas to emerge.

One by one they stood until Lucas was the only one still on the ground. "Get up," I willed, "get up!"

When he rolled over, and struggled to push himself up with his left arm, I knew something had happened to his right shoulder. It was still compromised from when I'd struck him with the water cart at training camp.

The team converged on him, but Thor was the first by his side, bringing him to his feet. By the time Lucas had stood, the medical staff had flown into action.

Watching him was terrifying, and my heart was nearly pounding out of my chest. He looked like he was in agony as he walked toward the sidelines, and all I wanted to do was run down there.

But I couldn't.

The quarter was back in play, and after kicking for the extra point, the Bears had just won the game, and they were going to the playoffs.

It was the first time in ten years, and I took a moment to glance at my father. Whether he was aware of the win or not, he wore a look of utter concern on his face as he hurried toward Lucas.

The minute the team physician had finished probing around his injury, I felt a whoosh of relief, but it didn't last. I could see, even from here, that his right arm was tilted at a disturbing angle.

Then he did something I never expected, he glanced at the scoreboard, and then his gaze shifted up to the box, the place I was sitting, and that easy smile crossed his lips.

My pulse raced. I knew he had to know I was up here. Was that smile for me, so I wouldn't worry?

After he huddled with the team, and then broke away, every fan in the stadium went wild, including me.

Standing.

Clapping.

Cheering.

Echoes of, "Lucas! Lucas! Lucas!" pulsed through Soldier Field as he thrust his fist in the air.

Holding his right arm, he ran toward the end zone, jumped the guardrail, and climbed up into the stands.

"Lucas! Lucas! Lucas! Lucas!" the crowd chanted.

My heart swelled, this was *his house*, *his time*, and suddenly I knew he had made the right decision in choosing football over me.

Jumping down from the ledge, he started running like he was hot stuff. And he was. He definitely was. Television cameras, photographers, and fans followed. They thought so too.

This was his victory lap, and it looked so good on him.

The team joined him, and by the time he made it all the way around the stadium, the team owner and my father were waiting for him.

My eyes welled up again.

"You must be Gillian."

I turned to see who I knew had to be Lucas's brother standing beside me. I was surprised he'd known who I was. "Yes, and you must be Nick."

He smiled. "Yeah, that's right. So what do you think?" he asked. "Is our boy going to be okay?"

Our boy?

He wasn't our boy, not anymore. I drew in a breath. "Well, I'm not a doctor, but it looks like he dislocated his shoulder. It's going to have to be popped back into place, but in a couple of weeks, with a lot of rehab, he should be fine."

"You should help him with that," Nick said, shoving his hands in his pockets.

"I . . . we . . ." I stumbled with my words. "We aren't together."

Nick shrugged, and he looked so much like Lucas when he did. It was that *I don't give a fuck* thing that Lucas wore so well. "Well, if you ask me, you should be."

I had a thousand questions to ask him. Why would he say that? What had Lucas said? Had Lucas moved on? I mean come on, women everywhere were dying to get near him.

Just as I opened my mouth to speak, I saw Lucas back on the bench with the team's physician, Dallas, and Aiden.

My stare had Nick whirling around.

And together we watched as the team physician extended Lucas's right arm and pulled it until I knew it had snapped back into place.

"Shit," Nick winced. "He's probably headed to the hospital. I'm going to see if I can get down there and ride along. It was nice to finally meet you, Gillian."

I nodded, tears stuck in my throat. "You too," I managed.

He walked away, but then turned, "Gillian," he called. I glanced over. "Don't let him try to convince you it was for football."

"What do you mean?" I asked.

His cryptic words hung in the air because then he was gone. I walked down the steps and pressed my face against the glass to look down.

I felt like a kid outside a candy store who was not allowed to go in.

When I found Lucas on the field, he was just entering the tunnel with Dallas and Aiden and even Drake by his side.

The need to be down there with them had never been so strong, and I felt a wave of anger surge through me like I never had. I was mad. Pissed. Furious even, that I wasn't.

I knew in this instant where I belonged.

And it wasn't Minnesota.

Thirty

CALLING THE PLAY

Gillian

THE INSIDE OF a luxury box had glass panels that could be opened. It also included a bar, televisions, a small seating area, and a private bathroom.

The boxes were catered with champagne, canapés, shrimp, and sushi among the many other food choices. For those of us who had season tickets, there were allocated parking spaces and access to the stadium by separate entrances, away from the general public gates.

This box, the executive team box, had emptied out without me even realizing it. And with my nose still pressed to the glass, I mourned the loss of what I loved—both football and Lucas.

This wasn't the place to break and shatter, but I couldn't stop myself from coming undone, not anymore. I'd held it together for long enough. I had to let go, let it out, and then I had to move on.

The tears came fierce and raw and so hard I felt like I couldn't breathe. Of course I couldn't breathe, my heart was down there, in that tunnel, and I didn't know how to get it back. I clutched my face and pressed my forehead harder against the glass to try to silence the cries, but I couldn't.

"Gilly?"

Startled, I turned to see my father just staring at me, and I tried to catch my breath, to wipe the tears away, to hide this ridiculous display of emotion from him, but it was too late.

"Gilly," he said again, this time his voice breaking. "Are you okay?"

The rush and rise of my tears wouldn't stop, not even in his presence. I was worn out from pretending I was okay. "No, I'm not."

He was in front of me and I never saw him move. He put a finger to my chin to lift my gaze to his. "Gillian, what is it?"

I shook my head, my voice stolen by emotion I had no idea how to face. Or how to put behind me.

"It's him, isn't it?" my father asked.

I nodded, not caring anymore that he didn't like what I had done. "I loved him, Daddy. No, not loved . . . I love him, and he just left me without even trying to see if we could work things out."

Despair lined his face.

Pushing out a breath, I spilled my feelings. "Like I was nothing to him. Like I meant nothing."

His hand fit neat under my elbow. "He didn't leave you because you meant nothing, he left you because you meant everything," my father said.

I stared at him. "What do you mean?"

Gently holding onto me, he started for the door. "He did what he did because I asked him to."

Anger spirited through me. "Why? Why would you do that to me?"

"Come to the office. We need to talk."

I dug my Converse-covered toes into the carpet. "I can't, Daddy,

I can't hear you tell me it's for the best because it's not. It's not for the best."

He rested his chin on my head, and I felt like a little girl again who had just skinned her knee. "That's not what I'm going to tell you." The dire tone of his voice told me this was serious, and I relaxed my body enough to move.

Trying to move through Bears headquarters was nearly impossible. It was a flurry of activity. People and press were everywhere, but the way my father moved, no one dared approach him.

Heading down the hall, I found myself staring at the framed clip-art drawings that lined the walls. They were of team uniforms through the years, dating back to the very first blue jerseys with tan colored vertical striping, all the way to today's Nike-designed orange and blue ones.

As we walked by the open door to the equipment room, I looked in. Cabinets were stocked from the floor to the ceiling with everything from chinstraps to sunflower seeds. The sign just inside read, "We Issue Everything Except Guts."

Guts weren't a problem in the NFL, maybe just for me.

The offices were just ahead.

Moving through the double doors etched with the team logo in frosted glass, I felt a sharp pain in my chest as we passed the locker room. Hard rock music was cranked up, which meant the players were still there. Was Lucas still here too, or had he already gone to the hospital? My father would know, but I didn't ask.

Once we were in his office, he closed the door behind him. The monitor behind his desk was still replaying a practice, most likely the very last one, and the bookshelves above it were lined with binders detailing every minute of every training camp he'd ever run.

Right now I knew my father should have been meeting with the press, standing on a platform in front of a throng of media just outside the entrance to the dining room, but instead he was here, with me.

He didn't go behind his desk like he usually did, instead he went over to the sofa and motioned for me to sit down on it. Only after I did, did he pull out his wallet and remove a piece of paper that looked worn.

I'd never seen it before and wondered what it was.

Once he sat down, he started to unfold it, but then stopped and looked me over. "Gillian, I have something to tell you that I should have told you a long time ago."

By the time he finished telling me what really happened the day I was born, that my mother hadn't been actually going to see him play, but rather she was leaving him, I was in such shock that I had to swallow over and over, hard, before I could force myself to speak without my voice crumbling.

That shame on his face was almost too much to bear, but hearing the guilt in his voice was enough to make me want to crumble all over again.

"Oh, Daddy." It was all I could say before I lunged across the sofa and threw my arms around his neck. "It wasn't your fault."

"You're wrong, Gilly, it was. I put football before her, and when I refused to change that, she died because of it." The unsteadiness of his voice scared me. He was always the one who held it together, no matter his temperament.

I pulled back and shook my head. "Life in the NFL might not have been for her, but what happened was an accident."

He handed me the letter. "I want you to read this and then maybe you will understand why I did what I did. I did it for you," he said. *"For her,"* he added softly.

With trembling fingers I took the worn piece of paper, and read the letter that the woman I had never met had penned to my father the day I was born.

My Dearest Jack,

I am writing this letter with so many regrets, but I can't go on like this. This is taking the cowardly way out, but I know I can't face you and see the disappointment on your face when I tell you I'm leaving you, because I feel that same disappointment in myself as well.

From the moment I heard your voice I knew that you were a special person. We talked for hours and shared our most intimate secrets. We laughed, played, and laughed some more. I remember our first kiss and the tingles that went through my body, from the top of my head, to the tips of my toes and straight to my heart. It was kismet.

The time we have spent together over the past ten years has been filled with both sorrow and joy, but it's the sorrow I can't live with. Our lives were never normal. They will never be normal. Life in the NFL is not normal.

Looking back, I can clearly see that over the years we grew apart. But by some miracle, we now have a daughter on the way, and those things I had been feeling before we she was conceived, suddenly seem like a mountain on my shoulders. A burden I can't bear. A weight I can no longer carry.

You know as well as I do, that as time has passed, the feelings we once felt for each other have slowly changed. While you have continued to ignore my pleas to change your lifestyle, I have grown more resentful of the time you are away.

This may sound selfish, but I want our daughter to have a normal life. I want to be able to go out for fish tacos whenever I crave them. I want a husband at home to be with me, love me, and do the same for this child I am carrying. In order to make that happen, I have to be selfish.

I know I sometimes took more than I gave. That I pouted when I should have understood. That I cried when I should have laughed. That I was angry when I should have been grateful. But I acted in those ways because I was unhappy.

I apologize to you because I did nothing to change that. Instead, I let my emotions get the best of me, and I spewed angry, hateful words that I cannot take back.

Our daughter will always be our daughter, as you will always be her father just as I will always be her mother. But she will need more than the woman I have become.

I know that in deciding to move back to Louisville, I have made severe and life altering decisions for the both of us. But I need to find the sunny day to what has been a night filled with angst and turmoil. I need to find normal, and give normal to our daughter. In order to do that, to be the best mother I can be, I have to leave you—for her. I'm putting her first. She deserves normal.

There is no proper way to say goodbye, so I'll end with, please understand.

Jill

There was so much I didn't know about in this letter, and yet I wasn't angry or upset, but I was sad. Sad for what they'd had and lost. Sad for her. Sad for him.

A tear slid down my check, followed by another. I glanced up at my father, and then back down to the letter.

The words written on the page gave me a glimpse into a marriage I never knew was troubled. They were brutally honest and heart wrenching at the same time. They were selfish and selfless. But most of all, the words written were in the past.

They had loved each other, but this life had driven a wedge between them. I hated that. I wanted to think what my parents had together had been more than a love that had been lost, so I re-read it.

This time slowly, carefully, pausing after every sentence. *Kismet*, she had called the love they once shared, and I found something profound in that.

But when I came to the words, *fish tacos*, for the second time, I knew Lucas had known something about my father and mother way before I had.

What, he knew, I wasn't sure. And why it mattered, I wasn't sure either. But I was certain that what we had was *kismet*, as well, and like my parents, it was lost, just for different reasons.

After I finished reading the letter one more time, I carefully folded it back up and set it on the table in front of my father.

I looked at him, at the lines on his face, the sadness in his eyes. I think he expected me to be angry. I think he expected me to look at him differently. I think his expectations were incorrect.

This time when I spoke, it was with the strength I had learned from him. "It was okay, Daddy—that this life wasn't for her. It's not for everyone. In fact, I bet it's not even for a small fraction of the people in this world. But it's okay that it was for you."

He blinked a few times and I could clearly see there were tears welling in his eyes. This was a man I'd never seen shed a single tear. "Do you understand now why I want for you what I couldn't give her?"

There it was, wasn't it? After all these years I finally knew the reason behind his need to give us a normal life. "Normal?"

He nodded.

"But Daddy, I don't want normal."

"You don't know that, Gillian. You haven't given it a chance."

"You're wrong, Daddy, I do know what I want and I know what I don't want. When I think of going to Minneapolis and working nine to five, I break out in a cold sweat. When I think of staying in one place for the rest of my life, it makes my stomach hurt. When I think about a life away from football, I feel like a black cloud is hovering over me. Normal is not what I want. I don't want the same things she wanted. I'm not her."

All he could do was stare at me.

"How can you not see," I whispered. "I'm not like her, I'm like you."

He blinked again, and this time swallowed.

I reached for his hand and squeezed it. "I want what you've

wanted your entire life—this life—football."

And then that one single tear slid down his face. "Then let's make it happen."

Now I was the one staring completely open mouthed.

"We. Can. Make. It. Happen," he said as a smile slowly spread across his mouth.

And then for the first time in almost five months, I laughed.

I actually laughed.

Thirty-One

DUAL THREAT QUARTERBACK

Lucas

I HAD BEEN knocked down, but not out.

Back on my feet, I found myself pacing, and not over my injury. My shoulder would be fine.

An MRI confirmed I hadn't torn the labrum and that there was no tear in the rotator cuff, which was the team physician's biggest concern after he had relocated my shoulder.

If either of those things had happened, there would have been a chance I'd never play football again, and just when I was getting started. Or I thought I was just getting started anyway.

That was until I had listened to that cryptic message Coach left on my voicemail. I should have answered the damn phone when it rang, but I hadn't. Then again, I had been out cold.

After refusing to ride in ambulance, because come on, I wasn't dying, Dallas drove me to the hospital. Four hours later, after numerous examinations and a lot of poking and prodding, I was released with instructions to follow up with the team physician. I was also given some pain meds to help ease the throbbing.

The drive back to my place seemed to take forever. Dallas said nothing. I didn't either. Everything was so raw.

What I'd done hadn't been smart, but it had won us the game and a place in the playoffs. This meant the Bears had a shot at the Super Bowl. Still, that didn't change the fact that I made a stupid play.

Of course, Gillian also weighed heavily on my mind, but that was nothing new. It was just catching sight of her walking through the stadium before the game had my head spinning. Seeing her and not being able to talk to her was like being punched in the gut over and over again.

"Take it easy the next couple of days," Dallas told me as I got out of his car.

I nodded in his direction. "I plan to do just that."

The minute I walked through the door, though, Thor jumped to his feet. "Hey, man, you're back. I've been waiting for you to go meet the guys."

I blinked a few times, trying to clear my head of Gillian. "Meet the guys?" I asked. "This late?"

He tossed his trademark grin. "Yeah, they're at that all-night strip club, and they really want you to join us in the victory celebration."

Of course he had already known my injury wasn't serious because we had been texting for hours, but still, he paused when I took my coat off and his eyes landed on my arm in a sling. "You sure you're okay?"

I nodded. "I'll be fine."

He grabbed his keys and wallet from a pile of stuff on the side table. "Okay, then come on."

Tossing my coat over the back of the sofa, I shook my head. "Sorry, not tonight."

"I had a feeling you'd say that." He clapped me on my good shoulder. "Call me if you need anything."

"Thanks, man, I will," I said, and headed to my room, stepping over

Thor's shoes, cleats, and helmet as I did.

He was proving to be a real slob.

The late night partying might have been the NFL lifestyle, but not for all of us. The job we did was so physically demanding, there was no way anyone could function if they overdid it. Maybe that was just me. But hell, I didn't even drink and if I went out, I still had issues the next day.

Besides, I was not only both mentally and physically exhausted, I was second guessing my decision to let Gillian lead that normal life her father wanted for her.

To keep myself from doing something stupid, like calling her. To stop thinking about her being back in Chicago and close enough to touch. To block out the white noise I felt from knowing she had been there watching what had happened to me and not being able to tell her I was okay—I took the prescribed painkillers and went to sleep.

I woke up to my phone ringing. While reaching for it, I made the decision to ignore it. I laid back down for another hour before I finally listened to the message.

It was a message from Coach, and as soon as I heard his voice, I jumped out of bed. The message was a summons to his office. A summons for tomorrow night at eight pm.

Nothing else.

Not a clue as to why.

That was not good.

Really not fucking good.

The season was almost over and after the dumb play I'd made last night, and everything else that happened this season, there was a chance he was going to trade me, and it was a pretty good one.

Shit, I didn't want to leave Chicago.

Talk about a turnaround from a year ago.

I just found my footing, and I wanted to stay. To prove who I was and to prove I could do this.

Do football.

Do Chicago.

I spent the day on the couch, but didn't take any more painkillers. The physical pain wasn't that bad. The emotional anguish was another story. Thor wasn't around, which was good because I didn't feel like talking. By nine, I went to bed. Unable to sleep, I woke up early, which only caused the day drag.

Now that it was time to discover my destiny, I didn't want to go. Still pacing the room, I wanted to call Coach and tell him to just get it over with on the phone, but he would never go for that.

This back and forth had to stop. I had to get my shit together. Being late would only cause his temper to flare, and I'd been on the receiving end of his wrath more than my share of times.

Since I'd stopped taking the painkillers yesterday, I knew I could drive without issue, well other than the damn sling, so I couldn't use that as an excuse for not showing up.

Darkness had fallen on the winter evening by the time I turned onto Lake Shore Drive. Snowflakes fell, and some seemed to be sticking to the ground. It would pile up soon. The parking lot at the stadium was deserted as I drove into Soldier Field and stopped at the guard shack.

Hawkins, the guard on duty, let me through and slowly I headed around to Halas Hall.

1920 Football Drive was a modern concrete building with a giant orange C on it. I used my code at the locked door on the side of the building to get in—at least I knew that still worked.

My stomach reeled as I walked through the corridor toward his office. The idea of being traded made my heart feel even heavier. It would mean breaking with *my* team. It would mean not having a connection to Gillian, and I hated the thought of both.

I still pictured her face when I walked into that hotel room. The life and joy in her eyes was gone, and that smile she always wore was nowhere to be found. I'd done that to her. Me. Every day since, the guilt had been eating me alive.

When I'd seen her in the parking lot before the game yesterday, I knew she hadn't seen me. As she walked into the stadium, I couldn't believe how damn beautiful she was. She took my breath away.

I'd gotten through the season by focusing on football and knowing she was doing what she had to do in order to make a life for herself.

A normal life.

It stung like a motherfucker.

And God, I still wanted her. Every single day. I was certain I would for the rest of my life.

Coach's door was closed when I reached his office, and I checked my watch to make sure I wasn't late. It was seven fifty-five. I was early, not late. Had I gotten the message wrong?

This wasn't like him.

I knocked on the door. Suddenly, I realized I probably looked like shit. Pulling my baseball cap lower, I waited, but there was no answer.

Just as I was about to pull my phone from my back pocket, the training room door opened and I heard *her* voice.

I twisted and there she was. Fingering the football shaped rock in my pocket, I devoured the sight of her. Seeing her was like the brightest ray of sun after the longest rain.

Wearing jeans, faded and worn, as if they were her favorite pair she couldn't part with, and a tight navy sweater with the Bears logo on the right chest, she looked thinner, and I hated that. Then again, I was too.

But when her eyes met mine, she became larger than life.

My eager gaze slid down her body and then back up in a way it shouldn't have. It was wrong. This was really wrong.

But then she smiled, and I knew the only thing this was, all it could be, was right.

"Hi," I said.

"Hi," she said back.

As she closed the distance between us, I felt my heart thunder in my chest. I had made a promise to Coach, but damn, I wasn't sure I could keep it anymore.

I missed her.

I wanted her.

I . . . I let that thought hang.

She stopped right in front of me and just looked at me. Her eyes bounced from my face to my arm and back. "Are you okay?"

I nodded. "I'll be fine."

Or so I hoped I would.

Doubt furrowed her brow, but then she gave me a slight smile and held her hand out. It was almost as if we hadn't broken up, hadn't been apart for more than four months, hadn't not talked since the day I left her alone in that damn hotel room. "Take a walk with me," she said.

I wanted to, but I couldn't. I heaved an unhappy sigh. "Gillian, I can't. Not right now. I have a meeting with your father."

The weight of the words on my tongue felt so heavy.

Her hand remained outstretched. "No, you don't."

I looked at her in confusion.

"He asked you to come here for me. He's not coming."

I leaned closer. My gaze was fixed on her, and curiosity flowed through my veins. "I don't understand."

She didn't back away. That magnetic pull between us was stronger than ever as she reached a little further and took my hand. "Take a walk with me and you will."

"What's this about?" I asked, uncertain.

"Do you trust me?"

I cocked one eyebrow. "I think you know I do."

Deep shadows under her eyes made her look like I felt—exhausted, but there was also an undeniable gleam in her green eyes. "Then just come with me," she coaxed, "and I'll tell you when we get there."

Drawing in a breath, I had a feeling this was a bad idea, but I went anyway. I couldn't resist her. I never could. She put her jacket on and then guided me toward the tunnel. The silence stretched between us, but it wasn't awkward. Being with her, next to her, only felt right.

"How's your shoulder?" she asked again, and I knew she didn't want the canned answer.

I rubbed it with the hand she'd let go of the minute I accepted her request, and then I glanced over at her. She was everything I ever wanted. She was all I needed. It took everything I had in me not to push her up against the wall and kiss her. I settled for honesty. "It hurts, but it's not throbbing anymore. And at least we don't play again for two more weeks, which should give me enough time to recover."

She opened the door that led to the tunnel. "Yes, it should, with the proper training and rehab."

Curious where we were going, I slowed my stride and shook my head at her. *So Gillian.*

"Congratulations, on the win, by the way," she said and then she stopped at the end of the tunnel where it met the field.

The wind blew harder and the snow fell heavier on the empty field. Gillian tugged her coat tighter around herself.

"Are you cold?" I asked, wanting to draw her closer, but knowing she wasn't mine anymore to do that. "You can take my coat."

She shook her head and drew in a deep breath. "I love watching the snow fall."

I tilted my face toward the sky so that the soft white flakes gathered on it. "Are you going to tell me why we're here?" I finally asked. "I'm sure it's not to talk about the weather."

With a slow glance around the field, it took her a moment to speak. "Do you see those goalposts over there?" she pointed.

I looked out at them in the pitch dark of the night. "Yeah, they look like yellow glow sticks," I joked.

She smiled, but I saw a tear slide down her cheek. "Yes, they do," she murmured, then said, "And do you see the white lines painted on the field?"

This one-arm thing was annoying, but I pivoted and placed a hand on her shoulder to turn her in my direction. "Gillian. What's going on?"

She ignored my question. "Do you see them?"

"Yes, I see them."

She kept talking. "Do you see all that snow-covered turf?"

I stepped closer. "I see it."

"And the scoreboard?" she asked, her voice unsteady.

Although I was uncertain what this about, I didn't question her anymore. I could hear the importance of this conversation in her tone. Instead, I offered her comfort. My fingers slid down her arm to her hand, and I laced our fingers together. "Yes, I see that too."

She was still looking at Soldier Field. "Everything that is here is what makes this a football field, right?"

I nodded, agreeing.

"And this place, it's a place you know you can't live without. Right?"

I stepped closer, still. "I never said that."

Finally, she turned to face me. "But you'd prefer not to, if you were given a choice, you wouldn't?"

I hesitated. "Yeah, I suppose that's true."

Hurt, and maybe a little anger, flashed in her eyes. "Then why would you think it was okay for me to live without it? Why would you think I'd ever want to?"

The questions caught me off-guard, and I blinked. Another tear slid down her cheek. This time I moved our hands and wiped it away. "Gillian—I don't know what to say."

She shook her head. "Tell me you know me. That you know who I am."

The desolation in her voice hit me deep. I ran my fingers down her cheek. "I do know you. I do know who you are," I answered quietly.

"Then why would you ever think I'd be better off away from this place? Away from football? Away from you?" She paused, and then said again, "Why?" and her voice was broken, sad, full of sorrow.

I stared at her for the longest time, and then finally I said, "He told you."

She nodded. "Everything. About my mother, the letter, and how he made you promise to let me live a normal life. How could you do that to me?"

I flinched and let our linked hands fall. "How could I do that to you? I did it *for* you," I insisted. "Do you think I wanted to end things? Hell no, I didn't. You are the only woman I have ever been in love with, and letting you go after proclaiming that love for you was the hardest thing I have done. But I did it *for* you."

There was anger on her face, there were tears sliding down her cheeks, and there was something hard in her gaze. "You did that *for* me? Or *for* you?"

I was angry now, and I couldn't stop my jaw from clenching or my lips from tightening. "You're wrong, Gillian. It wasn't for me. Nothing about that was for me. It was all for you."

She closed her eyes, and tilted her head toward the sky. "For me," she whispered and her voice was soft, gentle, as if the realization was almost too much to bear.

I had no idea what had transpired between Coach and Gillian, and to be honest, I really didn't give a fuck anymore. Screw my promise. I needed this woman, and I was pretty certain through that entire pissed-off attitude she was showing, she wanted me, maybe even needed me, too. I slid my one arm around her and dipped my head. "I love you so fucking much it hurts not to be near you. It physically hurts. Don't you know that?"

Her eyes flew open and tenderness softened her expression even more.

"I missed you, Strawberry Fields. Every Goddamn day, I thought about you, and it killed me not to call you, not to see you, hear your voice, not to be near you."

Shaking, she reached her hands up and cradled my face. "You weren't out partying with the guys?"

I shook my head. "Not once."

Her thumbs brushed over my cheeks. "Were you—?" she stopped, as if she would choke on her words.

I shook my head again. "I haven't been with anyone since you. You are the only one I want."

She burst out in a sob.

Closer. I needed to be closer. I leaned my forehead against hers. "Please, Gillian, tell me what I need to do to make things right and I'll do it. Anything. I swear."

With a tilt of her head, she gave me a smile that rocked my world. "You're already doing it."

What could I do but smile back at her? "Can I kiss you?"

She let out a slight laugh. "Since when do you have to ask?"

I kissed her then.

Hard.

And then harder.

I sucked on her tongue.

She moaned.

I did too. She tasted so good.

We stumbled back against the wall as we kissed each other like we were starved. And we were. I pressed against her. She pushed into me. I gripped her hip with my free hand while her fingers pressed deep into the muscles in my back.

Remembering the security cameras, I jerked back, shaking my head. "Can we get out of here before your father somehow sees the camera footage?"

She laughed. "He isn't everywhere."

"I'm not so sure about that. So is that a yes, or is there more of Soldier Field you want me to see?"

Her eyes were bright with lust and color was high on her cheeks. "I could show you the bleachers, smart-ass."

That grin I gave her felt like a thousand pound weight had been lifted from my shoulders. "Okay, Strawberry Fields, bleachers it is," I said and then bent to toss her over my left shoulder.

As I walked out onto the field, she kicked and squirmed. "Lucas Carrington, you only have one good arm. Put me down before you drop me."

"Girl," I said, "I don't care how many miles separate us, there's not a chance in hell I'm ever letting go of you again."

She stopped her assault. "I love you."

We were mid-field when I let her slide down my body, and once she was steady on her feet, I slung my left arm around her. "My truck is right out there." I pointed to the parking lot.

"Right over there?" she asked coyly. "Aren't there cameras out there too?"

"Yes, but I meant to get out of here and go somewhere quiet, not to fuck, smart-ass, but if you have something else in mind, please tell me."

Her grin spread across her face. "We could go to my father's apartment. It's not that far."

I contemplated this. Thor's place, my place, wasn't exactly the best option. "Is he there?" I asked.

She nodded. "Yes."

"Hell, no," I said. "The things I want to do to you are nothing I want him to hear."

Her laughter was all I needed to take all my pain away. "You have a point, but don't you have a roommate?"

I shrugged. "Thor will just have to deal. You're coming home with me, and not leaving for days."

Snow was falling all around as we walked out to the parking lot. Once we were in the Range Rover and I cranked the heat, she looked over at me. "Lucas," she said.

I glanced her way.

"We should get our own place."

I was confused. "But Dallas told me you got the job in Minnesota."

"I did," she said, "but I'm not taking it."

"Gillian, you wanted that job."

She shook her head. "No, that was the job my father wanted for me, but today I got the job I wanted. My dream job."

My heart fell a little. "That's great, Gillian. Wherever you go, we'll make this work."

Her grin was so wide I couldn't figure out why she was happy about us being apart until she said, "I'm taking Liam's position."

"With the Bears?" I asked in shock.

She nodded her head. "Yes, it became official earlier today. So do you want to make a home?"

"A home?" I asked, dumbly, as if I didn't know what that was.

"Yes, a home," she grinned. "Do you want to live with me, or what?"

"Come here," I said. She didn't hesitate. After she crawled over onto my lap, I took her mouth and kissed her slowly, tenderly, without hurry. "What do you think?"

"I don't know. You look a little dumbstruck."

"Dumbstruck? Did you really just say that?"

She nodded, and grew serious. "I don't mean where we live. I mean you and me and a place to call our own. That's home."

I closed my eyes, and then opened them. "I like that definition of home."

She nipped my lip. "So I take it that's a yes."

Kissing her harder this time, I didn't pull back until we were both breathless. "Yes, that's absolutely a yes."

Whimpering against my mouth, her body writhed against mine in need. "It won't be easy," she said.

I cupped her chin. "Gillian, it doesn't need to be easy. It just has to be right. And I promise you together we'll make our own normal."

Her tongue, hot and wild, met mine in a clash. "If I have to have normal in my life, you're the only normal I want."

"Me too, Strawberry Fields," I managed to say before I sucked her tongue deep, wanting to devour her whole.

Right here.

Right now.

But I wouldn't. I'd waited way too long to have her, to have it end quickly in this small space.

"Get in your seat and put your belt on," I told her.

She shivered against me. "Why?"

"I want you in my bed."

"Are you even serious right now?"

"Dead serious. I'm not taking you in my truck."

"Lucas." My name came out in a needy moan that had me grinning.

"Gillian," I said back.

And we both laughed.

In that moment when I looked at her, I couldn't help but think I was one lucky guy.

I guess luck was on my side after all.

Thirty-Two

RECOVER

Gillian

THERE WAS A sense of unreality as Lucas threaded his fingers through mine and brought my knuckles to his lips.

Was this actually happening?

The soft brush against my skin reassured me it was when a shiver ran down my spine. But the way he then led me through his apartment and to his room without so much as stopping to take his coat off, more than reaffirmed it because his actions had me trembling.

Lucas was a part of me. He was the blood running through my veins. The oxygen I needed to breath. The thing I didn't know I was missing in my life until I met him.

After first instructing me to remove my outerwear and then help him with his own, he eased me onto the edge of his bed.

My lips parted when I hit the mattress. "I want you."

Holding my gaze, with one hand he fumbled to unbutton my

jeans. "And I want you, Strawberry Fields."

I smiled, letting out a blissful sigh. "I like that."

"What do you like?" he asked, his voice going impossibly deep and low.

"When you call me that. It sounds so sweet."

"You are sweet," he replied, tugging my jeans down and tossing them aside before allowing his gaze to shift from my face to the lacey thong I was wearing, and sucking in a breath.

"Sweet enough to eat?" I asked, holding my arms up so he could pull my sweater over my head.

He licked his lips. "Every single bit."

Already I felt precariously close to coming, and he hadn't even touched me yet. It was the look in his eyes and the determination in his moves that had me already climbing a mountain that I hoped to never fully reach the top of anytime soon.

After removing my undergarments, I leaned back on my elbows and gazed at him in surreal wonder as he removed his own clothing. It seemed to take forever; then again, I always was impatient when it came to Lucas. "Hurry up," I said.

He shook his head in amusement, and then he pounced on the bed, landing on his left side, and finally he was lying beside me.

I reached for him.

He reached for me.

We mapped each other's bodies with our mouths, our tongues, and our teeth. I traced the lines of his abdominal muscles. He licked his tongue over and around my breasts. I kissed the inside of his elbows, the backs of his knees. He nipped at my ankles, my wrists.

His cock surged into my hand when I wrapped my fingers around it. I let out a breathy sigh that sent tingles from my head to my toes as he licked and devoured my nipples.

When his palm skimmed over my core, I started shaking. I couldn't wait another minute to have him inside me. "Come here,"

I whispered.

"I'm here," he breathed, as he quickly moved up my body.

I brought his face to mine, and fluttered my lashes against his skin, over and over, while he laughed softly. And then I kissed his closed eyes, threaded my fingers though his hair, and breathed him in.

It's strange how the things you miss most are the things you take for granted.

His smell, the taste of him, the feel of him. Then again, I missed everything about him. "Make love to me," I whispered.

He didn't wait.

Rolling onto his back, he urged me on top of him. I straddled him and he guided his cock right where it needed to be. As I slowly eased down, he pushed up, hard and deep.

I cried out.

Instantly, he could feel me. "That's it," he said, "let me in."

I cried out again, and let him in.

I would always let him in.

Moving slowly, he sucked in steadying breaths. I watched as he struggled to control himself, as he tried to make love to me instead of fucking me.

Leaning down to kiss him, I tasted sweat on his upper lip, and it tasted good.

Even when the pace got frantic, when I raked my nails down his chest, and he bit me hard enough to bruise, when the headboard creaked from how hard I was gripping it, the feeling of love was everywhere.

Closing his eyes as he withdrew, he opened them to look at me when he brought me down hard on top of him, burying himself deep inside me.

I bucked upward, my cry splintering the air. "I'm going to come."

His jaw clenched. "I'm almost there," he told me.

But I had already fallen. I closed my eyes and arched my back and allowed this wave of never-ending pleasure to wash over me.

At the same time, he thrust upwards one last time and held himself deep. I opened my eyes then to watch him. He was beautiful when he came.

With his chest heaving and his eyes wild and unfocused, he emptied himself into my body.

We were both struggling to catch our breath, to suck enough air into our lungs, but we were both smiling.

"I love you," he said.

"I love you," I replied in a dreamy voice.

I collapsed beside him, and he pulled me to him. After a few silent moments, he reached for my hand and placed it on his already hardening cock.

"Again?" I giggled.

"Again," he laughed.

His mouth found the spot that drove me wild at the base of my throat, and I moaned in ecstasy. He bit the slope of my bare shoulder, and I cried out. He moved along my skin with sureness of familiarity even after all these months apart, and I writhed under his touch.

Here he was, with me, touching me, wanting me, owning me, loving me, and it felt so good.

It felt so right.

It felt like home.

Thirty-Three

Riding the Bench

Gillian

THE PARTY HATS and noisemakers would have to wait.

This was New Year's Eve football style. The team arrived in Denver yesterday for the playoff game. And much to my delight I was on the plane with them as an official employee of the Chicago Bears.

The trip was fashioned in the way my father had always done it. We rode in a convoy of five buses, bypassing the main terminal and going directly to the tarmac. All of us were either in first class or business class. I sat next to Lucas and we thumbed through travel magazines, while the other players either slept, watched a movie, or played video games.

When we landed, my father remained in his seat and so did every non-player, including me, while the guys filed off. This was a thing my father did to let the players know they came first.

Police escorted us to the five-star hotel and once arriving there, two elevators were curtained off to take us to the reserved floors.

When on the road, unlike training camp, the players were re-warded with individual rooms. I would be staying with Lucas in his room because . . . well . . . that was what we both wanted. My father was not happy about our decision. Hey, he'd eventually have to realize I was no longer his little girl, but in the meantime, I really did try to make it easier on him, whenever I could.

After the usual pre-game routine, we all went to dinner and lights out early. Lucas fell asleep right away, I found myself staring at the ceiling. I was nervous. Really nervous. It was one thing to be an intern, but a full-fledged assistant trainer was another.

The morning came way too fast, and after I dressed in game attire, I left Lucas in the shower to meet with Dallas before the team breakfast. After we ate, it was time to say goodbye to Lucas and get to work.

While Dallas evaluated the injured players, Aiden and I checked through our gear one last time.

A nervous flutter whispered around my belly as we drove to the Sports Authority Field at Mile High. It was just about nine in the morning. Kick-off was at one and we had a whole lot to do in-between.

The drive was fast, and with the medical staff and supplies, I headed to the training room. The prepping of supplies, tape, tape, and more tape, fluids and more fluids, as well as the trunks of emergency equipment was done last night.

As soon as the buses unloaded with the players, it was *go time*. I was about put my sports medicine skills to use. While Aiden aggres-sively prepared the players with massage and Dallas used manual therapy techniques to increase joint range of motion, I taped ankles.

Two and a half hours later, I was out on the sideline, checking ev-ery trunk one last time. Dallas was grinding his teeth as he watched the injured players to see how they moved during warm-ups.

And then the game was on.

I hadn't seen much of Lucas since we arrived, but that was to be expected.

As I glanced around, I couldn't help but feel that I'd missed the opening act. I might have arrived to the show in time for the encore, but that was all right by me, because I was finally where I was always meant to be.

The temperature was around thirty degrees, but standing outside in the sunshine it felt a lot warmer. Then again I was also nervous. With the heat getting to me, I pulled my gloves and hat off and set them on the bench.

The game was mostly injury free, which was a good thing.

In the final few minutes of the game, I watched with baited breath from the sidelines as the team tried to make a comeback.

It hadn't been the best game for the Bears. Lucas had gotten sacked over and over again. I hated watching him go down, but breathed a sigh of relief every time he got back up.

He'd somehow managed to throw two interceptions, but they'd only totaled just over one hundred passing yards. The Bears as a whole had only scored ten points the entire game.

Things were not looking good.

My father was pacing back and forth, chewing his pen to bits and talking into his microphone at the same time. It was crazy how he could do that.

The announcer made a speculation that in these few final moments Jeb Burns, the quarterback backup, would finally be making his debut. But, needing a touchdown and two-point conversion to tie, my father left Lucas in place to lead the offense downfield.

There was always a chance, no matter how slight.

Of course, Lucas gave it all he had. As a last ditch effort he tried to thread a pass to a heavily covered Dion Reynolds, but it was intercepted.

My heart sank as I watched the players slouch on the bench.

That loss of the ball meant the game was over for the Bears, and it also meant the buck stopped here for them, for this year, anyway.

There would be no potential Super Bowl, but I knew that it would come very soon with the team my father had carefully assembled.

Down at the other end of the sideline, Lucas looked like a cocksure athlete humbled over the loss. I wanted to go down there and console him, but I was on the clock, working, and acting like his girlfriend was against the rules.

Yes, my father had added two rules to the team doctrine when it came to inter-team relationships.

First, I was not allowed to treat Lucas in a professional capacity unless it was absolutely necessary. This made sense. I was too invested and might think irrationally. I agreed with him.

And second, Lucas and I were not allowed to act as boyfriend and girlfriend on football time. This made me laugh. Obviously, he didn't want us kissing during practice or at games. After all, we were both employees of the Bears.

Other than that, he accepted our relationship. In fact, I think he rather liked that Lucas was in my life, and that we both joined him for Sunday dinners.

Lucas and I were moving into an apartment not far from Soldier Field next week, but then we would be off. We were going to spend the first week of the off-season snorkeling and whale watching in Hawaii. Backpacking in Europe was on our list, and of course Paris, but as the newbie athletic trainer, I didn't get that much time off, so those would have to wait.

The thump of music from the PA system was the prelude to the walk they would take up the semicircular ramp into the tunnel. The two teams wouldn't be mingling like they had before the game in the empty stadium while our players found their footing on the turf.

"Violent game, wasn't it?" Drake deadpanned as he started to pack up the gear.

I tore my eyes away from Lucas. "Yeah, it was."

"Guess we'll be rolling out."

"Looks that way."

It didn't matter that it was New Year's Eve. It didn't matter that this was their final game of the season. This was football, and we lost. There would be no celebrating.

In the locker room, the players would be silent. Angry. Deflated. I hated when we lost. Not just because we lost, but because of what it did to the team spirit.

As soon as the team was ready to leave, we'd be on a bus heading for the airport. At least they wouldn't have practice tomorrow.

When the team filed past us, of course I had to look, and much to my surprise, Lucas's penetrating eyes were on me. His hard body was covered in dirt and his hair was a sexy mess. He held his helmet in his hand and he wore a frown on his face.

"Hey, hot stuff," I mouthed.

And just like that he turned that frown upside down. It was that easy smile that made me weak in the knees each time I saw it.

A feeling coursed through me that everything in the world was somehow right.

And that's when I knew . . . *I really did have it all.*

Epilogue 1

BRAGGING RIGHTS

Three Years Later

Gillian

THE AIR FELT electrically charged. It was hard to believe that in a matter of minutes the eyes of over a million Americans would be watching what happened in this stadium in the Windy City.

And they would be focusing on Lucas, my father, the entire team, as well as the opposing team.

Lucas had dreamed of this his entire life, even if there were times he refused to admit it, and the time had come.

This was his house.

His time.

And it was more than deserved.

"Did you see this picture?" Drake asked, jolting me out of my heartfelt reflection.

I took his phone from his hand and rolled my eyes when I glanced at the screen. It was a picture of Lucas attached to a resistance band being held by Dallas as they walked the perimeter of the stadium.

Lucas wasn't a fancy dog—he was just getting a workout for goodness sake.

The photo that was snapped by the press just hours ago had already gone viral. I had to admit though as I glanced down at it again, he did look like was he being taken for a walk.

The chuckle I let out couldn't be helped.

All of a sudden Lucas started marching his team down the field, and when he looked at me, he narrowed his eyes.

How on earth did he know I was making fun of him?

All I could do was stand on the sidelines with my heart racing, and mouth "Good luck."

Just as the music for the National Anthem started piping through the stadium, I handed Drake his phone and placed my hand over my heart.

This was the Super Bowl. And the Bears had finally made it all the way.

All. The. Way. *As my father had said about five thousand times over the past five days.*

Lucas had an amazing season—the most touchdowns, the most passing yards, and the fewest interceptions.

He would be named MVP, for certain.

The coin was tossed, and we won, which meant Lucas was up. He always preferred it that way, being first.

Imagine that.

The first quarter passed in the blink of an eye. We were ahead by 7. The second quarter ended and we were up 24–14. The third quarter was over with no additional points scored. And the fourth quarter went by in a flash. Amidst all the scoring by both teams, we were still up.

With a mere forty-five seconds left, all that remained was for us to run the clock out. Lucas broke the huddle and followed the center to the line of scrimmage.

What was he doing?

I closed my eyes. I couldn't watch. This game was so close, and at 34–28, anything could happen.

Then I heard it.

The whistle.

The applause.

The roar of the crowd.

The game was over.

We'd won.

Won!

I opened my eyes and listened to all the cheering. Scanning the field, I found Lucas on his knees. The tears that fell from my eyes couldn't be withheld. This was his moment, and he deserved it.

My gaze quickly shifted to my father, who was headed to the field toward Lucas. I started crying even harder when he brought him to his feet. This was his moment too, and he too deserved it.

I stood with my hands over my mouth to try to quiet my sobs.

Orange and blue confetti came raining down as the men in my life embraced each other right there on the field.

I blinked in surprise when a spotlight bounced overhead and then directly landed on me, illuminating me to the crowd of cheering of fans.

What the what?

The announcer's crisp, clean voice came over the speakers. "Miss Whitney," he boomed, "Lucas Carrington would like you to join him on the field."

My mouth gaped open and heat shot to my cheeks. And then the entire stadium quieted, and I found myself shaking.

What was going on?

Aiden strode over and nudged me. "You better get moving."

I glared at him.

"Now," he grinned.

Somehow I found myself walking on shaky legs toward Lucas and my father.

As soon as I had gotten about five feet away, Lucas removed his helmet and tossed it to the ground. Our gazes locked, and with his blue-eyed stare fixed on me, I put one foot in front of the other. When I reached him, I felt like I couldn't feel my legs. I was that nervous.

"I was wrong," my father whispered when I was close enough.

I gave him a confused look.

"A guy can play ball and have a life."

I blinked at him. But then the spotlight found the three of us, and as soon as it did, I saw my father slip Lucas a small velvet box.

Once it was in Lucas's big palm, he dropped down onto one knee.

This couldn't be happening!

I felt like I was in a dream.

The lights.

The confetti.

The cheers.

There was no way this was real.

He looked up at me and smiled, slow and sexy, his eyes knowing. I gave him a tender smile, but my pulse was racing.

Around us, flashes went off and people yelled. There was cheering from the fans and sneering from the women who didn't want him off the market. Didn't they realize he had been for a very long time? It didn't matter.

I knew he was mine.

The crowd applauded as he opened the box. "I love you, Gillian Whitney. Will you marry me?" he asked in a husky voice.

I shut out the noise all around us and I dropped to my knees in front of him. I stared at the gorgeous diamond ring in awe. It sparkled and caught the lights from above, dazzling me with its brilliance, the same way Lucas had the first time I saw him on the field.

Leaning forward, I cupped his face in my hands. "Yes, Lucas, I'll marry you," I breathed, my voice shaky and filled with emotion.

That easy smile spread across his lips as he slipped the glittering diamond onto my ring finger.

The crowd erupted all around us, but the only person I was looking at was him. I wasn't expecting this. We hadn't talked about marriage. But sometimes unexpected, was best.

Lucas pulled me into his embrace, his mouth hard and fierce over mine. I clung to this Super Bowl champion just as fiercely.

Our journey was far from over, but we had been gifted with the greatest page turning script in life . . . each other.

And we were going to give that gift the most perfect ending . . . together.

Epilogue 2

Gillian

I'D FINALLY MADE it, and I'm not going to lie, I was giddy about it.

Since I was a little girl, I had dreamed about coming to this city. Strolling along the curve of the Seine, walking through the Arc de Triomphe, and yes, albeit cliché, eating croissants near the Champs-Élysées.

From our hotel room, the sleek metal bars of the Eiffel Tower crisscrossed in the distance in such a way that I imagined I could slide my wrists through the openings.

"What are you doing?" Lucas asked, his voice husky, deep, intoxicating.

I glanced over my shoulder, and when I did, the white silk fabric of my nightgown ruffled as the cool air cascaded beneath it and wrapped around my naked body.

I didn't care.

The sleepy sight before me was magnificent—tall, dark, and

handsome. Sexy as hell with his mussed up hair and low hanging sweat pants, he was shirtless. And I swore I could see every inch of the muscled lines and the contours of his body.

I bit my lip and turned back around. "Come over here, and I'll show you."

Lucas stood beside me and I caught his gaze just as he looked over at me with those penetrating eyes.

"Watch," I said, and I held my thumb and forefinger up with one hand, and this time pretended to pinch the Eiffel Tower.

He tossed me that easy grin that I could look at for a thousand lifetimes, and then he lifted his hand to mimic mine.

I smiled back at him. With his recently acquired Super Bowl ring on one hand and his wedding ring on the other, he too pretended to pinch the Eiffel Tower.

"See," I said, placing my free hand beneath the one extended, "it's like it fits in the palm of your hand."

With a chuckle, he shook his head. He always found me so curious. I loved that about him. Then again, I loved everything about my new husband.

The Eiffel Tower might have been looming impressively before us, but that didn't stop me from leaning over to kiss Lucas.

I couldn't help myself.

And I guess neither could he because he abandoned our play and pulled me close to him. His cock was in a state of semi-arousal. Long and thick between his legs, it was rising from his pants very quickly.

I panted, wet and needy, into his mouth.

Manhandling me, he gripped my thighs, wrapping my legs around his hips so he could grind his erection into me.

Clinging to him, I tried to remember why I had gotten out of bed at all. But it was difficult enough to breathe, let alone think, as he thrust his hips between my legs.

There had been a chill in the air, but with his warm hard body pressed up tight against mine, I no longer felt it. Lost to him, I tossed my head back as his lips dropped to my throat.

He peppered kisses down my throat. "I don't like waking up and not seeing you beside me."

My hands slid up his back so my fingers could curl in his hair. "I'll try to remember that, but honestly, I think I like it when you miss me."

His mouth made its way down to the silk garment that covered my breasts and I relaxed into his touch with a groan. "Vixen," he breathed.

I laughed, but then suddenly stopped as arousal took control of my body. Last night we'd made love for hours, and yet my chest still fluttered at the thought of having him inside me right now.

I was crazy hot for this man, and he was mine.

Mine.

I still couldn't believe it.

The thin spaghetti strap over my shoulder fell to the side, allowing him to easily suck on one of my nipples. I tossed my head back as his touch sent electricity pulsing through my body, and I drew my nails down his back in anticipation.

All the while this was taking place, his erection was pulsing hot between our bellies. His chest heaved and each exhale was ragged and erotic. I loved it. I loved him.

Soon, he started moving, and then we were inside and I was on the bed looking up at him as he stood before me. "Stay right where you are," I told him.

I never could get enough of his body, so while I had the opportunity, I began tracing every line of his six-pack, and then I used my tongue to trace a similar pattern.

Every muscle in his body coiled tightly, and he quivered under my touch. I glanced up at him and when I did, I found his gaze locked on me. Lust and desire blazed in it, and I knew what I had to do.

I lowered my mouth to the waistband of his sweats and teased him a little. A long hiss escaped his lips when I started to pull it down, but just then the alarm on my phone started to chirp, and I remembered why I'd gotten up early.

"Should I turn that off," he said with a groan.

"Yes, and we have to hurry. We have to meet our families for breakfast," I managed to say. My voice cracking as arousal overtook me.

Lucas jerked away from the bed. "Shit, your father is going to be waiting for us." He took my hand. "Come on, hurry up, we can't be late."

I yanked him back toward me, and circled my lips with my tongue. "We can be a little late. I was just getting started."

He shook his head.

"Lucas," I said, but he was already halfway to the shower.

I couldn't help but laugh.

Some things were never going to change, and one of them would be that my father, his father-in-law, would always be Coach to my husband.

Lucas and I had gotten married yesterday, right here in Paris.

It had been only four weeks since the Bears' Super Bowl win, and our engagement, but Lucas insisted we tie the knot before the next season started up.

Elopement seemed to be the only option, but then he suggested Paris, and of course I swooned.

My father and his wife of two years, Mallory Harlow, flew to France with us. Turned out my father was sneaking around with the cheerleading coach while I was sneaking around with my now new husband. He told Lucas and I about his relationship with Mallory shortly after Lucas and I got back together.

Lucas used his own version of the coined phrase, "Like daughter, like father," that he loved to use. He taunted me with it as soon we found out, but refrained from saying a word to my father.

In truth, he was still a little afraid of the man.

That was never going to change, no matter how many meals we shared or holidays we spent together.

Nick, his wife, and six kids, also came to witness the event. Believe it or not, Lucas even invited his father. He seemed to have come to terms with who his father was, and to accept him.

And then, of course, Thor and Dallas wouldn't have missed it for the world, and they all flew in too.

The wedding took place on the Le Bretagne—a luxury yacht that offered a stunning view of the Eiffel Tower while we said our vows.

It was everything I could have ever imagined and more.

It was perfect.

And what else was there to say . . . other than we were going to live *happily-ever-after*.

THE END

Look for these two stories in

The Sexy Jerk World . . .

Sexy Jerk

When a Chicago playboy agrees to help babysit his best friend's son, he knows he won't be doing it alone. Unfortunately, the other half of the babysitting duo is completely oblivious. And there's only one small problem with that—she thinks Nick Carrington is a jerk.

Big Shot

Jace Bennett was the type of man you would love forever. Tall, dark, and brooding, there was just something about him that drew you in and captured your heart. It might have been that slow, sexy smile or his filthy, dirty mouth. Or it might have just been him.

What I didn't know back then was that although I'd love him forever, I wouldn't be the one sharing his bed, the one having his children, or the one he adored.

But then—that was because of me—not him.

Wasn't it?

About the Author

KIM KARR IS a *New York Times* and *USA Today* bestselling author.

She grew up in Rochester, New York, and now lives in Florida with her husband and four kids. She's always had a love for reading books and writing. Being an English major in college, she wanted to teach at the college level, but that was not to be. She went on to receive an MBA and became a project manager until quitting to raise her family. Kim currently works part-time with her husband and recently decided to embrace one of her biggest passions—writing.

Kim wears a lot of hats: writer, book-lover, wife, soccer mom, taxi driver, and the all-around go-to person of her family. However, she always finds time to read. One of her favorite family outings when her kids were little was taking them to the bookstore or the library. Today, Kim's oldest child is twenty-one and no longer goes with her on these now rare and infrequent outings. She finds that she doesn't need to go on them anymore because she has the greatest device ever invented—a Kindle.

Kim likes to believe in soul mates, kindred spirits, true friends, and happily-ever-afters. She loves to drink champagne and listen to music, and hopes to always stay young at heart.

www.authorkimkarr.com
Facebook, Twitter, Instagram, Amazon

also by
NEW YORK TIMES BESTSELLING AUTHOR
Kim Karr

CPSIA information can be obtained
at www.ICGtesting.com
Printed in the USA
FSOW03n2347060318
45391FS

9 781974 506606